Help us Rate this book...
Put your initials on the
Left side and your rating
on the right side.
1 = Didn't care for
2 = It was O.K.
3 = It was <u>great</u>

DATE DUE

Initials	Rating			
mc,	1 2 ③	OCT 0 5 2018		
dn	1 2 ③	OCT 2 7 2018		
LR	1 2 ③	DEC 1 1 2018		
DV	1 2 ③+	JAN 1 7 2019		
mc	1 2 ③+	FEB - 1 2019		
MK	1 2 ③	FEB 1 8 2019		
	1 2 3	MAR 0 2 2019		
	1 2 3	MAR 2 2019		
	1 2 3	SEP 2019		
	1 2 3			
	1 2 3			
	1 2 3			
	1 2 3			
	1 2 3			
	1 2 3			

PRINTED IN U.S.A.

**This Large Print Book carries the
Seal of Approval of N.A.V.H.**

The HOPE *of* AZURE SPRINGS

Center Point
Large Print

The
HOPE
of AZURE
SPRINGS

RACHEL
FORDHAM

CENTER POINT LARGE PRINT
THORNDIKE, MAINE

This Center Point Large Print edition
is published in the year 2018 by arrangement with
Revell, a division of Baker Publishing Group.

The text of this Large Print edition is unabridged.
In other aspects, this book may vary
from the original edition.
Printed in the United States of America
on permanent paper.
Set in 16-point Times New Roman type.

ISBN: 978-1-68324-887-3

Library of Congress Cataloging-in-Publication Data

Names: Fordham, Rachel, 1984- author.
Title: The hope of Azure Springs / Rachel Fordham.
Description: Center Point Large Print edition. | Thorndike, Maine :
    Center Point Large Print, 2018.
Identifiers: LCCN 2018017455 | ISBN 9781683248873
    (hardcover : alk. paper)
Subjects: LCSH: Single women—Fiction. | Sisters—Fiction. |
    Large type books. | GSAFD: Western stories. | Historical fiction. |
    Love stories.
Classification: LCC PS3606.O747335 H67 2018b | DDC 813/.6—dc23
LC record available at https://lccn.loc.gov/2018017455

For Tyler—
who never doubted.
I love you forever.

Prologue

Iowa, 1881

"She dead?"

Em heard a man's voice from somewhere above her. A strange thumping pulsed through her with each word he spoke. Her throat burned, screaming for water, but she could not cry out.

"There's life in her. Not much of it though," a second, raspier voice answered. She felt a hand press against her throat and then move over her body, gently probing. "She's bleeding pretty bad."

"Gunshot?" the first voice asked.

If only her eyes would open and she could see them. Straining, she struggled to pull her heavy eyelids open. Finally, bits of light darted in front of her eyes, but she could not focus. The faces above her were fuzzy and indiscernible.

Fear swept through her, suddenly waking her battered body. Afraid the men from before had returned, she opened her eyes wide, finding strength that only moments before she had lacked. With thrashing arms she flailed at the men. Her arms flopped about but offered little defense—she was too weak from blood loss. And then they moved no longer, subdued by large, strong hands.

"Easy, girl. We aren't going to hurt you. We just want to help. Take you into town, that's all. There's a good doctor there." The man's deep voice sounded gentle, but still she did not trust him. Voices could be deceiving. Arms could hurt as well as help. She knew these things well.

Soon she felt her body being raised above the ground, and moments later the hard planks of a wagon became the resting place for her injured frame. Too weak to move, she lay looking at the sky, wishing there were a way to end the agony, but knowing that for Lucy she would fight on.

Once the wagon lurched forward, she lost track of everything again. The wheels bouncing over ruts made her pain so intense that everything closed around her and then faded to black.

One

I'm sorry to come by unannounced, but this business with the girl's been put off long enough," Sheriff Caleb Reynolds said while standing in the doorway of the Howells' home. "I'd have come by sooner, but Doc Jones said she'd need time."

"I reckon that's fine." Abraham scratched his balding head. Then he reached into his pocket and took out his handkerchief. After blowing his nose, he said, "She's been sleeping pretty hard for two days. I think we could rouse her. I know we'd worry less if we knew the whole story." He opened the door wider, admitting Caleb inside.

"Thank you," Caleb said, trying not to sound too eager. In the years Caleb had known Abraham, the man had never spoken quickly. "Most folks wouldn't have taken her in. It was good of you."

"It's no problem." Abraham smiled as they made their way inside. "Eliza was a bit put out giving up her bed, but the rest of us haven't minded a bit. The girl hasn't asked for anything. Mostly she just sleeps. Follow me. I'll take you to her."

They proceeded through the well-lit house. Caleb couldn't help admiring the details as he walked. Dark decorative paneling. A massive stone fireplace. Large, deep chairs that begged to be sat in. He hoped to have a home like this someday. An involuntary sigh escaped him. A place like this would make his father proud.

Abraham's quiet words came again as they walked toward the room. "Abigail is in there. She rarely leaves the girl's side. She's been so worried that we'd lose her. Even after the doctor told us the wound wasn't serious, she's still worrying."

"It's not a bad wound?"

"Doctor said she's lucky the bullet didn't hit anything important. It should heal up fine. But she lost a lot of blood. My Abigail has been by her side since. Nursing seems to be in her blood—and in her heart." Abraham spoke of Abigail's current nursing, but Caleb wondered if he was remembering. A few years back the whole town had suffered from fevers. The Howells had lost two sons. Grief sat heavy on the town, but no one had mourned quite like Abigail Howell.

Focusing on the current circumstances, Caleb readied himself for another glimpse of the waif.

For just a moment he'd seen the girl when the wagon lurched into town two days before. She was a sorry excuse for a girl—unconscious, seeping blood, dirty, and smelling like something pulled from the bottom of a privy. He had been near the wagon and had heard the doctor shouting his request for someone to take her in.

"Who'll house her?" the good doctor had shouted into the growing crowd. "She needs a place to stay. Somewhere safe to convalesce."

No one had volunteered. No one but Abraham, who happened to be returning home from his store, his books tucked under his arm as they were every night when he locked up and walked the short distance back to his home and family. Stopping to see what the commotion was, he had quietly offered his roof to the girl. The crowd had murmured among themselves, but none seemed surprised by Abraham's offer.

Caleb had been ready to wake the girl and go after whoever did this. No one was going to get away with shooting a pitiful girl in his territory. Before he'd been able to shake her and get the details he needed, Doc Jones had stopped him. "She's not well enough to be questioned," he'd said. "Give her a couple days."

Caleb had questioned the men who had found her, but they'd been no help. When he'd walked back to the jail, he had nothing to show for his efforts but questions. Now here he was. He'd followed the doctor's orders and waited two days, but it was time to figure out this mess.

"Em, try to wake up. The sheriff's here. He wants to help you. Can you wake up and talk to him?" Abigail gently nudged the girl's shoulder. Abraham stood near his wife, silently spectating.

The effect was slow, but the girl did open her eyes. Blue eyes met his own. It was obvious that the Howells had attempted to clean her up, but she was in need of a good dunk in a tub.

"Em, is it?" Caleb asked, trying to sound gentle, not wanting to scare the girl off. *Em,* he said again in his mind. *A mighty plain name for a mighty plain girl.*

"That's my name. What do you want?" Though the girl's voice quivered, it still carried a hint of defensiveness.

"I want to find out who shot you and what I can do to help." He leaned in a little closer and tapped his badge. "I'm the sheriff of this town, and it's my job to catch whoever did this. You tell me what you can and we'll keep you safe. I need to know everything you remember." He'd dealt with youngsters before, often enough to know that a gentle voice helped them stay calm. After years of questioning people, he'd also learned other tricks: Never let them know you're caught off guard. Always keep control. "Go ahead, tell me what you can."

She raised herself up a little, her eyes meeting

12

his. "Why are you talking to me like I'm a child?"

"How old are you?" He was okay starting with her age—at least it was something.

"Nineteen. Nearly twenty."

He could find no words. So much for keeping control. Staring hard at the girl, he tried to decide if he believed her. Upon closer inspection, he thought perhaps she was right. She was so thin, terribly thin, her frame *looked* childlike. Perhaps it was lack of food rather than age that caused her to look so young and small.

Finally, clearing his throat, he spoke, making sure he was using a voice appropriate for an adult. "I apologize. I'm not the best at guessing a *woman's* age. Can you tell me who shot you?"

"I'll tell you, but it won't do you much good. Three men came to the house, yelling and knocking things around, and then they started shooting." Pausing, Em took a ragged breath. "I'm sure they thought I was dead. They just stepped over me, cursing and searching the house for something. I just lay there in my own blood, waiting for them to leave."

"Did you see their faces?" He opened his notepad. "Did you know any of them? Do you know what they were looking for?"

Em's eyes darted around, and her breathing sounded more labored. Abigail put a hand on her shoulder. "It's all right, Em. Just one thing at a time." Turning to the sheriff, she said, "Perhaps one question at a time. She's been through so much already. I think we need to take it slow."

He fought the urge to remind them that he'd already waited two days.

Em took several slow breaths while Abigail wiped her perspiring brow. "Shhh," she soothed. "It's all going to be all right. We'll keep you safe, and Sheriff Reynolds will find whoever did this."

Em turned toward him. "I never saw them before, but I did get a good look at them. I'd know them if I ever saw them again. I don't know what they were after, but if you could take me back there, I might have an idea where to find it."

"Where to find what?" he asked, his voice rising. She was only further confusing him. What he needed were answers, not more questions.

"I said I don't know. What I do know is whenever George came back from one of his trapping trips, he always went to a certain spot, tucked away on our land. Like he was checking on something. I never thought much of it. He was a quiet man, and this was not his only strange habit. But I'm guessing whatever they were looking for is there."

Caleb nodded and reached for his hat, relieved that this would have an easy solution. *A quick ride to an old homestead and—*

"I see what you're thinking, Sheriff Reynolds, but she can't go anywhere—not yet. Doctor said she's to take it easy for a couple weeks." Abigail's eyebrows pulled together, and her eyes did not leave his until he set his hat back down. For being a kind woman, Abigail Howell could be intimidating.

"I'm not staying in bed for a couple weeks," Em said. "I can't stay here. I've already been here too long." As she sat up higher in bed, the blanket fell away from her arm. Caleb was surprised to see wrinkled, discolored skin all along its surface. He was no doctor, but he was fairly certain the grim marks were from an old burn.

Abigail again put a reassuring hand on Em's shoulder. "Hush, dear. We were happy to take you in. We volunteered and haven't regretted it for a moment. The doctor says you have a bit of a recovery ahead, and I'm not about to cross the doctor." Abigail pursed her lips into a tight line and waited.

Caleb hoped that Em knew when to admit defeat. Despite Abigail's resolute look, he saw the good woman's tenderness and concern.

Abigail Howell was as near a saint as there was in Azure Springs. This girl in her sorry shape could not have landed in a better home.

"I second what Abby said. You're welcome here," Abraham said, crossing his arms over his pudgy belly. Abraham Howell always stood by his wife. "Now, if you will excuse me, I have work to do. Good day to you, Sheriff, ladies." He

15

stood deliberately, nodded, and then turned and left.

"I'm not one to put things off that need to be done. But I'll follow the doctor's orders and wait to take you back out there," Caleb said.

"Her recovery will be much quicker if she takes it easy," Abigail said.

"I'll trust her to your care. But I can't just sit around here waiting. I'll head out there myself and see what I can find. Those men might have left clues. There's no reason for me to wait."

"If you head out there, you could bring back her clothes and some of her essentials." Abigail turned to Em. "Are there any personal items you would like the sheriff to bring?"

"Won't find much by way of essentials," Em said. "The dress I was wearing is my only dress. I know it's not much to look at, but it's the only one I have. If you do head that way, there's something I could use your help with." Avoiding eye contact, she turned her head toward the wall, her hand fiddling with the edge of the quilt. "Would you bury George? I hadn't meant to leave him, but I knew I had to get away."

"George? You mentioned him before. Who is he?" Caleb's voice again rose as he spoke. He had not expected to hear that someone else had been shot. Someone killed. Why hadn't she told him that first? Caleb rubbed the dark stubble on his chin, giving himself a moment to calm down. "Tell me about George."

Em's voice was softer now, barely above a whisper. "George is the owner of the homestead. I lived with him—in a way."

Caleb looked from Em to Abigail, hoping to understand. "You lived with him? Was he your brother, father?"

"I think we should slow down. These have been a taxing few days." Abigail came to the rescue again. "I'm sure Em can explain it all. But you must give her time."

Em spoke up. "It's all right, Abigail. I'll tell what I can. I suppose you could say I worked there. Though I wasn't paid. And yes, he's dead. They shot him more than once in the chest before they shot me. I checked before I left and he was dead. I wouldn't have left him if he hadn't been. He needs someone to bury him. It's not right, him rotting aboveground. I'd do it myself if I could, and I will if you won't."

Caleb pictured those frail limbs digging a grave and dragging a grown man into it. He doubted she possessed the strength, and even if she did, it would be a daunting task. It wouldn't be a pleasant job for him—dealing with death never was—but he'd had years of good meals to run on and he did not want for muscle.

"I'll bury him, don't worry yourself about that. But this is more serious than I thought.

17

Depending on what these men were after, they may be back." He scratched at the back of his neck, then stood and paced the room. "When they return, if they return, they'll know you're still alive and may come looking for you. Seeing as you are a witness to George's death, they might want you dead. I've been sheriff long enough to know there's a breed of men who hates a witness."

He felt Abigail's and Em's eyes trailing him as he walked back and forth. They said nothing.

"Judging by the wound in your side, they're not afraid of pulling the trigger. If they're smart, they'll know you may be able to identify them." He ran his hands through his hair. He hadn't anticipated anyone coming after this pitiful girl. For two days he'd assumed that she was merely the victim of some senseless crime. Never had it crossed his mind that this might have been a planned attack. The longer he talked to her, the more he was convinced this was not just a matter of her being in the wrong place at the wrong time. These men were after something.

"I don't even know where I am. How will they know?" Em asked. "I took a horse when I left. I rode it a long way before I fell off."

"Even if there's no trail of blood, there aren't many towns around. If someone wants to find you, they will. It'd be best for all of us to be cautious. We don't know what lengths they'll go

18

to in order to find you. I don't want you leaving this house, not yet anyway. Not until those men are behind bars. I'll enlist some men to help me keep a watch around this home, and we'll spread the word to others to be careful."

Abigail jumped into the conversation again. "In another day or two we'll give her a real bath. I'll find her some of Eliza's clothes to wear. A little freshening up will change her appearance. I'm certain that will help. Already she's improving."

Caleb took in Em's disheveled and ragged appearance—her hair caked with dirt and oil, a layer of filth covering her skin. Never had he seen a face so thin. The bones in her cheeks looked harsh and sharp, the skin pulled tight around them. No man would look twice at her for her beauty. But if a man were looking for the plainest, thinnest waif of a girl, she would not be hard to pick from a crowd.

"A good bath and clean clothes couldn't hurt, but it still won't be hard to track her down. Half the town saw her come in on the back of that wagon. All those men would have to do is ask a few questions around Main Street and she'd be found. I'll spread word to everyone I see, but it's best if she stays put, away from people. Guarding one house will be easier than watching the whole of Azure Springs. I'll get to the bottom of this and then she'll be free to go."

Turning his attention from Abigail and back to

Em, he said, "I know you can't talk long today, but can you give me descriptions of the men and tell me where your place is?"

Em's eyes were looking weary, but she nodded. In a tired voice, she gave him details. Specifics most people would overlook came pouring out of her. He wished everyone he interviewed remembered the little things the way she did.

"One man had a scar running along his left cheek," she said. "It was red, like it was new. Another had red hair, deep red, and he was missing a front tooth. The third man had fair hair and bushy eyebrows. He didn't talk much—just followed orders."

The images of all three of the men came alive, the details vivid, as Caleb scrambled to keep up with her, frantically writing notes.

"I don't know where I am now, but I know George's place is next to Hollow Creek, about a mile south of where it meets the Eagle River. It's tucked in the back of a little clearing. It's not much to look at, but I think you'll be able to find it."

Clutching his notes, he stood. "Thank you, Em. I'll let you rest now. I'll be back soon to talk. Please think hard about what these men could have been after."

He made his way through the house and was reaching for the handle of the front door when Abigail said, "Sheriff?"

Caleb turned around to see her standing in the front room. "Yes, ma'am?"

"I've heard of a man living back along that creek. I remember the preacher saying he'd tried visiting before, but the man had sent him away without letting him in. And I think the Walkers have mentioned a strange man back there. They live out that way. It's pretty secluded, but you know Ruth Walker, she likes knowing what's going on. But I've never heard of a girl back there, not from Ruth or the preacher or anyone. And this man, George, no one really knows him." Creased worry lines formed on Abigail's face.

Caleb wished he could ease her mind somehow. "I've never heard of anyone living on Hollow Creek. I try to know everyone, but I've never heard a single mention of George. I'll head out there as soon as I can. I don't know how the pieces will come together, but they always do. Let me know if she tells you anything else."

"I will." Abigail took a few steps toward Em's room before turning back. "I hardly know the girl. It's strange, but already I care for her. Please stop these men. I want Em to be safe. I know she's frightened. She hasn't said she is, but I can sense an uneasiness. You have to stop these men. She deserves a chance." With that she stepped back into the sickroom.

Caleb put his hat on and left. James, the town's land agent, would have a detailed map of the area and any land deeds. With his long arms swinging at his sides, Caleb made his way toward the land office, his mind working like the gears in a clock. Who was George and what kind of arrangement did the girl have with him? The few ideas he conjured up sickened him. He hoped for a simple, untainted explanation.

Em was plain looking, with her stringy, straw-colored hair, freckled nose, and thin frame—no denying that. But she was quick and alert. The details she'd provided told him she had a keen mind. *What's her story? Who would shoot a girl like that? What reason could they have?* Lost in thought, he was startled to hear his own name.

"Sheriff Reynolds. Pleasure running into you." Eliza Howell approached from the side. He stopped. Skirts swaying, she moved closer until she stood very near, smiling up at him through long lashes. He found himself staring at her perfectly rosy cheeks. He couldn't help admiring her curled blond hair with just a hint of red. The land office did not seem so urgent now.

Caleb stepped out of the way as several men passed by. He watched as the men's eyes drifted to Eliza and lingered on her. Everything about Eliza turned heads, including his.

"Miss Eliza. What has you out and about in Azure Springs?" Caleb asked the local beauty.

"I walked in to meet Olivia. She wanted to visit Miss Caroline because she was expecting a new order of lace today. Olivia's still looking. I think she might stay all day trying to decide which she likes best. I saw you passing by and thought a quick hello would break up the monotony of my day. Besides, Miss Caroline has already talked my ear off long enough about Mr. Norbert. Poor old maid, someday she'll realize no one is interested in a spinster." Eliza reached up and brushed at the shoulder of his jacket. "Seems you picked up some dust from these dry roads."

He offered his arm and walked her along the street toward the dress shop. "I'm glad you stopped me," he said. "I was just over at your place. I met Em. It's a puzzling case." He felt the pull of his conscience at the mention of Em. "I won't be able to visit long. I need to do some digging around and see what I can learn about her."

"That horrible, dirty girl is in my bed and I'm upstairs with Mae and Millicent. Have you ever seen a dirtier creature in all your life? It's rather disgusting." She scrunched up her nose. "I'll have to boil the entire bed to get the smell out. Even then I'm afraid I'll catch something she left in it. Let's talk of other things. I'm so tired of everyone talking about Em and worrying over her."

Caleb stared a moment, surprised such ugly words could come from someone so beautiful. Odds were she hadn't meant to sound so harsh.

"She was a sight. I don't think she's had enough to eat in a long time. Gets me wondering what kind of life she was leading." Drawn back into his reverie, he wiped his brow absently and looked off into the distance. "Whatever her story is, it's my duty to help her. If I don't, those men could hurt others. You, even."

"We all rest easier knowing you're the sheriff. Always our valiant man in arms." Eliza's voice was playful, but he liked the image she painted of him. He'd been too young to fight in the war. Sheriff was the closest he could come to being a hero.

"I know you'll take care of us all." She squeezed his arm a little tighter.

Olivia stepped out of the shop just as they approached. Olivia Bingham was eighteen, a year younger than Eliza. She was dark haired and fair skinned. The two were often together. Everywhere they went the pair drew attention. More men talked about these two than any other females in the county.

"So nice to see you, Sheriff," Olivia said when they approached. "About time you took Eliza for a stroll. I was beginning to think you'd never ask her. Don't stop on my account. I can turn right around and buy more lace. The shipment today is better than any other. I plan to have a new frock made just so I can trim it with ivory lace."

Caleb dragged his foot around in the dry dirt.

"A stroll would be pleasant. To be honest, it sounds much more appealing than the day I have waiting for me. I can't stay though. I have to see James over at the land office. But I'll look forward to seeing your new frock. I'll let you two go and pick out lace." Caleb reluctantly unwound Eliza's arm from his own, then turned and stepped away. "Good day, ladies."

Smiling back at the pair of them, he forced his legs into motion and headed south. A few steps later he allowed himself one more backward glance. The women had linked arms and were whispering together, smiles lighting their faces, both carefree and radiant. Spending the afternoon with them would have been enjoyable. But he had a job to fulfill, and now was as good a time as any. Being a sheriff was an honor and a responsibility he took seriously. Still, there were days he wanted to walk away from the demands. Lead the quiet life he'd once dreamed of.

Caleb put all thoughts of Eliza from his mind as he walked to the land office. Once there, he pushed open the heavy wooden door and looked around for James. Cigar smoke filled the air, mixing with the smell of musty paper, the same smell that always greeted Caleb when he stopped by. At the sound of the door, James stood, put his half-smoked cigar down, and walked over.

"Sheriff Reynolds, what brings you here?" James's voice was big and hoarse, as always, and he sounded as if he had something trapped in his throat. "Can I get you something?"

"I need you to help me dig up a claim. I want to see who owns a stretch of land." Caleb fumbled through papers in the top drawer of an old desk. He pulled out several maps before finding the one he was looking for.

"Hollow Creek area?" James asked after giving the map only a glance.

Caleb nodded but didn't look up. At last he pointed to the section he was sure was George's land. "This bit here. I don't know how big the claim is, but this is it. Can you tell me who owns it?"

"It'll take me some time. I don't recall anyone buying up any land there for years, but I can find out for you. I've got the records around here somewhere. When do you need them by?" James was already shuffling through papers, his head bent low, eyes racing across faded lines of scrawled handwriting.

Caleb wondered how he knew where anything was. There seemed to be no system, no organization. "The quicker the better. I'm going to ride out there as soon as I can. I'd go today if I could, but it's too late. Tomorrow I have to take the Strafford boy in to the county judge. There and back will take me the whole day. I'd have someone else take him, but there's no one."

Caleb scratched at his collar. "I'll probably

head out the next day before dawn. Do you think you could have it for me by then?" He knew James would find it by then, probably much sooner. Whenever he asked a favor of him, he managed to find a way to help.

"I'll have it before you head out. Come by tomorrow when you get back in town." James bent over and fought the frog that seemed to live in his throat. When it was finally suppressed, he asked, "Is this about that girl? The one they brought in half dead a couple days back?"

"Yeah. Not sure what the story is yet, but it might end up being a big one." Caleb walked back toward the door. "Thank you, James. I'll come by tomorrow evening and see what you've found."

Caleb opened the door and stepped outside, away from the stench of the stale cigar smoke. He felt grateful for his position and his shiny star. People were eager to help, and depending on how the next couple of days went, he might need that help. Already his gut was telling him this was no usual crime.

Two

E m, you look so improved. You have some color in your cheeks again. I've been meaning to stop in and visit with you, but I didn't want to disturb you." Eliza seated herself next to Em's bed. "Are you feeling well enough to move upstairs? There is a lovely room up there. It would be perfect for you." She spoke quickly. "You'll just love it, I know you will. Mae and Millicent are so sweet. They would just be delighted with your company." Her eyes darted toward the door. The two were alone for the first time, at least that Em had been conscious for.

Studying Eliza, Em wondered if the two would become friends. Could they become friends? It seemed unlikely. Girls like Eliza had never cared much for Em. But what did she know? She had little experience with peers. "Is this your room? I didn't realize—"

"It is, and I haven't minded you being here. Honest, I haven't. But the bed upstairs is terribly uncomfortable on my back. It really would be much better for me if I could have my own bed again. When you're ready, of course." Eliza

28

smiled prettily at her, her right hand rubbing her back.

Em doubted Eliza's back could hurt nearly as badly as the tender gunshot wound she was struggling to recover from, but living off charity kept her from saying so. "I'll gladly sleep upstairs. I think I could manage the stairs even now. I feel up to it."

"Oh, thank you. You're a gem." Eliza squeezed her arm. "I'm certain you'll like it. The girls are so energetic. They'll be great company. When my mother returns, be sure to tell her that you *really* want to be up there."

Em fought the chuckle that tried to escape. "I'll let her know that I'll enjoy the girls' company," she said. She had shared a room with a little girl before—with Lucy. The thought of that sweet girl brought a new ache, different from the gunshot wound but just as real and just as tender.

That afternoon when Abigail came to Em's room to sit with her, one of the little girls peeked her head into the room and waved. Em waved back, motioning for her to come in. The little girl tiptoed into the room.

"Mae, you can't come in. You know Em must rest," Abigail said from her seat beside the bed.

Mae took a swift step toward the door.

Em jumped to her rescue. "If it's all right with you," she said, addressing Abigail, "I'd enjoy her company."

Abigail looked at the girl and then back at Em. "If you're certain."

"I am." As soon as the words were out, Abigail gave a nod in Mae's direction. The child looked more carefree now as she approached. Her brown curls bounced with each step. Mae put a hand on top of Em's and smiled.

"I'm Mae," she said.

"Hello, Mae. Thank you for visiting me. It's been much too quiet for me in here." Returning her gaze to Abigail, she said, "In fact, I was hoping once I was cleaned up I could move out of this room and bunk somewhere else. I feel awful having this big room all to myself. Perhaps I could move in with the girls. If that's all right with you."

"Did Eliza put you up to this? Of course she did, that girl." Abigail pursed her lips. "You don't have to move though. This room is so quiet and there are no stairs."

"I'd love to be with the girls. It's been far too long since I've spent time with little ones. I'd enjoy it very much. In fact, I think I *would* be happier there."

"Eliza is used to having her own space, so she's not much fun for the girls. If you think you would be happy there, then I'll ready the room for you. But only if you're certain." Em bobbed her head, prompting Abigail to continue. "The stairs are not steep, but you must promise to have assistance. I would feel just terrible if you took a fall." She rose from her seat. "First, I'll go and heat water for a bath. I think a good scrub in the tub will be excellent medicine. I dare say you don't need any—you look better each time I enter this room. But a bath is soothing, and according to the doctor it couldn't hurt as long as we are mindful of your injury."

A tingling sensation began near Em's eyes. Rubbing at them with the back of her hands, she tried to fight off the feeling. But tears of joy threatened to creep from their edges. She'd not taken a bath, with warm water, since—she couldn't remember when. George didn't have a tub. A sponge bath or dip in the cold creek were her choices. No matter how nice it sounded, it wasn't worth crying over, so she held the tears back. Seven years ago she had cried her last tears. Seven years. Seven long years. There would be no crying today.

Instead, she turned toward little Mae. "Miss Mae, it seems you and I are going to be bunking together."

"Did you share at the last place you lived?"

"I did, but I shared a barn with a few smelly animals! Sharing a room with you and Millicent will be much more fun."

"Maybe the barn was better. I bet sleeping with animals would be fun. I love our horse, Nelly. I'll have to ask Papa if I can spend a night near her."

Mae's eyes were large and spirited. "Besides, sometimes Millicent talks when she's supposed to be sleeping. And once, not long ago, she had a dream she was using the privy and we had to air out our mattress the next morning. But that won't be so bad for you, since you'll have a bed to yourself." Mae's voice was clear and easy to understand. She had the slightest touch of a lisp, just enough to remind those around her that she was still a child.

"Sounds like your room is full of adventure. It's a bit too quiet in this room for me. I think I shall prefer the upstairs bedroom."

"I'm going to go tell Milly that you and Eliza are switching spots. She'll be so glad. I know she will. Eliza isn't any fun. She just tells us to be quiet and not touch her things. You'll be much nicer, I can tell." With that she pranced out of the room.

The warm, fragrant water was just as nice as Em had anticipated. Abigail let her soak and encouraged her to stay in as long as she liked. Twice Abigail brought buckets of warm water and added them to the tub. The soap smelled sweet, like flowers and well-dressed women. Very unlike the harsh lye soap she'd used before, though she'd been grateful for that since so often there'd been no soap at all.

She scrubbed and soaked and scrubbed some

more, always being mindful of her tender wound site. She washed around the bandage, doing her best to protect it and keep it clean. When she finally stood, she held her hands palms up. The skin resembled sunbaked fruit—wrinkled but fresh. Staring at her arms, she could see freckles she'd forgotten existed. With the dirt gone, they boldly proclaimed themselves once more. The water was murky and a film of oil and grime coated the edge of the tub. Yes, Abigail was right—she had needed a good soak. It was astonishing how dirty she'd become. Never would she let herself get so filthy again, not if there was any other way.

Abigail had left a clean nightgown, undergarments, a fresh bandage, and a comb for her hair on a chair near the tub. Em stood looking at the bounty. Then reverently she ran her hand across the simple gown. There was no lace, no ribbons. Nothing but soft, clean fabric. She gathered it in her hands and brought it to her cheek. The smell of sunshine wafted from it. Em felt her chest tighten as she realized it was not just a nightdress, it was kindness. She allowed herself to feel nothing but gratitude. Later she would worry about repaying the Howells and the tremendous debt she owed them. Tonight she simply felt their goodness and savored it.

She removed the old bandage and for a moment looked at the red stitched skin. It was healing quickly, and someday it would be nothing more than a scar. One that when she looked at it would cause her to remember the night she was finally set free.

Em pulled the clean cloth over her head, letting it fall against her newly scrubbed skin. In an uncharacteristic moment of pure delight, she twirled around, letting herself pretend this life of luxury was hers and not something temporary. She was filled with joy and an involuntary smile spread across her face. Twirling did not last long. She stopped when she felt light-headed, the sharp pain in her side a reminder that this was not truly her life—at least not permanently. Soon enough she'd be back to merely surviving, but for now, in this moment, the world felt brighter.

Sitting on a stool, she caught her breath and regained her composure. She ran her fingers through her hair, which quickly became ensnared in a mass of tangles. Then she began combing it, starting at the ends. She winced as she worked out the stubborn knots. At last the comb slid through her hair unimpeded. Her straw-colored locks were long and straight against her sides, reaching nearly to her waist. Mounted on the wall was a small mirror. Em stepped closer and watched her fingers work the long strands into a tight braid for the night.

Then her eyes met those of her reflection, and seeing herself in the glass flustered her. The quivering creek had been her only mirror for seven long years. The last time she'd looked in a real mirror she'd been a child; now she was a woman.

Stepping closer, she looked hard at her face, hoping to see a little of her mother staring back at her. Always she had wished when she grew up that she would look like her angel mother. Where was she? Not in her dull hair. Not in her freckles or harsh cheek bones. Em closed her eyes, longing to find the loving image in her mind and heart.

It had been so long, but she could picture her mother's arms around her, her face looking down at her own. Her pink lips smiling at her. Soft blue eyes—the color of a cloudless summer sky—met hers. Em touched her forehead where her mother had planted so many kisses. She allowed herself a long moment to savor the feeling of love that had once been a regular part of her life.

At last she opened her eyes. Again she saw her plain face looking back at her, and the warmth of the past drifted from her like vapor rising from a smoldering log. Turning away from the mirror, she finished quickly, wrapping a fresh bandage around her wound and readying herself to leave the room.

A rapid knock sounded at the door. "Em, are you clean? I heard you're going to move to our room," a little girl's voice called from outside the door.

"I'm clean. I'll be out in just a moment. Will you show me where your room is?"

"I will. I'll go get Mae—she'll want to come too." Millicent padded away from the door.

With her health rapidly improving, Em hoped she would get to know the two small girls better. Now that they'd be sharing a room, it could hardly be avoided.

Glancing back at the mirror one last time, she accepted the face that looked back at her. It wasn't a beautiful face and she couldn't change that. No prince would ever sweep her off her feet and ease her burdens. Hard work was how she'd always survived, and she'd go on that way. This was no time to lament a body she had no way of changing. She opened the door, determined to embrace whatever was ahead.

"You look different. You were so dirty before, and now you smell better too." The two girls were looking at her, studying the change. Both faces equally rosy and full of life. "Come with us!" the girl on the right said.

Em had not seen them together until now. They looked so much alike, both round-faced little cherubs.

"I'm so glad you've come to show me the way to your room. First, you must remind me which of you is Mae and which is Millicent."

"She is Mae and I'm Milly," said the girl on the left.

"Are you twins?"

"Yes," they said at the same time.

Em pretended to be thinking hard. "And let me guess, you are both . . . fourteen?"

The girls giggled infectious little-girl giggles. "We're seven. When we had our birthday, we had real ice cream with berries in it. It's a shame you weren't here. We'll have to ask Mother if we can have it again."

Seven. Just like Lucy. The last time Em had seen Lucy, she'd just had her seventh birthday. Em had wanted to do something special for her. She had wished she could bake her a sweet or buy her a doll. All little girls loved dolls and sweets. They were what she'd longed for herself at seven. But she had not been able to give those gifts to Lucy. Instead, she'd taken her for a very long walk to a small park, tucked among the tall buildings. They had spent the afternoon making little people out of sticks and leaves, laughing and smiling the hours away. Lucy had said it was the grandest day. On the walk back Em had picked her a daisy, tucked it behind the small girl's ear, and whispered, "Happy birthday, princess."

And now here she stood with two seven-year-olds. "My, my, seven years old. Well, that's halfway to fourteen. You'll be there before you know it. But don't grow too fast. Seven is a magical age."

Using wisdom beyond their years, they walked slowly, making it easy for the still-recovering Em to keep up. They went up the stairs, one on each side of her, and led her to the right. Em glanced to the left and saw another door.

The girls noticed her gaze. "That's the boys' room. We have a boy room and a girl room up here," Mae said.

"A boy room?" Em had not heard of or seen any boys.

"We had brothers. But they died from a fever." Millicent spoke matter-of-factly. "We were little, but we know Mama thought they were the best boys. She cries whenever she goes in there. Usually, she just leaves the door closed and tells us we are not to play or go inside. I don't know why she goes in at all. It just makes her sad."

Em wondered if Lucy was as resilient as these girls or if she had a locked-up wound like Abigail. A wound that ached whenever the door swung open but that begged to be opened when closed.

Mae led the way into the girls' room. It was a big room with two beds, each covered with a brightly colored patchwork quilt. One bed was bigger than the other and had two pillows on it. Em guessed that was Mae and Milly's bed.

A small window looking out toward the road

was cut into one wall and violet curtains hung along each side of it. A rocking horse and a little table with two little chairs sat in the corner. On the table were two little teacups and saucers. On each chair sat a rag doll—one with brown hair and one with yellow. Em's gaze lingered on the dolls. She was surprised to feel emotion rising to her eyes again. Fighting the traitorous tears, she smiled at the two little girls, grateful that they were enjoying being children. Feeling happy for them was better than feeling sorry for what could never be.

"We share this big bed and Ma put new linens on the other bed for you," Millicent said.

"That will be perfect. It's a beautiful room and that bed looks so soft. I'm sure I'll be happy in this room." Em wished she could fall into the inviting bed right then. She was so tired. "Thank you for letting me stay here."

"Ma says you don't have to go to bed when we do. But if you want to, you can," Mae said.

"Hmmm. What would you think about me coming up here when you go to sleep and telling you a story? Then I could go help your mama with anything she needs and come back quietly later."

"You know stories?" Millicent shrieked, her big brown eyes dancing.

"I know a few. I might know a story you've never heard before."

"Will you tell us one now?" Mae asked. The two of them looked at her with such pleading eyes that even if Em had wanted to, she would not have been able to say no. Em climbed onto the big bed and a girl curled up on both sides of her.

"Once I went for a long ride on a train. There were many, many children on the train. To entertain ourselves we told all the stories we could remember." Em forced a smile, even though the memory was dark. "When we were little, we'd all been tucked into bed by our own mamas. Each night we'd listened to different tales. So when we all got together, we sat around on the bumpy train and shared the stories we'd learned."

"You rode a train with all your friends? I've longed to ride a train. Tell us what it's like. Was it fast? Was it fancy?" Millicent asked.

"I thought you wished for a story?" Em said, hoping to avoid sharing the details of that fateful train ride.

"I suppose we did. But you must tell us all about trains another day. You're so lucky to have done something exciting," Millicent said. "We never do anything exciting."

"Hush, Milly. I want to hear her story," Mae said.

"Do you want one about a princess? I knew a little girl once who loved stories about princesses."

"Yes!" the children said together.

"Very well. I remember a story about a prince in need of a princess to marry. He had trouble finding a *real* princess. He decided he must find a way to test the women to see if they were indeed princesses . . ." Em told the story of the princess and the pea. The two girls listened, hanging on every word. She finished by saying, "When the girl woke covered in bruises from the one tiny pea, they knew she must be a real princess. The prince and his princess soon married and lived happily ever after."

When the tale was complete, the two girls sighed.

Mae, who was curled against Em's right side, said, "That was a very good story. I hope to meet a prince someday, a real prince that lives in Azure Springs. I don't want to move too far from Mama and Papa, but I do want to marry a prince."

Millicent spoke then. "Do you think Eliza is a princess? She always complained about that bed."

The girls started giggling.

"Enough stories." All three looked up to see Abigail smiling from the doorway. "It's time to tuck you girls into bed."

Then, turning to Em, she said, "You look refreshed."

"The bath was wonderful. Thank you for your kindness."

"And thank you for telling these two girls a story. It's been years since I heard the tale of the princess and the pea."

Em listened as the two girls said their prayers. They both thanked the Lord for Em and for her story. Em prayed a special prayer that night for her new little friends. She prayed their dreams of princes would come true, or at least be broken softly. Earnestly, she prayed that Lucy had been tucked into a warm bed and told stories. That she'd been loved.

Three

For at least eight miles Caleb had been riding along Hollow Creek. According to the deed James had given him, the house should be right around here. Trees, tall grasses, and a rushing creek caught his eye, but there was no sign of human life.

Normally the beautiful country full of rolling hills, tree-lined creek bottoms, and swaying grasses would be a welcome change from town life. Today was different. He felt little pleasure in his ride and struggled to see beauty in the surroundings. Even the warm sun on his back did little to soothe his soul. Knowing a dead man who needed burial days ago awaited him left little room for tranquility. He felt only anxiety about what he would find—if he could ever find the home. It didn't help that yesterday he'd ridden from dawn until dusk taking a rowdy teenager to the county courthouse. And here he was back in the saddle again.

George Oliver, the deed said, paid in full eight years ago. But where was the house? Em said she'd lived there too. There ought to be signs of life by now. Frustrated, he urged Amos on.

Caleb reasoned with himself as he rode, perplexed by the mystery of it all. If George had been living there for eight years, Em couldn't be his wife, not unless he'd married her later. She said she had worked for him but had received no wages. How did the two end up together? Caleb loved and hated mysteries. Loved solving them, hated being stumped by them.

Trodden grass caught his eye. Looking closer, he knew he'd arrived—a well-worn path led from the creek toward the clearing. Slowing Amos, he turned cautiously up the narrow trail. His heart beat wildly inside his chest, and he could hear it thudding, pulsing through him. He had to remind himself that despite its rhythmic thumping, he alone could hear it.

After jumping off Amos, he walked the path. He took each step slowly, easing his foot down as gently as possible. Looking down at his feet to check his footing, he saw stains upon the grass. Blood.

Up ahead he caught sight of a charred dugout. Early settlers lived in dugouts, usually only for a season until they could get a house built but sometimes longer. He hadn't seen too many of them around anymore. The few he'd seen were not used as homes. A barn or a chicken coop perhaps, but no one he knew lived in a dugout.

Off to the side of the primitive home stood a

small, dilapidated barn. It leaned heavily to one side like an old man bent from age. A sudden gust of wind would surely knock the bedraggled building off its feet. He decided to check it out first. With his rifle tight against his shoulder, he stepped inside only to be greeted by the vile smell of rotting animal dung and something dead. Looking behind a half wall, he saw the remains of a small calf. Caleb stepped back quickly at the site of vermin crawling across the corpse.

Covering his face, he took a few gulps of air and then looked over the rest of the building. There were no signs of any other animals. Nothing remarkable. Tools were few, feed was scarce, and the walls were so full of gaping holes he doubted the structure had provided any real shelter to the animals it had housed.

He left the barn and headed for the dugout. It was collapsing on itself. Blackened earth lay in mounds all around it. The air carried the smell of burned wood—the pathetic dugout had been the victim of a fire.

Caleb approached cautiously, prepared to meet anyone who lurked about. He entered the dugout and no villains pounced on him, but the darkness did assault him. He waited while his eyes adjusted, giving them time to find what light they could. The single room had only one small window. Even after several minutes, his eyes still had trouble determining what the room held.

Using his hands to aid his eyes, he felt around the tiny space. A couple steps in and he was already touching the back wall of the small room.

Remnants of furniture were all the fire had left. There had been a table and at least a few dishes, which lay broken on the floor next to the remaining table leg. On the other side of the room he made out what was left of a fire pit cut into the earth.

Caleb kicked his booted foot hard into the wall. It wasn't right—the pieces were supposed to come together. He was supposed to be able to make sense of it all, but there were no real clues. There was blood on the grass, more and more of it as he walked and explored. A tragedy had happened here. The blood and charred wood testified of it.

Caleb stepped away from the dugout, grateful for the light from the afternoon sun, but even it could not shake the darkness he felt inside. He began walking the property, attempting to regain control of his temper. Convinced he was alone, he stormed about upright and clumsily.

This was his job, and he'd always done it well. Calming his racing heart, he slowed down and let his eyes wander the property looking for anything he'd missed.

A bird caught his eye. It flew through the trees, black wings spread wide. Gliding among the branches. Graceful. Serene. Caleb's eyes followed the bird until he caught sight of a far-less-enchanting scene. A crawling sensation worked up his spine, followed by an involuntary shiver.

George.

At least he suspected it was George. High in an old oak tree, a blood-stained man was hanging, swaying slightly in the breeze. Bile rose in Caleb's throat, threatening to escape. He spit the putrid taste from his mouth and instructed himself to stay in control.

Everyone dies, he reminded himself. He'd seen death before. He didn't like it, but he'd seen it and he'd taken care of it. Today would be no different.

Up the tree he crawled, armed with a knife to cut the man down and a pistol in case whoever had the audacity to do this returned. Getting to George was no easy task—the tree branches weaved around one another, braided in the most inconvenient way. Whoever had taken the time to do this vile act was trying to accomplish something or send a powerful message. Or was it a threat? Caleb didn't know what the men were *trying* to say, but what he read was, *This isn't over.*

Once he got George cut down from the tree, Caleb went to work digging a grave. He picked a spot close by but not in the way of the paths. Minutes became hours before he had a hole large and deep enough to house the man's body.

Caleb's muscles were burning, sweat dripped from his forehead. The work of digging a grave was no easy task. He found a meager amount of humor picturing that scrawny girl digging. She'd thought she could do it. Maybe she could have, but he had trouble believing it.

Before throwing dirt on the body, he took a thorough look at it. No pleasure came from it—in fact, the sight of death always left him with a sinking feeling. But being able to tell Em what the man looked like would confirm that it was George. He had gray hair and green eyes. A thick scar ran under his jaw; it was old and had mended itself poorly. He looked to be in his fifties, maybe even sixties, and just like Em had said, multiple bullet wounds dotted his chest. In the man's pockets Caleb found nothing but a piece of tobacco. Unable to find anything else on the man, Caleb laid him to rest, covering him in both dirt and rocks to keep the animals away. Then he marked the grave so Em could return and mourn if she so desired. The burial had taken longer than Caleb had wanted, but it needed doing and he'd done it.

Down by the creek he bent low and splashed water on his face and hands. He scrubbed them hoping to wash away the scent of death. Then he turned back and looked at the house and the land. Whoever had killed George and shot Em might know she was still alive. This was all more serious than he'd thought—his town, his people could be in trouble.

He left the creek and walked back in the house hoping he'd missed a clue, but there was nothing. Not one blasted thing. He always found something, usually something everyone else had overlooked. "That sheriff can solve puzzles no one else can," the men around town would say. The pieces just had a way of coming together for him. Today was different. Lots of pieces, but no way to attach them. There had to be something. Something he'd missed.

Back in the barn, he spotted a small loft and crawled up into it. Mindful of its bent frame, he proceeded slowly. A well-worn blanket and folded nightshirt sat on the dusty floor. He grabbed the nightshirt, stuffing it into his pack. Two people had lived on this piece of land for years, so there had to be more.

A bit of straw lay in a mound near the loft's wall. Brushing at the straw, he searched through it and discovered a pile of sticks. He picked them up and realized they *were* sticks, but they were no ordinary ones. Little twigs wound around one another in the shape of little people. He had found so little worth taking back and had room for these, so he put them in his pack with the dirty nightshirt. Hoping to find something else, some clue in the hay, he moved it all around, sifting through it bit by bit, but there was nothing else.

Unsure where to look or what he was looking for, Caleb began walking the property for the spot Em had mentioned—the place George would go when he returned from his trips. He searched for hours but found only trees and grass, rocks and shrubs. The sun was creeping low on the horizon and he knew he had to either camp for the night or head back. Reluctantly, he mounted Amos. A fresh grave, a tattered nightshirt, and a bundle of sticks. That was all he had to show for his day.

"Let's go, Amos," he said as he coaxed the horse away from the property.

"Uh . . . hello . . . Eliza," Caleb said. "I'm sorry to come by so late. I didn't mean to disturb you. I . . . I've come to see Em. Is she around?" Caleb leaned against the door frame, watching the light from the oil lamp dance across Eliza's face.

"Of course she is. She doesn't leave the house. But why must you speak to *her* at this hour?" Eliza drew her lips into a tight line. "Nothing has changed since you saw her last except that she has finally left her sickbed and taken a bath."

"I didn't come to check on her health. I've been out to her place and need to ask her some questions. It's important, too important to wait."

Footsteps sounded from inside the house, growing louder as someone approached the open door.

"Eliza! I told you not to open the door for any-

50

one. Not while Em is here and the town's not safe." Abigail gave a gentle rebuke.

"Oh, Mama, I'm not a child. Besides, it's the sheriff. We've never been safer." Eliza's voice carried no hint of remorse.

Abigail shook her head but said no more against her daughter.

"Ma'am, I've come to see Em. I'm sorry to come at such a late hour." Caleb questioned his own impatience. Perhaps he should have waited until morning.

"You're always welcome regardless of the hour. We just want to be cautious. You must understand that," Abigail said from inside.

"Your mother's right," Caleb said to Eliza. "Until this is settled, you can't be too careful."

Eliza laughed. "I knew it was you or I never would have opened the door."

"Please, come in. I'll get Em for you." Abigail gestured inside.

Eliza reached for his arm and led him into the house. She continued holding his arm as he stood waiting for Em.

"Are you going to come to the social? I have a new dress I'm saving to wear. You really must see it," Eliza said.

"A new dress? Well, now, I wouldn't miss that. Better save me a dance or two so I can see how it looks spinning around the dance floor."

"I'll do my best, but in this dress I'm sure to be

noticed a little more than normal." Eliza batted her eyes at him. She knew how to get attention in any dress. "But if you ask real nice, I'll tell the other boys I've promised you a dance."

"I haven't been to a social yet where you haven't had a whole string of men waiting to lead you onto the dance floor. Lucky I'm seeing you now before I have to stand in line."

"They're all just the boys I grew up with. Dancing with you is much more exciting." She squeezed his arm. "You are always my favorite partner."

"My mama would be happy to hear it. She was always telling me that someday I'd be glad I knew how to dance. I'd be honored to dance with you at the coming social."

"I'll tell all the other boys you asked me before the dance even started. They will be green with envy. It'll be such fun. Find me early though. I can't promise to save you every dance, and I hate to be stuck sitting out because you haven't found me."

He smiled down at her. "I'll find you first thing." He certainly hadn't come to the house expecting this piece of luck. "I'll be counting down the days."

Abigail returned, her eyes drifting to the arm Eliza still had linked through the sheriff's. "Eliza, why haven't you asked our guest to sit?"

"Sorry, Mama. We just got carried away talking

about the coming social. Do sit down, Sheriff."

"Em has been retiring early. Her strength is slowly coming back. I woke her and she'll be down in just a moment." Abigail smoothed her skirt as she sat.

"I'm sorry you had to wake her. I didn't mean to cause a problem." He shifted from side to side. "Where's Abraham?"

"He received a new shipment late in the afternoon and wanted to have the shelves stocked before he opens in the morning. It was a big order. A bit of everything. He is always worried someone will need something and he won't have it. I expect him to be along shortly."

"He works too hard. I hope he at least knows we are all grateful that he does carry a bit of everything." Caleb fiddled with the band on his hat. "If he's not back when I finish here, I'll stop off at the store and see if I can give him a hand."

"That's very kind of you. He so often does more heavy lifting than he should." A fog of sadness passed across the good woman's face. "If only the boys were here to help."

A door creaked above them. Abigail rose. "I'll help her down the stairs. I worry so about her falling and reinjuring herself. The dear girl is so frail. It just breaks my heart thinking of the life she must have led."

Abigail looked worn and tired. Caleb stood quickly. "Allow me," he said and then proceeded to the stairs without waiting for a response.

Em stood at the top of the stairs about to descend.

"Hold up, Em. I'm here to give you a hand. Hasn't even been a week yet since you were hurt." In three giant steps Caleb was up the stairs and at her side. Holding her arm, he could think nothing but how fragile it was—just skin and bones, like a delicate bird. His hands were so large, so strong. He'd dug a grave and felt little effect from it. How different he was from her. Ever so carefully, he held her arm as he guided her down the stairs.

"Thank you, Sheriff. I'm certain I could manage fine, but Abigail worries, and I hate to cause her any grief. She's been so kind to me." Her arms remained thin and weak, but her voice was stronger than before.

At the bottom of the stairs Em turned to face him. She was wearing a dress he presumed was one of Eliza's. Deep blue with little white flowers. The fabric hung on her. She lacked the comely curves of Eliza. Her hair was braided and looked different, not as dull as before. He could tell from its gleam that she had washed the layers of dirt from it. Good feminine soap had left a trace of its flowery scent with her. Still the same girl but improved.

"I was out at your place today. I know it's late, but I think we should talk."

"All right. I'll tell you what I can, but like I said before, there isn't much to tell."

Abigail and Eliza approached.

"Would you two like to sit at the dining table? Come this way. It'll be quieter in there, and I'll bring another lamp. We'll let you two talk. Eliza can help me in the other room with my yarn."

Once seated, Caleb was ready for some answers. It wasn't every day that he found an old man hanging in a tree. The horror of finding him there came back to him. The revulsion he'd felt only spurred his need for answers.

"Like I said, I was out at your place. Took me the whole morning to find it. I did though. The dugout was just a charcoaled ruin. I searched inside and found nothing but an old table leg and a few bits of broken dishes," he said, his voice rising. "You lived there. You must know something about all of this." He brought his fist down hard on the table. "They burned the place and you act like you know nothing. You've got to know something about all this."

Putting a finger to her lips, Em spoke. "You'll wake the girls if you keep talking like that. You're right. I did live there. I lived there for nearly seven years. I slept in the barn, fixed the man meals from whatever food I could find or that he brought in when he was around. We rarely spoke, and when we did it was just about the laundry or the animals. I know nothing."

Em pulled her long braid over her shoulder and twirled the end back and forth in her hand. "I've no reason to keep anything from you."

"How did you end up there? Why of all places would you live *there?* In a barn? Was he a relative?"

Why wouldn't she tell him more?

"What does that have to do with any of this?" Em snapped back at him.

"If I don't know the whole story, how am I supposed to figure this mess out?" He set his hat on the table. "Look, it's my job to keep this town safe. A person's dead. I found him swinging in a tree. You told me yourself that you were shot and left for dead. Everyone's at risk until I take care of this. So start thinking." He wrung his hands together.

"Swinging in a tree?" She put a hand over her mouth. "He was lying facedown when I left. They were back. They know . . . they know I'm gone."

"Who are *they?* Why do they care about an old man and . . . and . . ."

"Why would they care about me?" She pressed a hand to her chest. "Why would they care about a girl who's not much to look at? If I were a beauty it might make more sense. Is that it? Am I right?"

"Yes—no. Yes, I suppose. No. That's not what I mean." Caleb couldn't meet her eyes. Frustration filled him. This conversation was not going how he needed it to. An entire day spent on this and he'd gotten nowhere and now this. It was vexing.

Em sucked her lip in and sat very still. He watched her, surprised by the look on her face. No longer expressionless, her face was marred in pain. He had never hurt anyone. Sure, he'd raised his voice from time to time, but she didn't need to fear him. Then he heard his words over in his head. He'd said yes when he should have disagreed. But she'd been the one to label herself. He pressed his hands against his throbbing temple. "I didn't mean what I said. It's just— you don't look like you've eaten enough in some time. That's all."

He stood up, pushed his hands into his pockets, and paced the room. "I can go and we'll talk about this another time. It's been a long day and we aren't getting anywhere right now."

How could I be so rude? he lamented as he continued to pace.

"No, sit," she said quietly without meeting his gaze. "Just sit down and I'll try to help." She paused a moment before continuing, her voice quieter. "I am plain. I got a good look at myself in the mirror the other day. Even with a few square meals in me, I'm still plain. I don't expect I'll ever be anything more. But I'm certain that's not what you came to talk about."

Caleb wished he could put the words back into his mouth. He wished he hadn't agreed with her even if there was a measure of truth to it all.

He cleared his throat. There was no going back in time, so he pressed on. "When I got to your place, the dugout was burned and George was swinging. He had been shot just like you said. I cut him down and buried him. I marked the grave so you'll be able to find it. It's covered good, so there's no need to worry about animals. I'm pretty sure it was George, but just to be sure, did George have green eyes and a scar under his jaw?" He ran a hand along his own square jaw.

"That's him. I often wondered where he earned that mark."

"You won't be asking him now. The man's dead and buried. My guess is there are quite a few questions that would have been easier to ask him when he was standing on his own two feet."

"Only I didn't know to ask them then. Thank you for burying him. It was the right thing to do and I am grateful. It wouldn't be fitting just leaving him."

"I can't say I enjoyed it, but it was my duty."

She looked up then and found his eyes. "Thank you."

"The barn was still standing. I found a few things in the loft." He reached in his pack and pulled out the nightshirt. She snatched it from him and tucked it on her lap under the table. Her downcast cheeks flushed a soft pink.

Then he pulled out the sticks and set them on the table.

Her pink cheeks turned crimson. She reached for one of the stick people, running her frail finger over the curve of the wood. He wanted her to look up. He hoped to be able to read something in her eyes. Moments passed, neither of them speaking.

At last he asked, "Was there anything else you were hoping to have? I looked but found nothing else."

"No. This is all."

Making sure his voice was gentle, reminding himself that this was not just a crime to her, it was personal, he said, "You say you were there seven years. Did you live in the barn the whole time? Even through the winter?" No one deserved such treatment.

"I did. It was not so unbearable when there were animals in there. The smell was bad, but they added some warmth."

"I imagine your time with the Howells has been a welcome change?" Caleb wanted more answers, but something inside him told him to tread softly.

"It has been indeed. I've spoken more in the last four days than in the last seven years combined. How could I not with Mae and Milly around? It's strange to think I spent so many years wondering when I'd be able to leave and where I would go, only to suddenly find myself here in this beautiful house with the kindest people." Em brightened as she spoke. The blue of her eyes matched the color of the azurite the town displayed so fondly in the civic building. "It's like a dream."

"I wish you could live the dream and not think of the past." He leaned toward her. "Tell me, though, when George was gone, where did he go?"

"Usually he said he was going to check his traps. He never came back with much. I'm not sure where he went." She shrugged. "I kept my distance and it worked out all right."

"Why didn't you leave? Why stay?" Caleb rested his elbows on the table.

"I did once, but I was so lost I ended up back where I had started. I didn't know my way around there at all. I had no map, no supplies, no money. I used to be able to navigate the big city, but put me in a grove of trees and they all look the same. George never knew I had tried to get away. He told me if I stayed until he died, he'd leave me his land and money. Although I doubt there is much money, considering how little we usually had to eat. I suppose I stayed because I didn't know how to leave. Besides, there are not many ways for a girl to get land and money. I passed the time dreaming and praying about a life away from there. I never thought it'd be a gunshot wound that would finally lead me away."

"I've never seen a gunshot wound as a blessing. In your case, though, perhaps it was." He smiled. "Did he bring friends home with him ever?"

"Not often. When he did, I stayed out of the way. I've seen what men can do when they're drunk or lonely. I stuck to the barn. I wish I could tell you more. Honest I do. But the truth is, I lived a lonely life these last seven years. The days were pretty much the same for me. I was just surviving until I could find Lu—whatever was next for me. Surviving, it's what I do."

"The Howells won't let you settle for just surviving. Better get used to the idea that you're living now."

He pushed himself away from the table and stood. Amos needed a bucket of oats and he still had to check in with the deputy. And before all that, he'd committed to helping Abraham unload his delivery.

"Has the doctor told you when you'll be up to traveling?"

"He said two weeks when he first came, but he's been pleased with my progress, so it could be sooner." Em stood.

"We need to get back out there and search the spot you say George would go to. There's got to be a clue out there somewhere." And maybe along the way she'd fill in the many blanks about her own story.

"I'll do all I can to help you. I don't wish any harm on anyone. The Howells have been so good to me. I'd never want anything to happen to them—not ever, but especially not because of me," she said, her eyes professing her sincerity.

"We'll get to the bottom of it. I'll watch out for you and for them." He picked up his hat. "You work on getting yourself well."

"I will."

They said their goodbyes. Then she silently headed for the stairs, insisting no one needed to assist her.

Caleb apologized again for the late hour and reached for the door only to have Eliza sneak in by his side. Having her so close, he felt less tired. Reluctant to leave but knowing he should, he said, "Miss Eliza, Amos needs me, but I'll be looking forward to that dance at the social."

Four

"D̲id you and Caleb make progress on the case?" Abigail asked after breakfast the next morning.

"We talked about it some. I wish I could help more—I feel so useless. I want it to be over for everyone's sake, but I don't know how to fix it." Em stopped stacking dirty dishes. "There were moments last night when Caleb seemed so upset. Angry that I couldn't help more. What kind of man is he?"

"A good man. Once when Abraham promised the farmers a shipment of wheat seed, it came three weeks late. It rolled into town days after the farmers should have started planting. For a week he stormed through the house." Abigail laughed a little. "The memory of it is so funny now, but back then I worried. I didn't realize what had come over him. I questioned so many truths I knew about him."

Em listened, unsure how the story related to Caleb's character.

"What I'm trying to say is that even though it wasn't right for Abraham to storm about, it didn't mean he was a bad man. It simply meant he was a man. A man who took his job very seriously. A man who has his own burdens and pain to carry. But Abraham is a good man, and Caleb is a good man too. He can be very serious, especially about this town and keeping it safe. Perhaps he wants to set this right so badly that he forgot himself. But you can trust him. He will help you and he won't hurt you. You don't have to be afraid of him."

"I've so little experience with men . . . with any of this."

Abigail took the dirty dishes from Em's hands and sank them into the water. "Don't worry. You'll settle down and life will work itself out. And when you feel overwhelmed by it all, come to me. I'll answer anything."

Accepting the invitation, Em asked, "Do you know where Beckford, Iowa, is?"

"I believe I've heard of it. I think it's on the east side of the state. Do you know someone there?"

"I did once. I've been meaning to get there so I can find her. I just haven't had any way of going." Em had never spoken so much to anyone of her dream of getting to Beckford.

Lucy was there, or at least she thought she was. The last time she'd seen her was on the train platform in Beckford. Since that day, there had been nowhere Em had wanted to be more than with her sister.

"We could write a letter, try to find your friend. If it's been a long time, it might be best to know whether she's still there before you go. When did you see her last?" Abigail dried her hands and motioned for Em to follow her from the kitchen.

"It's been seven years, ma'am."

"It's Abigail, remember?" Abigail brushed a piece of Em's hair from her face. The gesture was so tender it felt foreign to Em. She flinched but did not run. "Seven years is a long time."

Em nodded her head, but her resolve remained firm.

Abigail pulled a sheet of paper from the secretary desk and offered it to Em. "Write your letter and I'll see that it gets posted. We'll help you find her."

Em took the paper and held it between her fingers. Then she handed it back. "That's all right, Abigail. I think I'll just go and look for her. I don't have anything keeping me here. Beckford is as good a place for me to go as any." She continued to hold out the paper as it bent under its own weight. "Do you know how much train passage is?"

Abigail eyed her suspiciously before taking the paper. "I don't know how much a ticket is, but we could find out. Don't be rushing off too fast though. The doctor says you need to take it easy for some time. Plus, Mae and Milly will be heartbroken if you leave and they haven't heard all your stories." Then, placing a hand on Em's shoulder, she waited a moment before saying, "I know we don't know you well. But you're welcome to stay here as long as you like. We want you to stay."

Em's throat tightened. "I appreciate that. I may need to stay for some time. I have to earn money for the train passage, and I want to pay you back for your kindness. Once I have enough, I'll be on my way." Em did care for these people, more than she had imagined she would. Leaving was best, though, because already her debt to them would be impossible to repay in full.

The back door slammed shut and footsteps thudded down the hall. Mae and Millicent came bounding into the room.

"Mama, did you hear? There was a stagecoach robbery, just outside of our town. We were walking with Papa to the store when the news came. The sheriff is heading out. He's going to get the awful men and bring them in." Mae was talking fast, her cheeks flushed with excitement. "I can't wait to see him ride back with the men all tied up."

Pulling the two girls to her sides, Abigail said, "Oh dear, we don't need more trouble around here. You two stay in the house for now. I don't want you in the store or the yard until I know it's safe."

"Oh, Mama, what will we do in the house all

day? Let us go out. We want to see the sheriff when he brings the awful men in. They might have eye patches and peg legs. Please don't force us to stay in. If we stay in, we'll never know," Milly said, speaking almost faster than Em could keep up with.

"Yes, Mama, let us go and watch for the sheriff. We want to see him bring the wicked crooks in. But there won't be any peg legs or eye patches. That's what pirates look like, not bandits," Mae said, sounding proud that she knew the difference.

Abigail's face was marred with lines of worry and fear.

"It may not be as exciting in the house, but if you will stay in and keep me company, I'll tell you more of the stories I remember. I may even know a story about a bandit or a pirate." Em bent down in front of the girls. "Will you stay and listen to my stories while your mama makes sure it's safe?"

The two girls looked at each other, silently conversing as only twins do. At last two eager faces turned toward her. "Will you tell us the one about the princess and the toad again?" Mae asked.

"No, Mae. I want her to tell us a new one we've never heard before."

"But I love the one with the princess and the toad. Why do you always get to decide?" Mae's voice rose above Milly's as she crossed her plump little arms over her chest.

Em stood and put her hands on her hips, waiting for the two to stop. "If we are in the house all day, I'm certain we will have time for several stories. But I cannot begin if the two of you are quarrelling."

Abigail turned from the window where she'd stood watching the street. "Thank you, Em. Sometimes I don't know what to do with those two." Crouching down in front of the little girls, she said, "Girls, behave yourselves and be sure that you do not wear Miss Em out. Make it easy on her."

"Yes, Mama," the girls said together. Their argument over, they both smiled at their mother.

Abigail grabbed a few things and then headed for the door, destined for the store to talk to Abraham. "I'll be back soon. Thank you, Em, for watching the girls for me."

Milly and Mae ran to the window and watched as their mother crossed the street.

"Who would like to hear the story of the three dwarfs in the woods?" Em asked, trying to distract the girls.

"Does it have a princess in it?" Milly asked.

"I'll tell the story and you can find out! Come on, let's sit together."

Reluctantly, they followed, dragging their feet as they turned from the window. The three sat down together on the sofa. Em pulled them close and began telling them story after story, embellishing each one so they took even more time. During her fifth story, she was startled from the fantasy world of ogres and princes by an urgent banging at the back door.

"Run upstairs and don't come down until I tell you to," Em whispered. "Now!" Without an argument, they went.

Em grabbed a wooden walking stick from near the front door and carried it through the house to the back door, where the sound was coming from. Careful not to bump the furniture or step on a creaking board, she moved silently through the house. The knocking grew louder. Her heart seemed to be pulsing with the rhythm of the banging—her heartbeat echoing through her head and ears. Taking a deep breath, she pulled the curtain to the side just a little, all the while reassuring herself with the thought that bandits did not knock on doors. If they wanted to come in, they simply came. Still, she feared for the girls hiding upstairs.

Through the opening in the curtains she saw a flushed and sweaty Sheriff Reynolds standing at the door, his hand fisted and ready to pound once more. She quickly unlatched the door and swung it wide open for him. His hand stopped midknock. A look of relief washed across his face at the same time that her heart finally started to slow.

He skipped his usual greeting and good

manners and went right into questioning. "Where is everyone? Are they all right?"

"The girls are upstairs, Abigail is with Abraham at the store, and Eliza left this morning for Olivia's."

"No one was here? No one came to the house looking for you?" He wiped at his forehead with the back of his arm. "You're all safe?"

"We're safe. All of us. We've been alone all day." She leaned the stick against the wall. "No one can come here looking for me. There are little girls that live here. Those men, they'd hurt them. We can't let anyone hurt them."

"Today the stagecoach was robbed. I lost their trail, but I got close and caught sight of one of them. He had red hair and a missing front tooth. I'm sure he's the man from your place. There was something vile about him. Even from a distance I saw it." Caleb sat down heavily in a kitchen chair. He took his hat off his head and smacked it against his leg. "I lost them. I lost their trail."

Em felt at a loss. Unsure how to help, she stood and just stared at him, watching him struggle to control himself. He ran both hands through his hair and sighed deeply. When the ticking hand on the clock made a complete circle and the silence persisted, she moved from her spot and filled a glass with cool water and offered it to him. He took it and drank.

"We need to get out to your place." His voice

was steady now but still just as urgent. "We need to know how this all connects. You, George, whatever the men were looking for. I've searched and I have nothing to go on. We need to go back out there. Are you able to travel? Can you do it?"

Em had regained much of her strength in the six days since the bullet had grazed her side. Often, though, she struggled to catch her breath, and even a set of stairs could leave her winded. But if it would help to go, she would. "I'll be fine," she said. "I'm feeling much improved. I can't leave the girls now, though, and by the time I fetch Abigail it might be too late to start out."

"I know, I thought the same thing. I'll come by before first light tomorrow. That way we'll have the entire day to look for clues. Can you be ready then?" His eyes begged her to say yes. They pleaded with her. "Can you?"

"Of course. I want to help. I'll be ready. But the Howells, will they be safe?"

"I'm posting men throughout town tonight. I'm also spreading the word that you have moved and don't live here anymore. You can stay tonight, but then I'll find another place for you until this is taken care of." He stood, his long legs solid beneath him. He looked directly at her with intense brown eyes. "I'm sorry I stormed in here. I'm sorry about it all. There's nothing fair about this happening to you. I'll do my best to make it right, I can promise you that."

She felt the strangest sensation when he looked intently into her eyes. Something long dead seemed to come alive. Years of living to survive had taught her to never trust anyone. Now, looking into his eyes, she felt that he truly meant it—that he cared about her safety. She wanted to trust him, to believe his words.

"Thank you." She took his glass. "Thank you for helping me. I'll be ready in the morning when you come."

He left and Em returned to the girls. She put an arm around each one and reassured them. "Everything is all right. Sheriff Reynolds is taking care of everything. You needn't worry."

Mae reached both arms around Em and held her tight. "Is Sheriff Reynolds a prince?" she asked, her face tucked into Em's shoulder. "The Prince of Azure Springs?"

Five

Em stood on the front porch, quietly looking heavenward. The sun had yet to rise. The only light came from one lantern and the lustrous night lights that had not yet bowed to the morning sun. Sheriff Reynolds rode toward her, the sound of his horse drawing her eyes back down to the earth.

"You didn't need to stand outside waiting for me. I would've fetched you." He tapped the brim of his hat.

She hadn't thought of that. She'd only thought of being ready and being silent so she wouldn't wake her little roommates. "I didn't mind waiting. Where is your wagon?" As if on cue, the giant horse whinnied in her direction.

"We'll go much faster on Amos." He patted the horse's side. "Besides, a wagon could hardly get through on those overgrown roads. Come over here and meet him. He's nothing but a gentle giant. I'll help you up. I'll be careful of your side." He swung himself out of the saddle. "Tell me if I hurt you," he said as he slowly placed his hands on her waist. "Is that all right?"

She struggled to breathe. "Yes. My injury is lower than that." She took a step closer, preparing herself to be lifted onto the animal.

"Are you sure I'm not gonna hurt you?" he asked while standing with his hands on her waist.

"It hurts less all the time." Amos snorted then, making Em's already racing heart increase its pace. Uncomfortable with the idea of riding the horse and the lingering touch of his hands, she broke free, putting space between them.

"I *can't* ride a horse. I did once when I left George's place. But I was desperate and even then I fell off. I don't remember the falling part, only waking in the woods afterward. I just don't know much about horses. Well, I know that I am supposed to give them hay and rub them down, but I don't know how to ride," she said. "I can't ride on him. I just can't."

Caleb stepped forward and took her hand. "It'll be all right, Em. I'll be right behind you. You won't fall off this time. Who knows, you may even enjoy it. Riding out to your place was a mighty pretty ride. And old Amos is a good, tall horse—you just can't beat the view from his back." He reached for her again. She darted back a step. He waited.

There she stood in the shadows, unsure what to do next. The seconds ticked by. After a long moment of silence, he reached for her once more. "Trust me. I won't let anything happen to you."

Oh, how she wanted to. She wanted to have someone to trust again.

Do I dare?

Can I?

From inside the Howells' home she heard the now-familiar sound of Abigail starting a fire in the kitchen. Soon she would fix breakfast for her family. They'd eat together, amiably talking about the coming day, and a verse of Scripture would be read before they parted. For the Howells and their safety, she would do this hard thing.

She nodded as she stepped close to Caleb and the mighty animal. His hands came around her waist again. He lifted her up a bit, but she winced.

"I'm sorry." He set her back on her feet. "I don't want to hurt you."

He led her and Amos near the front steps. With Amos close to the steps and them on the top one, he was able to cradle her like a child and set her carefully into the saddle. She fumbled around on the horse trying to find a comfortable way to sit. As she adjusted her dress the best she could, she wondered how one was supposed to sit modestly while riding a horse. Still fixing her skirts, she felt Caleb swing up behind her in one graceful movement.

She thought she'd been uncomfortable on the horse before, but now, with him so close, she could hardly breathe. Never had she sat so close to a man, his body touching hers. He took the reins in one hand and put his free arm around her, steadying her and stealing her breath at the same time.

With a click of his tongue, Caleb commanded the beast forward. Out of town they went, away from Azure Springs, away from the Howells, away from the new life she'd found. Em soon forgot about the arm around her waist and the Prince of Azure Springs sitting behind her. She felt as though she were floating through magical woods. She could almost believe she'd stepped into one of her own stories as they soared across the dimly lit landscape. Wind brushed her cheek and worked its way through her hair. Fresh, cool morning air seeped into her lungs, and with it came life and energy. She sighed, overwhelmed by it all.

"Riding in the early morning is my favorite," Caleb said. "There's something about the world as it wakes and comes alive that I like. When I was small, my brothers and I often slept out under the stars. All the frightening night noises were worth it for this moment at dawn. Did you ever do that?"

"I was a child in a city that never sleeps. New York is rarely peaceful." She remembered the morning noises of New York. The milkman, the women yelling, the babies crying. "I don't remember ever enjoying a morning like this."

"Why did you leave the city?"

The fresh air, the dreamlike landscape, the peace all seemed to disappear as she thought back to those days of desperation that had pushed her from her city. "I left because there was no way for me to stay. Survival demanded it."

"Did you run away? Is that how you came to live with George? You can tell me." His voice coming from behind her sounded so kind. She wanted to tell him her sad tale, but something else pulled at her to keep it all locked up.

She squirmed in the saddle, feeling like a trapped animal. She thought of Caleb's outstretched hand and words of trust and forced herself to talk, to fight against the urge to keep her story locked away. "I came by train when I was twelve. Have you heard of orphan trains?"

"Orphan trains?" Without seeing him, she knew he was shaking his head. "No. Never."

"They're trains that come from the city. They're full of children who don't have homes. They stop in all the towns along the way. Most places the preacher in the town helps coordinate families for the children. At least that's how it's supposed to be. That's how I came to live with George." Em wished she could hide. Wished she could be off the back of the giant beast—alone, not here, with him. But she was not alone, and now she knew a slew of questions would follow and the past would be fresh again.

"They do that? They just put children on a train and let anyone take them?" Caleb asked.

Em grasped the saddle tightly, her knuckles turning white. "Not just anyone. At least it isn't supposed to be just anyone. Most places there are rules. I just happened to end up in a town with a preacher who didn't care. I don't even know the name of the town I was in. George was passing through when he picked me up. It was all a long time ago. It doesn't matter now."

Her shoulders shuddered as she remembered that fateful, wretched day. She'd stood with her number pinned to her dress just like she had at all the stops. Eager parents gathered around the children. Some scrutinizing from a distance. Others approaching. Some were even so bold as to look at the children's teeth as though they were animals at auction. One by one, occasionally two at a time, the children were ushered off the stage. A few customary papers were signed and the children disappeared with the adults who had claimed them.

There she stood. Her still-fresh burns ached in the heat of the sun and sweat ran down her face. She stood straight and tall, a smile plastered on her face just like the women of the Aid Society had prompted her to do. Promising them good homes if they would only comply. But her heart was not in it.

There had been so many stops and always she

had been ushered back onto the train. Only a few children were left and everyone was eager to be done with this trip west. She too was ready to be done, vowing never to set foot on a platform or train again. Hating the scrutiny. Hating the rejection. Hating the ache that lived inside of her.

The voices of the women from the Aid Society and the preacher found their way to her ears. "Can you not find homes for these last few?" one woman asked the preacher. "This trip has already taken so long. We need to get back to the city."

The preacher glanced Em's way, scanning her up and down, then said loud enough for her to hear, "I don't think I'll be able to find anyone willing to take her. I'll do what I can with the others." He left then and meandered through the crowd, stopping to talk to several couples in his path. Em watched as some nodded their heads yes, others no. Soon all the children who had stood beside her had found hands to hold. And there she stood. Alone. Unwanted.

Never in all Em's years of struggle had she felt so small. So unloved. So worthless. From the shadows of a tall maple stepped an older man. He was dirty, his clothes nearly threadbare. He didn't smile or meet her eyes. With a slow tread, he walked to the preacher. Neither man seemed to care if they were overheard.

"I'll take the girl," the man, George, said. The preacher said no to him, that the children were to go to families. George put up no fight but simply turned and started walking away.

Then Em heard the preacher say, "Well, all right, then. You look decent enough." And that was that. She walked away with the stranger. The exciting new life the Aid Society had promised turned out to be a pile of straw in a barn, working for a man who rarely talked and provided little by way of nourishment.

Why was it all coming back now? She knew she shouldn't talk about her past. It only made her remember, and remembering hurt. Caleb must have felt her tense with emotion. His arm tightened ever so slightly around her middle. Then, swiftly, he changed the subject. "I'm sure the Howells told you about the coming social. Everyone attends. Are you looking forward to it?"

"Eliza talks of it often. She has a new dress she plans to wear. But I have no notion of attending, nor any desire to."

"You might have to go. Not *have* to, I suppose, but you shouldn't be alone and *everyone* attends. I think you'll like it. There are a lot of good people in our town." Caleb stopped then and slid out of the saddle. He reached up and helped her down.

She watched silently as he took the horse to the creek and let the animal drink. When he looked back at her, she knew he was waiting for some sort of a reply.

"I've never been to a social. I don't plan to attend now. It might be better if you taught me to shoot and left me with a pistol. I think I would stand a better chance against the bandits than at a social."

"Teaching you to shoot isn't a half-bad idea. But leaving you isn't going to happen." He spoke firmly but kindly. Again she felt that he meant it and wondered what kind of a man Caleb Reynolds truly was. "Maybe I'll let you take a shot or two this afternoon after we find what we are looking for."

"I'd like that. I sure could've used a gun all those years at George's." Humor crept into her voice, but Caleb didn't seem to hear it.

He walked to her. His large hands grasped her shoulders and turned her toward him. Fire flashed in his eyes. "To protect yourself from him?"

"No. No, George was never mean. Neglectful and careless but not harsh. I stayed clear of him if he'd been drinking and kept in the barn whenever I could. I saw how men can treat women when I lived in the city. I knew how to make myself scarce. I never needed a gun with George. I would have hunted with one. As it was, I had to be resourceful and create my own means of catching dinner." Em smiled then. She stood a little straighter. She may not have eaten well, but she had managed to survive largely due to her own tactics.

Caleb laughed then. A big, body-shaking laugh. Rich and deep.

Slowly it stopped, and soon only his shoulders shuddered and his eyes gleamed. "I'm sorry, Em, but the image of tiny you out making traps and catching critters. I never would have thought an itty-bitty thing like you could manage. What did you do when you caught something?"

Being laughed at was not new to Em. Always it had cut at her, but this time it didn't. Rather than causing her to shrink away or lash out in anger, it made her smile. "When I caught something, I killed it, usually with sharpened sticks or rocks. It was hard at first, seeing as I never did anything like that before. It got easier with time, but I would not miss it if I never had to live like that again."

"You surprise me, Em. A regular frontiersman—sorry, woman—you are." He led Amos to a fallen tree and using it as a stepping stool, he lifted Em gently back into the saddle. Before urging Amos on, he said, "Know this, not all men treat women the way you saw in the city. There are good ones out there."

Em didn't reply. But she thought on his words.

Em's peculiar life tale kept him entertained as he led Amos onward. Never had he heard of orphan trains or pictured a girl out trapping critters with homemade traps. She was different, there was no denying it. He wanted to ask her more. He wanted to pry the secrets of her past out of her, make sense of it all, but he had felt her closing up on him and didn't want to lose what little trust he'd gained.

The ride itself had been swift and easy. Em weighed next to nothing and didn't seem to slow Amos at all. She was new in a saddle and hadn't learned to sway with the horse yet. But she was tough. Not once did she complain about the ride. A little practice and she would be a regular horsewoman.

Warm morning sun penetrated their backs as they approached the burnt dugout and barn that Em had called home for so many years. The thought of it made him angry. What kind of a preacher would let a little girl leave into the woods with a strange man and let her live so desperately for so long? Given the chance, he sure would like to meet that preacher—and George too. He'd give them a piece of his mind or a piece of his fist. But there'd be no vengeance. George's fate was in the Lord's hands.

Caleb hopped off the horse and then carefully helped Em down. Her eyes judiciously scanned the area. He saw no fear in her and heard no fear when she spoke. "Sheriff, do you think we're alone?"

He too assessed the area, ears and eyes focused as he searched the surroundings. "I think we are.

I don't see any signs of others. Here, take this." He handed her his pistol and took his rifle from its sleeve. "Just in case."

"I don't know how to shoot," she whispered as she took the weapon.

"Pull this back, aim for your target, and pull the trigger," he said as he pointed to the different parts of the gun. "I'll give you a better lesson later, but at least you'll stand a chance with that in your hands. Just don't point it at me—even if I do say something I shouldn't." Still bothered by his own heartlessness the other night, he longed to apologize. But he couldn't bear to bring it up. Em didn't seem to be holding a grudge—he was grateful for that olive branch. Grateful she was different from other girls, girls who took joy in making a man grovel.

The two walked the path toward the house and barn. Neither speaking. Their steps noiseless, stealthy.

"Stay here and I'll check the house and barn. If it's clear, we'll go in together," he said softly over his shoulder.

Em nodded and crouched behind an enormous tree, gun held ready. Then quickly he made his way back through the house and barn only to find that they looked the same as when he'd been there last. He saw no new prints on the ground, and even George's grave was untouched. "Come on out, Em. It's clear."

Her skirts blew in the breeze as she walked up the path toward him. "I passed George's grave. Thank you again for burying him."

He nodded in the direction of the grave. "You lead the way—let's see this place where George used to go."

Em stepped in front of him and led him down a crude path that ran along the edge of a small valley. Caleb held Amos's reins and together they made their way across George's land. On the far side, they turned and walked up the side of the bluff. She stopped and pointed to a tree. "See there, that's the remains of one of my traps."

A bit of rope was dangling over a tree branch, set with a stick and looped. He'd seen snares before and even used them as a boy. His pa had taught his brothers how to tie them and they'd taught him. He couldn't imagine figuring it out on his own. Fingering the frayed rope, he inspected it. "This is a fine snare. Even my brothers, who could be hard to please, would applaud you."

"It worked fairly well. Just for small animals. Rabbit mostly. I caught rats and squirrels in the barn." She pointed to a large flat rock. "I would also prop up a flat rock like that one with a stick and put a morsel of food under it. I only did it at night though. The rock usually killed them and I'd have to take care of them right away when I heard the rock fall."

Never had he been hungry enough to eat rat. In fact, he'd never truly gone hungry before. Sure, he'd run in after a long day in the sun and told his ma he was starving. But in truth he'd rarely ever missed a meal. Living off rats and squirrels and other vermin, no wonder this girl was as small as she was.

She stopped near the top of the bluff. "Just over the edge on the other side of the bluff is a cluster of trees. When George would come home, he always went there first. I saw him a few times but never investigated much. The only time George got real mad at me was when he saw me sitting in the bluff after he had visited the grove. I didn't mean anything by it. I didn't even know he would be home. He was madder than I ever saw him. Just cussing and pacing, kicking at the ground. I stayed pretty clear of this portion of land from then on. Whenever I felt myself getting just about curious enough to risk his anger and go exploring, I focused on dreams I still hoped to live for."

"See, you were more than surviving," Caleb said. "It's safe now. No angry George is going to stop us from exploring. Let's see what we can find."

The towering cottonwoods and oak trees created a canopy from the sun. It felt cooler, secretive among the trees. Caleb figured in this cluster were thirty to forty big trees, countless other smaller ones, and a slew of fallen dead ones or standing stumps. Not knowing what he was looking for, it could be a long day.

"Let's start at different ends and see if we can search faster that way. I sure wish we knew what we were looking for," he said as he walked to the far end of the grove.

Time rushed by as he became busy searching. He walked by each tree, looking it up and down. Normally a puzzle like this got him anxious. He became eager to solve it as quickly as possible, restless until he was at the bottom of it. Today he found himself whistling as he walked among the trees. It was perfect late-spring weather, not the blistering heat of summer or the chill of winter. Em was easy company. She hadn't complained once about the long ride or the seemingly impossible task they'd undertaken. She wasn't someone he'd ever bring home to his parents, but she was nice enough to be around.

When the sun's position declared it was past noonday, he walked over to her. She had not heard him approach, so he watched her for a moment. A large, leafy oak was before her. With eyes focused, she scanned it from near the base to all the way up its tall trunk. She walked around the tree, even stooping down and running her hand through the dirt by the roots. Standing back, she put her hands on her practically nonexistent hips and sighed.

He cleared his throat, drawing her attention to him. "Nothing on that one?"

"No, not a thing." She stood tall and brushed her hands on the sides of her dress. "I haven't seen anything unusual all morning. What if I was wrong?"

"Let's stop for an afternoon meal. Then we'll tackle the rest of this grove."

"I'll just keep looking. You go ahead and eat without me."

"You are as thin as a rail and now you are going to skip a meal? I won't have it. Come and eat." He headed toward the clearing he'd left Amos in. Looking back, he saw she hadn't followed. "Do I have to come and carry you over?" he shouted.

And then he saw it written on her face. Something about the way she bit her bottom lip and shifted her weight from side to side told him— she hadn't packed a meal. Of course she hadn't.

"I packed enough for two. I knew we would get hungry." He was lying. "Come eat so I have someone other than Amos for company."

Hesitantly, she made her way to him. They sat side by side on a log. He split what he'd brought and handed it to her.

"Thank you," she whispered and nibbled at the bread in her hand. Midbite, she stood. "We have to find it today. Whatever it is. If we don't, then they will. Even a poor tracker will know we were looking for something in this grove." She set her half-eaten bread and cheese down and headed back toward the trees, determination written across her half-starved face. "We have to find it."

Caleb flew to his feet. "Hold up! I'm not about to let your scrawny little hide back over there until you've eaten."

"I'm fine, really. I want to find what we're looking for. I want to stop all of this."

"Don't even think about it." He took her wrist in his hand, his fingers encircling it, and pulled gently, hoping his touch didn't scare her.

A smile worked its way to the corners of her mouth. "All right, I'll eat. A week ago I couldn't imagine ever being forced to eat." She stomped back to the log, sat down next to him, and shoved a few bites of bread and cheese into her mouth. Her manners were anything but ladylike as she took one enormous bite after another. With her mouth full, she started laughing at herself. Once she started laughing, she couldn't stop.

Crumbs flew through the air, landing unceremoniously on herself and on Caleb. The mess she was making only caused her to laugh more. He could tell she was trying to stop but couldn't. Making a show of it, he brushed crumbs off his own pant leg. He too started laughing, choking on his own food. There was something fun about spending a day with a girl who didn't know anything about being a lady.

Caleb handed her a handkerchief and she

attempted to clean her face. "See what you did to me, forcing too much in me? It all just came right back out."

"You're blaming me for this mess of crumbs?" He moved his gaze to the ground, eyeing the bits of bread.

"Of course I am. If not for you, I would be in the trees discovering whatever it was George was hiding." She stood, smoothing her skirt like a proper girl should. Then she turned on one heel, dipped a ridiculous curtsy, and marched back to the spot where she'd left off.

He stood up and walked to put the saddle-bags back on Amos, laughing under his breath the whole time. When was the last time he had laughed so hard? Years at least. He used to laugh with his brothers, but that was before. Before the war that changed everything. Since then he'd spent all his time focusing on being successful, making his parents proud.

He patted Amos on the back and then headed for the tree where he'd left off searching, but halfway there he changed course and headed toward Em. "Let's work together," he said. "We can make sure we don't overlook anything."

"Very well. As long as you don't insist I eat." Her azure eyes had a new twinkle in them. One he'd not seen when he had first met her.

"Amos is guarding the food. You're safe. He's easier to get along with than I am."

"In that case, I agree to letting you work by me." Pointing, she said, "I have already looked around all the trees to my left. Let's try over here."

Caleb followed her lead as they walked a bit to the right and began their inspections, talking easily as they went. "I had three brothers," Caleb said. "My oldest brother, Reggie, could climb a tree like this faster than anyone I ever saw. I was the little brother. He was so patient as he taught me important skills like tree climbing. He never made me feel bad when I went too high and didn't know how to get down. Were there trees to climb in the city?"

"No. I never climbed trees until I lived out here. I figured it out pretty well for having no teacher."

"Shall we race? Pretend we're children again? We could make it interesting. Whoever wins can ask the other three questions and they have to answer them honestly." He felt younger than his twenty-eight years today. Young enough to climb a towering oak.

"Three questions?"

"Yep. And you'll have to answer. Anyone loses a bet to me, I expect them to honor the terms." Caleb nudged her. "You brave enough?"

"You won't go telling Eliza, will you? I think we may become friends yet, but it's unlikely if she hears I've been off climbing trees and spitting my food all over you. Her manners are so refined. I feel like a heathen beside her. I believe she finds me rather shocking."

Picturing Eliza's reaction brought a new smile to his face. "Eliza won't hear a word about it. It'll be our secret."

"Which tree?" she asked.

He pointed to a tall oak with branches low enough for her to reach. Taking a step toward it, he was surprised to see the wisp of a girl running full speed for the tree. Her wiry limbs grabbed the lowest branch and she started up. Competition. He liked it. Real competition.

Grabbing a large branch, he heaved his body up. Being taller, he went for higher branches. But she was quick. Up they went, higher than he had been in a tree since he was a boy. He remembered all his brothers up in the trees, laughing and feeling like the kings of the world. The memories were so vivid today, the memories of the fun. Memories of something other than the pain of losing them.

She stopped moving up—the next branch was too far for her to reach. His extra height allowed him to scale higher than she could. From a perch above her, he waved down. "You ought to see the view from up here."

"I like it fine where I am. This was the branch we were racing to, was it not?" She sounded innocent enough, but he knew he had her beat.

"Funny, Em. Admit defeat. And I'll admit you climb better than most boys I know."

"I suppose that is a compliment?"

"Of course it is. It should be every girl's goal in life to climb better than the boys."

"Very well. I thank you for your fine compliment and I admit defeat." She straightened her leg, ready to move back down the branches.

Not wanting the fun to end, he called down to her. "Wait, Em, take in the view first. I'm sure we have time for that."

She resettled on her perch and gazed across the horizon. "It's beautiful. The rolling hills go on forever. I lived here so long and yet I never saw it as beautiful. It was a prison then. Today it feels so different."

It was beautiful, all of it. The sturdy trees, the rolling hills, the sunshine, the laughter.

Slowly, reluctantly, the two made their way back down to the ground. Resting his back against the tree, he caught his breath and tried to decide which question he would ask her first. He had so many.

"There, over there." Em's voice sounded from beside him as she raced to a tall stump. Meeting her there, he tried to see what she saw. Before him was a rotting stump much like the others in the grove. He'd guess this tree fell years and years ago. Weather, animals, and time had worn it down. A large crack ran down the side from the top of the stump to the grass at the base. Em slipped her hand into the stump and pulled out a leather bag. "There's more," she said as she stuck her hand back in and then pulled out a metal box.

"You found it! This has to be it." Caleb felt adrenaline pumping through him. "We did it."

It felt like a grand victory—a splendid finish to a sublime day—having the leather bag and metal box in hand. Before undoing the latch on the leather bag, he looked at Em. This was her victory too. "Perhaps you should be the one to open them," he said.

"You take it. I need to catch my breath," Em said, taking a step away. Next to a sturdy tree trunk, she slid to the ground and curled into a ball. Her skin pale, her breath uneven. How could he have challenged her to climb the tree? What a fool he'd been. He was supposed to protect others, not endanger them. A week is all it had been since she had been shot and here he was pushing her in the heat of the day.

He secured the unopened bag and box onto Amos and went for Em. Crouching in front of her, he took her in his arms. "We'll look inside later. Let's get you back. It's been too long a day already."

"I'll be fine," she said. "I just have to catch my breath. Don't worry about me." She spoke quietly, her brow furrowed and glistening with sweat.

"No, I'm taking you back." As he carried her in his arms to Amos, sadness overtook him. She weighed nothing. She had nothing. Why had no one looked after her before?

Her head fell against his chest and he pulled her closer. "I'll make this right for you. You won't ever have to live like that again. Never. I promise you." Her body lay limp in his arms. "I'll keep my word. You won't live like that again."

Em's only response was a soft, pitiful moan.

There was no way or time to be careful. He laid her weak body across Amos, then pulled himself up and did all he could to hold her in such a way as to ease her pain and not add to it. The trip back was not the carefree ride they'd shared in the early hours of dawn. Em slipped in and out of consciousness as they rode. Whenever her body went limp, he kicked Amos harder. Supporting her slight body most of the way home was not hard work, but it was a reminder of how careless he'd been. As the miles passed, his determination grew—she would get well.

Six

I'd thought of having her live in this room while we sorted this all out." Caleb stood just outside of the bedroom that was attached to the jailhouse. He looked toward the small room, his mind wandering to the woman who slept within. "I don't know what's best now. I thought she was doing better. I thought if I moved her here, then the Howells would be out of danger. But the whole ride here she barely spoke. She looked so pained."

"She needs another week at least with someone nearby at all times," Doc Jones said. "She's still recovering from the bullet wound. It's not a bad wound, but she did lose a lot of blood—she's lucky it hit her where it did. You or I would be better in no time, but throw in the fact that she hasn't had enough food in her for weeks, months, years even, and it could take her a while. I think the best place for her is with the Howells. If she falls unconscious, someone will be available to help her. I saw Abigail not long ago. She's fond of the girl. I don't think she minds having her. I'll stop by and check on her from time to time."

Caleb had no desire to injure Em further, so when the doctor gave orders that she stay and rest before returning to the Howells', he promised to obey.

Doc Jones picked up his leather bag and turned to go. "Even being weak as she is, she seemed happier today. Less afraid. Maybe being there with the Howells, having people care about her, is as good as any medicine I can give her."

It was true, she had seemed happy today. He couldn't help but picture her smile, bright and full of excitement, as she scaled tree branch after tree branch. For the first time since he'd met her, the tired eyes she arrived into town with looked alive.

Being back on the property, the place where she'd been little more than a slave, must have been difficult, but she'd been playful. He tried to imagine the other women he knew enduring what she had. No one he knew could bear her lot so well—certainly not Eliza or Olivia. They never would have been able to catch an animal, let alone skin and eat it. Em was decidedly different.

"I'm a survivor," she had told him. But after spending the day with her, he believed she was more alive than she knew. Not a moment—not a single moment of the day—was lost on self-pity. This frail, bedraggled girl would be going places, not wallowing. Where she would go, he had no idea, but she'd make something of herself—he knew she would.

Once the crime was set right, she could go as she pleased. Where does a caged animal go when it is set free? Knowing the Howells, they'd probably help her get somewhere good, a place where survival would not be her main concern. She deserved that, and he would help if he could. He'd promised her that.

With his thumbs tucked into his belt loops, he stepped back into the room and paced, pondering the box and the bag they'd found. What secrets did they contain? Did they hold the clue to Em's freedom? He'd planned to wait to open them, but curiosity's pull was too strong, so he took the bag from under the table and heaved it onto the worn tabletop.

Little cracks ran like veins all over the dark surface of the thick, aged leather, and water marks marred the sides, leaving it stiff and uneven. He stared at it momentarily before moving forward. Getting it open took more effort than he'd anticipated. With his hands he worked the leather, kneading it in an attempt to loosen the stiff straps. He wondered what Em would say when she found out he'd not waited. Did it matter?

Minutes ticked by on the old wind-up clock that hung on the back wall of the jail. Had George ever opened the bag or did he merely look in the log whenever he was around to make sure it was still there? Judging by the condition of the bag, no one had pried it opened in months—maybe longer.

Caleb felt the leather slowly softening with each movement. When he finally opened the bag and caught a glimpse inside, he froze, uncertain what to do. Stacks of bills sat in neat little piles just like a bank would keep them, separated and tidy. The money nearest the opening was misshapen and warped from moisture, but considering its hiding place, he was amazed most of the bills looked as good as they did. He picked up one neat stack and fanned the money out as he tried to guess how much there was. There could easily be ten thousand dollars, if not more, in the sack. Never had he held so much money in his hands.

Digging deeper, he hoped to find something else, something that would tell him the money's story. He couldn't feel anything different. Just money. A great big bag of money. Who has this much money and lives like George did? Why didn't he spend it, get a real house, or at least stock his cellar with decent food?

Flustered, he set the money aside and picked up the metal box. A small keyed lock held the lid tightly shut. He tried picking it but had no success. Breaking it open would be easy, but then Em would know he had not waited. Instead, he took both treasures and put them in the safe at the back of the jail. The safe had housed many watches and a few pieces of jewelry, and once a man insisted that his hat spend the night inside, safely locked away. Not once since Caleb had been sheriff had it held more than a few hundred dollars.

With the valuables securely tucked away, he peered in at Em. Her slight frame just barely moved the blanket with each sleeping breath. Listening, he heard not a single noise. Stepping closer, he dared to look at her marred arm. A savage scar ran along most of her forearm. Pink-and-red ridges of puckered skin spread like spiderwebs all across it. How did it happen? Did it pain her?

The climbing contest—he had three questions, which he still had every intention of asking. He could know about her arm if he chose.

Caleb took a chair from the main room, brought it into the tiny bedroom, and seated himself. Watching her sleep peacefully, he made a mental list of details he'd like to know. The list grew and grew. He was grateful now that he hadn't asked the first three questions that had come to his mind. No, he would not waste these questions. After all, he'd earned them fair, and no excuses were going to keep her from answering them.

Before long he eased himself deeper into his chair. Tipping his head back, he allowed himself the luxury of closing his eyes. Moments later he too gave in to the pull of slumber.

Em was awake, she knew she was. But she didn't want to be. Keeping her eyes shut, she let her mind continue on in her dream. Riding high on a horse that looked a lot like Amos, she could feel the fresh breeze blowing around her. She wasn't afraid of the horse or of anything. Strong arms were around her, a prince's from one of her stories. He bent over and whispered in her ear, "Shall we go faster?"

The two set off across a dew-laden meadow faster than she'd thought possible. The tiny drops of moisture twinkled in the sunlight, and oranges and greens sparkled around her. It was a fantasy world, but it felt so real.

Life and excitement flowed through her. A happiness she'd not felt since she was a small child overpowered her. The horse slowed to a steady walk. It was easier to talk now. Her prince asked her if she was ready to go get Lucy.

"Where is she?" Em asked. Her prince told her he would take her to the child. Em's heart pounded in her chest as they headed over a small rise. There on the other side was little Lucy, waiting. She was picking beautiful summer flowers. Under the soft glow of sunlight, she danced from one flower to the next in the most carefree way. Unburdened and joyful. When she saw them, she bent and picked up a porcelain doll, then ran toward them. Em and her prince jumped off the horse. He took her hand and together they ran to Lucy. The reunion, the warm embrace, the completeness were before her . . .

The sound of chair legs scraping the floor chased the perfect dream from her mind. With her heart still racing, she turned toward the sound. There was Caleb Reynolds sitting—head back, shifting slightly in his sleep—in a wooden chair. Alone in a room with a man, she knew she should feel vulnerable. Afraid. But she did not. Instead she watched him while he slept.

Mussed, dark hair lay haphazardly across his forehead. Strong hands rested easily in his lap. His hat sat on the floor. Each breath came in long, even intervals—with it a soft, fluttering sound. Never had she watched a man sleep like this. He seemed peaceful now, so different from when he was awake. Awake he was always a storm of energy—laughter, frustration, fire.

The twins had asked if he was a prince. Looking at him now without worry of him seeing her, she could tell why Eliza was so smitten with him. He was no sleek city boy. So different from the men the girls at the Aid Society had admired from their second-story window. Caleb was no clean-cut boy in a tailored suit. He was handsome in a different way. He rode horses, carried a pistol, and protected the town from outlaws. In his own rugged, dust-covered way, he was princely. It was more than his physique that captured her. Something about him seemed to proclaim his character, announce that he was honorable and good. All traits of the finest princes.

She lay back flat at the sound of the chair creaking again. When she heard no other sounds, she dared a glance in his direction and saw him looking intently back at her. "Hello, Em."

She fought to keep her own voice equally casual. "Have I been sleeping long?"

"You slept most of the ride home, and it's been a couple hours now since the doctor checked you over and ordered rest. Doc said to take you back to the Howells'. He thinks you need to have people around all the time for a few more days. I'll see if they'll let me bunk there as well. I'd like to keep an extra watch on the place." She appreciated him telling her the plan. So often in her life she'd had to guess what was coming next.

"Would it be all right if we opened the box and bag first? Unless, of course, you already have." Em propped herself up on one elbow.

"I was hoping you would be up to that. Wait here."

Moments later he returned with the bag, the metal box, and a hammer. "The bag is money. Lots of money." He pulled it open and showed it to her. "I'd say old George was killed over this."

A gasp escaped her lips. Never had she seen

more than a few coins together. Shaking her head in disbelief, she reached out and touched it. A handful of that money would get her to Beckford and leave enough for her to live a modest life. Just a handful of it. The whole bag would make her as rich as a real princess.

"Where is it from?" Em asked. "Whose is it?"

Caleb shook his head. "I don't know. I wish I could tell you it was yours. But I'm guessing it wasn't George's to begin with. Until we know its story, it stays locked away and you and I keep it our secret."

"I won't tell anyone." She watched as he closed up the bag. "You can trust me," she said. "I can keep a secret."

"I don't doubt it," he said, the corner of his mouth rising into a half smile as he slid the metal box in front of him. "This box has a lock on it. I tried to pick it earlier but had no luck." A guilty look spread across his face. "I guess I was meant to wait for you."

"I'm glad you did. Can you open it now?"

Thud. He brought the hammer down hard on the lock, bending it slightly. *Smack.* This time it fell away from the box. Taking the box in one hand, he grabbed his chair with the other and moved it closer to her before sitting down. She sat up in the bed, barely noticing the pain in her side.

"Ready?" he asked.

Nodding emphatically, she watched. He swung

the lid open to expose a box filled with papers. Papers. Nothing but papers. Few things were more useless to Em than papers.

Caleb's reaction was the very opposite of hers. He smiled wide at her and dug in.

"Look here, Em, this one is the deed to his property. And here's a marriage certificate. Did you know he was married to a Gerda Lourne? It was in Boston thirty-five years ago." Caleb spoke quickly, his hands thumbing through the papers. "Old George left us a box of clues. Maybe some of your questions will finally be answered."

"I expect you'll know more about him than I do by the time you finish digging through the box."

"What is it, Em? Do you not think this is exciting? Rather be climbing trees? Or were you hoping for more money?"

"It is exciting. I'm merely tired." Pursing her lips, she turned away.

Caleb stopped shuffling the papers. "We can wait. I don't want to leave you out."

"You go ahead and go through it. Tell me what you find." She lay back, but as her head hit the pillow, she caught sight of a worn packet in Caleb's hand.

"That's mine." She shot back up, wincing slightly, and reached for the packet. "I remember this. It was in my pack before I rode the train. I never knew what happened to it."

He placed it in her hands and with it memories,

so many memories. Her mother had kept this packet with them when they moved tenements. When she died, Em put it with her few belongings before leaving. If it was important to her mother, she wanted to keep it. It was all she had from her. Someone must have put it in her file. Now, after seven years, it was back in her hands. She fingered the worn paper, feeling the same yearning she'd felt when she'd held it before. The longing to know what it was.

Caleb's voice was soft. "What is it?"

Oh, how she hated admitting what a stupid girl she was. "I don't know what it is." It seemed impossible for her voice to sound any softer, but it did. "I don't know how to read." She looked away then, unable to meet his gaze. "My mother kept those papers with her. When she died, I took them. I didn't know what had become of them. I always meant to learn to read so I could know what the papers said. I do think I could learn. I just haven't been taught."

Caleb shifted in his chair until he was squarely facing her. "I never would have guessed. You talk like someone who knows how to read. You sound like someone with years of schooling."

"My mother would be glad to hear that. She was a maid in a fancy house. She insisted we speak proper English. She meant for us to learn to read as well, but circumstances kept her from having the time to teach us. Over the last several years I often talked to her, even though she wasn't with me. In a way I suppose I was honoring her by speaking as properly as I could. At least in that way I wasn't letting her down." Em picked at her thumbnail. "Just her and God and the hope of something more. That's what got me through those long years."

"Do you want me to read those papers to you? Or do you want to wait and read them when you are able to yourself?" Caleb put a large, calloused hand under her chin and turned her head toward him. "I could teach you. You could learn."

Em sucked in her lip, trying to control the emotion she felt. "You would do that? You'd teach me?"

"Sure. Once you're feeling better and living in this room, we could have lessons in the evening. I've never taught anyone before. We could learn together."

"Why? Why would you do that?" No one had ever offered to teach her anything before.

"Well, I guess I figure everyone deserves a chance to read. Books, newspapers—it's not fair that they make no sense to you. I have years of schooling behind me. I might as well use it for something. Besides, my evenings around here are pretty quiet."

"Could I write too?" Em asked. Then suddenly feeling shy, she wished she could capture the words and lock them back inside. Surely she'd asked too much. "But you don't need to teach me. I was just wondering if it was hard, that's all."

"I'll teach you that too. Reading and writing go together." He closed the box and reached out a hand to her. "Let's head over to the Howells' now. The doctor was going to let them know you would be coming, so they'll be expecting you. I'll probably get an earful from Abigail about taking you out today. I might as well get that over with."

Taking her hand in his, he eased her off the bed. On shaky legs, she stood motionless for a moment, hoping the dizzy feeling would pass. Bracing herself on the chair, she waited. When the room stopped spinning, she took a step toward the door.

"Wait." Caleb offered his arm. "Let me help you."

Staring at it, she hesitated.

Caleb winked at her, then reached out and took her arm. Looping it through his own, he led her through the jail and out the door just the way a prince from her story would lead a fair maiden.

Seven

A week had passed, and now when Em touched her face, she felt a new softness. Gazing into the small mirror that hung on the Howells' wall, she looked at the plain features that stared back at her. They were the same and yet they were different. The eyes that looked back at her were brighter, the cheeks less sunken. Even the coloring of her skin seemed altered. The time at the Howells' had been good for her. Her once savage wound, though tender, was healing. She often looked at it and in a strange way felt gratitude for it—it'd brought her from her prison in the woods to this good home.

Inside she felt different too. Food and rest were good medicine—she was proof of that. But it was more than the food and the rest. The Howells were kind to her. Always helping her and caring for her. Looking at her like a real person who mattered. When she spoke, they listened.

Little Mae and Milly adored her, and she adored them. They followed her around, always begging for stories and wanting to sit at her side. They *wanted* her near them. Being wanted, truly wanted, made getting up each day easy. Was this what living felt like?

Caleb Reynolds had been staying at the Howells' home, sleeping on the back porch on the warmer nights and in the front room when a storm blew through. Eliza clung to him whenever he was near. He didn't flirt as obviously as Eliza, but Em thought he liked her attention just fine. She often watched the pair, quietly assessing them. A more handsome couple she could not imagine. Caleb was a man whom the Howells would cherish as a son if the two ever chose to make their relationship lasting.

Somehow he found time to spend with Em. He'd talk to her about what was happening with the case or tease her about climbing trees or make quiet jokes about her putting too much food in her mouth. During the first evening meal he'd shared with the family, he'd leaned over to Em and whispered, "Are you sure you should be taking such large bites?" The smile in his eyes and the memory had caused her to nearly repeat the past. It had taken great control to swallow. His shoulders had shaken in silent delight when he saw the affect he had on her. When he was around, Em never knew what to expect, but she knew one thing—she enjoyed his company.

A week of his near-constant presence and it felt normal having him at the table with the rest of the family.

With everyone gathered around the table, Abigail served dinner. The night had begun much like the others they'd enjoyed together. Mouth-watering food, lively stories from the twins, and easy conversation.

"There's been another robbery," Caleb said when there was a lull. "A telegram came today. Witnesses believe it's our men. Red hair and a missing tooth." Caleb set down his fork. Everyone stopped eating and stared, waiting for him to say more. "I'll be heading out after them. Alvin, my deputy, will look after the town while I'm away. He'll keep special watch on your home."

Eliza looked near tears. "Oh, you will be safe, won't you? I couldn't bear it if something happened to you." Daintily, she dabbed at her eyes with her napkin. "I'll be thinking of you while you're away."

"I'm going with a group of lawmen from all over western Iowa. These men know what they're doing. We won't do anything without a plan, and we'll be careful. There aren't better men out there. I could be gone a couple weeks, depending on how it all plays out. We're fairly confident that the bandits headed south." Caleb set down his fork and looked around the table. "I don't anticipate trouble in town while we're away. Other than the normal saloon brawl. But there is the small chance the men will evade us and come looking for Em. Be careful while I'm away."

Heads nodded in agreement. An eerie gloom dominated the once cheery atmosphere.

"Em, I don't expect you to stay in the house all the time. Not with you feeling so much better. There are still several hours of daylight left. I'd like to teach you a little about shooting a gun. I'll leave one with you so you'll have some means of defense." Caleb stood. "I'd feel better leaving knowing you had it."

Abraham cleared his throat, letting everyone know he was about to speak. Then his slow words came. "I think that's a good idea. A right fine idea. Our Em shouldn't have to hide out in the house all the time."

Em stared at Abraham. The kindhearted man had called her "our Em" as though she were part of the family.

Before she could say anything in response, Abigail said, "Em, you go ahead and leave the dishes to the girls and me. You go on out with Caleb."

Em rose from her chair. "Thank you for a lovely meal."

Abigail smiled back at her—a motherly smile that made Em feel warm deep inside. Em looked to Eliza. She found no familial affection in her eyes. Still hoping the two would become friends, she said, "Eliza would you like to join us? If that's all right with Caleb, of course."

"I'll need Eliza here. You two go along now." Abigail shooed them away.

Caleb led her from the table. Before they turned the corner, they heard Eliza's indignant "But Mama . . ."

Once they were out of earshot, Em said to Caleb, "I can't seem to get anything right with Eliza."

Caleb just laughed. "Don't mind her. She might think she wants to shoot, but I doubt it's for her. Don't worry over Eliza. I'll smooth it over with her later."

Once they were outside, Em greeted Amos. The horse put his head near hers, allowing her to pet his soft nose. She let him nuzzle her cheek, an intimate gesture she once never imagined she would experience with the gentle giant. She was no longer afraid. In fact, many recent nights she'd found herself dreaming of being on the back of a big horse just like him.

Up she went into the saddle.

"Not nearly as light as you once were," Caleb said, dramatically shaking his arms. "Not sure I'll be able to lift you much longer."

She laughed as he hopped up onto the horse and sat behind her. "Must be everyone forcing food down me. I've never eaten like this in my entire life. I can't walk through a room without someone saying, 'Em sit down and eat this' or 'I made this special for you—you really must eat.' "

"It's been good for you." He wasn't jesting now—she knew it. "I think by the time I return I won't recognize you." Caleb took the reins and clicked to signal for Amos to move forward.

He slipped his arm comfortably around her and they started off, away from the town. With Caleb's arm around her waist, sitting high on Amos, Em imagined she was in her dream again—the one where she was more than just plain Em. Closing her eyes while they rode away, she reveled in the thought.

"Em, I haven't had more than a minute or two alone with you this past week, and I've been eager to ask you one of the three questions that I earned." Darn, she'd hoped he'd forgotten. Life was so pleasant now, and she didn't want to dig up the past again.

She slowly opened her eyes and sighed. "I suppose we should get those questions out of the way and behind us. What do you want to know?"

"I want to know lots of things, but I'll only ask one tonight. That way you'll have something to look forward to when I come back. That and reading lessons."

The anticipation of learning to read, of reading the papers her mother had saved, brought a brilliant smile to her face. She imagined even Caleb could see it, creeping up at the corners all the way to her eyes, as he sat behind her.

"I am excited for the reading lessons, but I plan to get a job soon. I need to earn money. I hope I'll still have time for reading." She turned her head toward him. "Do you know of any jobs?"

"Why do you need money? You wanting a new dress for the social?"

"Is that one of your questions?"

"That's just a friend making conversation."

A friend. She'd longed for a friend. Why didn't her heart soar like she'd imagined it would? "Well, I can't very well live with the Howells forever. Plus, I have somewhere I need to go."

"Always so mysterious. One of these days I'll ask you a question and you'll trust me enough to answer it without leaving me wondering what in the world you aren't telling me."

"I'll tell you this. It's not a new dress that I am hoping to earn money for. I feel rather spoiled as it is, having so many of Eliza's castoffs to wear. Every time Abigail brings me one, I have to fight off tears."

Caleb stopped Amos and they climbed down. Together they walked to an open field where a cluster of trees dotted the edge of the grass. They were not far outside of town but far enough that they were alone.

"Wait here," he said.

She watched as he went to the trees and hung an old, worn bandanna from a branch. She admired his long stride as he walked back toward her, crossing the field in no time at all.

"What happened to your parents? That's question number one."

That was a big question, but she would answer it. While he loaded the gun, she tried to decide where to begin.

"My parents were John and Viviette Cooper. Everyone called my ma Vi. When I was very young, we lived in a one-bedroom tenement all to ourselves. I'm not sure where we were before, but I remember the day we moved in. My pa was so proud. He opened the door, taking his time with the lock." Closing her eyes, she could almost hear the jingle of the key.

"Then he pulled it open, picked me up in his arms, and swung me around in the open room. My ma laughed the most carefree laugh I've ever heard. Pa set me down then, walked right up to Ma, and kissed her square on the lips." Em turned away, embarrassed by the intimate detail she'd shared. "Life was good then."

Caleb moved around Em to face her again. "I remember when my parents were happy too. They were more discrete with their affection though." He laughed. "When the four of us brothers would play in the giant oak in front of our home, they would come out and sit on the porch. They had two rockers there and they would sit near each other. When they thought we were too caught up in our playing to notice, my pa would reach over and take my ma's hand. Just like this." He reached out and took her hand. She knew he meant nothing by it, but still, heat raced through her. She struggled to focus as he kept talking. "Sometimes my ma would lean her head on my pa's shoulder. Once, high in a tree, my brother Sam asked if I saw them. I said I did. Then he told me someday he would meet a girl that would sit, holding his hand just like that. His dream was so simple, but I remember thinking it was what I wanted too."

Caleb let go and Em realized she had been holding her breath. Filling her lungs, she took the hand he had held and pulled it to her chest.

Caleb took his hat off his head and ran his hand through his hair. "He never did though. Sam never got to sit with a wife like that. He died in the war. All my brothers did. One by one they left home. Nobly fighting for the North. They'd hoped to come home heroes, but they never came home. They were heroes though—even before the war they were my heroes. The war ended, and I was too young to fight. I was only twelve. I was the one who stayed home." He shrugged. "Maybe that's why I became a sheriff. Anyway, my parents stopped holding hands and laughing then."

The smile he wore was to convince her he was at peace with his past, but other more subtle signs told her he was not. His breathing was different now and his eyes held a faraway look, a longing look. He was hurting. She knew he was. The deep-inside ache that comes from missing someone, from wishing for a way to change something there is no way to change. She was all too acquainted with that feeling. "I'm sorry about your brothers and your parents. Having you must have been a comfort to them. No doubt they thank the Lord nightly that you're still with them."

He shook his head. "I've never been a comfort. I've been trying to be, and someday I know when I visit they'll be smiling again and proud of their remaining son."

If she'd been bolder she would have reached out and offered a hand of comfort, but she didn't dare act on the instinct. Instead, she just listened.

"What happened to your parents? That was the real question. I'm not sure how we started talking about me." He let out a terse chuckle and Em knew he was trying to change the mood. "Tell me the rest. What happened after they got their new home?"

"My pa worked at the docks in New York. My ma took in sewing and laundry. Everyone worked hard, but we were happy. One day, when I was about eight, he died. I don't know how exactly—something fell during unloading. Our lives changed then. We moved into a hot and smelly shared tenement where babies always cried. Sewing from home no longer brought in enough money for us to live, so my ma went to work as a maid. For three years she worked in a wealthy home, until a new employee brought sickness to the house. All the maids were dismissed. The owner feared they were all sick and rather than call a doctor, she let them all go. Ma came home with no job, and within a few days she too was sick. She wouldn't let us near her." Em brushed a stray strand of hair from her face. "And then she died. And our world fell completely apart. I don't know what it was that took her, but I wished I could do something. Often I wished it had taken me too." Em shrugged. "That's what happened to my parents. They died, and I've been without them since."

Em picked up the pistol he had set down, hoping the conversation had ended. One painful question behind her.

"You said 'our world.' You said that she would not let 'us' near her. Who else? Did you have brothers or sisters?" Caleb put a gentle hand on her shoulder. "Did you lose them too?"

Trying to smile, she said, "Are you asking another question?"

Silence.

Em busied herself by studying the gun.

"No, I suppose not. Not today anyway." He pressed his lips together into a firm line. "Thank you for telling me about your parents. They must have taught you well. No one I know could have handled all you have."

It was the nicest compliment she'd ever received. And yet Em was not sure she had handled any of it well. Too often she lay awake at night wondering if she should have done things differently.

There was so much more. So many days and sleepless nights he did not know about. Too easily he handed out his praise. Regrets started creeping into her mind. Why had life turned out how it had? Lucy was her responsibility. A vault inside her was opening. She could not go there, not now. She took a deep breath and closed it all back up again. Locked away until she could no longer contain the urge to revisit it.

They shot then, neither mentioning the pain from their pasts. Em missed completely the first three times, but on her fourth shot she put a hole in the bandanna. By her tenth shot she was hitting it consistently. And she was enjoying doing so.

"Are you ready for another competition?"

"Is that what you and your brothers did? Compete all the time?" She took a seat in the sweet-smelling grass, picturing four boys that all looked like Caleb running around together.

"We sure did." Then he told her about the time he and his brothers competed to see who could walk the farthest on the fence around the pigpen, which resulted in a severe scolding from their mother. There was the time they competed to eat the pies they had stolen from their mother the fastest, which resulted in no dinner for any of them. He went on laughing as he told stories about the mischief and competition he had shared with his brothers.

"So, Em, you can see I have a long history of competing and just as long a history of losing. Being the youngest son was a hard position to be in. And now I have found a friend willing to compete with me, and the best part is I stand a fair chance at winning. I need some wins after all those years of losing, don't you think?" He was sitting beside her on the grass now, his hands casually resting on his bent knees.

What fun it must have been to have all those brothers. "I will compete and likely I'll lose," she said. "I did *just* learn to shoot. Someday I'll win, though, at something."

"Unlikely, but I like your spirit."

"Just you wait, Caleb Reynolds. I'm past due for a victory myself. I'll win something, someday."

"You sound mighty confident." He stood and pulled her up from the ground. "We will each shoot five times and whoever hits the bandanna the most wins. Simple?"

Em scrunched up her face. "But you must shoot from farther away."

"I suppose that's fair. The loser gets more questions?"

He didn't sound serious. But just to be sure, Em said, "No. No more questions. Unless I win—then I get to ask you questions."

"You think you get to decide all the rules, do you?"

"If you will let me."

"Of course I won't. If you win, you may ask me three questions. If I win, you . . . hmmmm . . . you must come to the social. It's in two weeks and I know you're planning on hiding out somewhere, but you would have to come. No matter what."

What Caleb didn't know was that Abigail had already insisted she attend the social and Em had not known how to say no.

"I suppose I could agree to that," Em said, making it sound as though it were a big price to pay. "If you insist."

Reaching a strong hand toward her, he said, "Shake on it?"

Her hand felt lost in his. All too soon he let go and then they shot. He went first, hitting the bandanna all five times. She hit it four times.

"Let's hope you shoot that well if Mr. Redhead-No-Front-Tooth returns. You're a fast learner. You had me worried for a moment. I was afraid you'd pull off a victory. I did win though. Looks like you will get to meet everyone at the social."

She made a face at him. He elbowed her. "I think you'll enjoy it."

Em rolled her eyes. He seemed to enjoy her company well enough, but that didn't mean everyone would. The thought of the social made her skin crawl and her stomach queasy. "I won't enjoy it a bit."

"Just you wait. I'll introduce you to everyone. It'll be like a coming out party for you."

She shook her head. She wasn't the type of girl to have a coming out party, not before and not now. "I'll go. I'll keep my word, but I won't like it."

Back on Amos, they started for the Howells'. The sun was setting, painting the sky with oranges and pinks as it went. They rode in content silence, lost in the beauty of the evening.

After stopping Amos in front of the house, Caleb jumped down, turned, and reached for her. When her feet hit the ground, he left a hand on the side of her waist that was not tender. "I'll be gone early, before the house is up and moving. Be careful while I'm away."

"I will. I'll be careful . . . don't . . . don't worry about me. You be careful too." The feel of his hand distracted her. "Thank you . . . for teaching me to shoot."

He let go and she felt colder. She'd known Caleb for only two weeks, but already he was one of the dearest friends she'd ever had. Being near him did something to her. Something she couldn't explain, not even to herself.

She knew he didn't find her attractive—he'd as good as called her plain. Never had she expected him or anyone else to be attracted to her. Had she been elegant and graceful, she would not have ridden the train for so long. Someone would have wanted her. She knew she was still that same girl. Caleb was kind, though, and he made her laugh and feel young and carefree.

A horse needed caring for and Em needed to go inside. Yet neither of them moved. When the silence grew longer, he took one step closer and ran the tip of his finger over her cheekbone. "Keep eating whatever Abigail puts in front of you."

Then he walked Amos back toward the Howells' barn. Em stood alone, listening to the sound of him leaving, her face warm where he'd touched her. Putting a hand to her cheek, she savored the moment. So rarely had she been touched or held. The smallest acts seemed to send life rushing through her. Smiling into the darkness, she felt the happiness of the moment seep into her very soul.

Eight

Abigail had taught Em to curl her hair in the latest fashion during her slow days of recovery. Now, with the doctor's permission, Em was ready to find a job. He'd been pleased with her progress—amazed, even, at the swiftness of it. Today was the first day Em had fixed her hair all by herself. Inspecting her work in the little mirror, she was pleased with what she saw. She was not a striking beauty like Eliza, but she did not see the same plain girl she had viewed only weeks ago. Little curls framed Em's face under the borrowed red bonnet. Never had she felt this close to beautiful. Hopefully the difference in her appearance would help her find a job.

The prospect of venturing into town on her own had her wringing her hands together and biting her lip. Lifting the layer of cloth in the bottom of her basket to take a peek, she reassured herself that the pistol Caleb had loaned her would be going with her. How kind it had been of him to leave it.

"Abigail," Em said, stepping into the front room, "I plan to stop at the dressmaker's and see if she needs any help. I'll also try at the hotel and with Mrs. Norbert. Can you think of any others who may need me?" Em fidgeted with the bonnet's bow, tying and then retying it.

Abigail stopped braiding Mae's hair. "Oh, look at you, Em. Your hair turned out so well." Em had never worried about the sin of vanity until that very moment. Putting her hands to her cheeks, she felt heat rise to them. Despite the looming threat of three murderous bandits, she was happy. She fought to hide a smile.

"Abraham said there were no jobs posted on the store's board. That would have been my first suggestion," Abigail said. "Margaret may hire help with the meals at the boardinghouse. Her daughter just married and moved away, leaving the burden all on her. You may want to check there. I'll keep thinking and asking around. Something will turn up for you."

"Thank you, Abigail. Mae, you look beautiful. I think your hair has grown—soon it will be as long as Rapunzel's." She bent and kissed the ecstatic girl on the cheek. Mae quickly wrapped her arms around Em's neck and hugged her tight. Those little arms had no idea the joy they were giving her.

"If you do get a job, will you still have time to tell me and Milly stories?" Mae asked, holding her tight.

"Of course I will. It's one of my favorite parts

of the day. I'll see you later, little Mae-berry."
The arms released her, but the warmth they had
brought her went with her as she headed into
town.

"Oh, miss, I'm sorry to tell you, but business
is slow enough that I don't need any more help
right now. You're welcome to check back with
me another time if you'd like," the spinster
dressmaker, Miss Caroline, said.

Em masked her disappointment the best she
could and thanked her for her time. She admired
the beautiful dresses as she made her way to the
door. Abigail had told her that Miss Caroline
made most of the dresses when a request came
in, but she always kept a few premade dresses on
hand. To think Em had owned only one ragged
dress and here was a shop full of fine cloth, lace,
and gowns. It would have been a joy working
around so many fine things, but it was not to
be.

Miss Caroline had smiled at her sweetly, but
behind her eyes Em sensed sadness. In a few
years, when she was Miss Caroline's age, would
her eyes be lonely and sad too? Long ago she'd
accepted her fate. She knew she'd become a
spinster, an independent woman. Today the
thought made her feel heavy.

But right now finding a job was what mattered, so Em hurried toward the hotel. Women

working in the front of a hotel was unconventional, but there was a chance. Before pushing open the heavy door, Em adjusted her dress and straightened her bonnet. She hoped she appeared confident as she stood tall and walked into the hotel.

"Hello, sir. I've come to see if you needed any help. I was told you were short a front office worker." Em's voice quivered slightly as she spoke. Imitating Eliza, she smiled at the man behind the front desk. "I'm looking for work and I know I could learn the job. You wouldn't be sorry."

Without speaking, the man looked her over. His eyes crept up and down her slowly. Any confidence she had mustered upon entering the hotel was leaving with haste. When he finally spoke, his deep voice seemed to bounce off the walls, carry through the building, and rumble out onto the street. "We don't hire women, and we especially don't hire little girls. Now get on out of here."

Em knew she should turn and go, ignore the man's heated words, but anger boiled in her. "I am not a little girl, sir. I *am* a woman, that much is true. But I can work just as hard as any man. You have no right to talk to me so or to look at me with eyes like a snake."

"I'll talk to you however I wish. This here is my property and I said I don't hire no girls. Get on out of here before I pick you up like some mangy dog and throw you out."

Just then a man walked in from the street. "Everything all right in here, Pete?"

Em turned toward the stranger. "Your *friend* Pete needs help in the front of his hotel. But not from me or any other *girl*." Face hot with frustration, she turned to leave.

"Wait." The strange man grabbed her arm. "You looking for work? It might be your lucky day." He flashed a dashing smile at her, his perfect teeth twinkling. "Come with me. I might know of just the job for you."

Em let the man take her arm in his and lead her out, away from Pete and his temper. Her curiosity grew with each step. Who was this man? Pete's wicked laughter boomed behind them as they walked. Was he laughing at her? The nerve. Safely out of range of the laughter, she realized how close she was to her rescuer. She pulled away, putting space between them.

When the pair had rounded a corner, the stranger gently turned Em to face him. "I'm Silas. I've been looking all over for a beautiful woman just like you. I'm desperate for some help. A beautiful, hard worker. That's what I'm after. You interested? I think you'd be mighty good at it."

Something deep inside her stomach twisted and turned. She had always longed to have a man call her *beautiful.* Hearing it now was nothing like she had expected. Why did she feel uneasy? Alarms sounded within her, but she wanted a job. She needed a job. Money meant Beckford. Money meant Lucy. Learning more couldn't hurt. After all, it wasn't every day that a job came so easily—she needed to at least see what this perfect job was.

"I'm interested. I'd like to know more about the job first before I give you an answer." Em inched a bit farther from the man.

He took a step toward her, closing the gap. "It's a job that takes the kind of spirit I saw back there with Pete. That was really something—you had fire in your eyes. No one does well working for me if they don't have a little spunk. The job's next door at the saloon." She jumped back, ready to reject him. Ready to turn and go. Again he stepped toward her. "Wait a second. I know what you're thinking. Saloons aren't all bad though. Lots of nice folks come in. All they want is a drink to cool themselves off. Most people aren't looking for any trouble. Someone has to serve them. Why not you?"

Why not me? Why not me? Because my mama would be heartbroken if she were alive and knew I was working at a saloon.

The dreaded saloon, with its dark exterior, was mere feet from them. Silas took her arm again and nudged her toward the swinging doors. Into the dim interior she stepped—cigar smoke filling her lungs, laughter accosting her ears. Not the joyful laughter she treasured from Mae and Millicent, but a different kind. A low, crude laughter.

Silas's hand was tight around her arm. "We pay well, and should you ever choose to, we offer more for working upstairs. But we don't need to worry about that now. Let me show you around."

As they walked farther into the dark saloon, she was able to make out the faces of a few of the morning customers. Silas's buttery voice sent a shiver down her spine. "It gets busier in the evenings and at night. You'll work then."

One of the men stood on wobbly legs. "Where you get that girl from? I ain't seen her before." He stepped near her. His eyes crept over her, inspecting her, leering at her. "Have I been drinking too much or is she the ugliest one you ever brought in here?" The man chuckled. "Where'd you find that one?"

"You been here all night, Bert. Sit down," Silas said in a friendly voice.

Bert ignored the suggestion. Instead, he reached out and put a hand on Em's shoulder and moved his thumb back and forth along her collarbone. His mouth inches from hers, he laughed in her face. Nauseous from the smell of the man or perhaps the terrible circumstances, Em yearned for fresh air.

"I'm sorry, Silas. This isn't the job for me."

She pushed the man's hand from her and stepped away.

Silas reached again and wrapped his hand tightly around her wrist. "Ignore him. You *are* perfect for the job. We'll get you a fancy dress and the girls upstairs will show you how to paint your face so the men won't think you're so plain. In fact, it won't be long before they are begging for your attention. You'll love it. The men always get excited about a new girl. You'll have more men after you than ever before." He ran his hand up and down her arm. The touch of his fingers only made her desire to leave grow stronger. "We get all kinds of men through here. There'll be plenty that'll like you when you're all dolled up."

Em had lived on the streets for months. She'd seen horrors she'd never wanted to see. All too clearly she knew what Silas was insinuating. Her ma had taught her better than that, and she would not choose this life. She'd find another way. Somehow she would.

She swatted Silas's hand from her wrist like it was an unwanted pest. Then, planting both palms on his chest, she shoved him as hard as she could. Because she was so small, she could tell he hadn't expected the force. He took a few steps backward before crashing into a chair and toppling over it. The men at the bar roared with laughter as Em dashed for the door.

Once freed from the saloon, Em allowed the fresh air to fill her lungs. Leaning against the outer wall, she waited as her racing heartbeat slowed. All the while her mind was reeling. *How dare they?* And then the depressing thought, *Why did I think it would be any different?*

With a heavy heart, she walked away from the filthy establishment. The man's words replayed over and over in her head. "The ugliest one," he'd called her. Had it been the liquor talking? She wanted to believe so, but she found herself wondering if he had been right. It was one thing to never have a man love her, but what if no one would even want to give her a job? Would the saloon be her only option? Feeling as though she was at a crossroads, she stopped walking. Should she quit or fight on?

Quitting was not an option. She would persevere—she had to. A job was what she was after, and somehow she would find one. For Lucy she would press on. Standing ever taller, she held her head high as she walked down the main street of the small town.

Mrs. Norbert and the boardinghouse were the only two remaining job prospects. Earlier in the week, Doc Jones had suggested she talk to Mrs. Norbert because of the woman's poor health and horrible children. Em hadn't met her children, but Abigail had politely told her they were unruly, while Eliza had classified them as horrible. In fact, she had called them "detestable" and "undeniably the worst children in town."

Which should she try first? Having little experience with unruly children, she decided to go to the boardinghouse.

Standing two stories tall, it was easy to locate. A widow named Margaret Anders owned the building.

Em had never met her, but she'd heard of the woman. Eliza called her eccentric. "Who else would paint a building on Main Street such a horrid shade of yellow?" Eliza had said. "Honestly, the building is brighter than a sunflower. She's so peculiar."

The more Eliza had said about Margaret, the more Em had wanted to meet her. The door of the boardinghouse was red. Bright red. Em walked to the door and offered one last silent prayer heavenward before knocking. *Let this be my route to Beckford,* she prayed.

Knock. Wait. Knock again. At last the door groaned open. Standing before Em was a woman who had to be the notorious Margaret Anders. Her dress was as outrageous as her house—bright pink trimmed in deep purple. Her hair was wildly curly. At some point in the morning she must have pinned it up, but now at least half of it was outside the pins. Tight brown curls soared in all directions.

"Don't tell me who you are. I believe I know.

You must be the local stray! I've been wanting to meet you." Mischief or something similar to that twinkled in her eyes. "Come in. Come in."

The saloon had made Em feel sick inside, but walking into Margaret's boardinghouse felt welcoming. Both were just buildings, yet there was a unique spirit about each. One dark and foreboding, the other bright and inviting. The boardinghouse was much less ostentatious on the inside. Simple, modern furnishings filled the front room. Ordinary paper—soft green with a floral pattern—covered the walls. Nothing garish or gaudy.

Margaret laughed. "Did you expect the inside to be bright yellow too? I wasn't sure my guests would like it. My room is much more fun than these stale ones." She gestured to a closed door down the hall. "What brings you here? Have you decided to leave the Howells? You looking for a room?"

"Oh, no. I'm very happy there. It's just I heard your daughter had married, and I thought perhaps you could use my help. I'm looking for work." Em held her breath as she waited for a response.

"Of course you're looking for a job. I'm surprised I didn't think of that when I opened the door. Have you had any luck yet?"

"None. Pete at the hotel practically threw me out. Miss Caroline is not busy enough to need help. The only offer I've had is from a scoundrel named Silas who tried to coax me into a job at the saloon. I am not nor will I ever be working there." The memory fresh, she bit her lip as she tried to control a laugh. "I am fairly certain he knew how I felt by the time I left."

Margaret twisted one of her wild curls in her hand. "A girl who can take care of herself—I like that. Anyone who can put her foot down to Silas is a friend of mine. That man is a close relative of the devil. All slick and handsome. Nothing but flattering words come out of his mouth. But don't let him fool you." Margaret's eyes were large as she spoke. "He tried getting my Scarlett to work upstairs in the saloon after her papa died. He tried awful hard. She didn't have your backbone. I had to step in." Her big eyes lit up like a cat's in the night, as though they were laughing at the memory. "Remind me to tell you that story sometime. Silas never knew what was coming and hasn't bothered me since." Tossing her head back, she let out a whoop. "Not once has he bothered me since. My guess is he will leave you alone now too. But be careful. Always be careful around that serpent."

Without another word, Margaret started walking from the room and turned down a side hall. Unsure if she should follow, Em stood waiting. Margaret's head poked back around the corner. "Are you coming? I'll show you around, let you know what I expect."

"I can work here?" Em could have thrown herself into the woman's arms. Making it to Beckford did not seem so far off anymore—not now that she had a job. For the first time in years she felt like she would actually get there.

Oh, Lucy, I am coming! I am coming!

"You can work here, but you'll have to work hard. Not too hard—nothing more than you can manage until you're all healed up. I treat my employees fairly, but I won't be paying you a penny if you don't earn it. I don't say that to scare you, but I believe a life is better lived when you know you've earned the things you have."

"The doctor is happy with my recovery. Don't worry on that account. I haven't felt this good in years. I'll work hard," Em said in her most confident voice. Hard work was all she had ever known. "I'll work so hard. Thank you for the job."

"We serve breakfast for those staying here. I can handle that myself—there aren't that many. I spend my afternoons cleaning and getting the big meal ready. In the evening, I open the front dining hall and we get all sorts in from the streets. It gets real busy some nights, and it's more than I can handle. You could begin at noon and work until six. When you first come, you'll be helping me clean. Then we'll prepare and serve the evening meal. After that it's a mountain of dishes. We serve the meal from four until five thirty. You're welcome to eat your evening meal here. My wages are fair. How does that all sound?"

"Mrs. Anders, it sounds like you are the answer to my prayers." Em blinked quickly, once again holding back unexpected tears. She wished she could start that very moment.

"Tomorrow then?"

"I'll be here at noon!" she said as she headed out the door.

Feeling ever so much lighter, Em glided down the street to the Howells'.

Mae and Milly met her at the door. "You've been gone forever. We missed you so much. Mama says we can't beg you for a story because you're probably tired. We aren't begging, but if you want to tell us one we would love it. Please." Mae was speaking, but Milly was there nodding along with every word she spoke. Em was fairly certain she would never be able to resist these two sweet girls.

"There is nothing I would like better. Come with me," Em said, heading for the back door.

"Where are we going?" the girls asked.

Rather than answer, she motioned for them to follow.

Em led the girls to the big tree behind the house. Feeling carefree, she helped the girls up onto the first branch and then hoisted herself up. They each climbed around until they found a branch that suited them. Once in her perch, she reclined back, resting her head against the tree's large trunk. "I'll tell you a story of a princess who started out as a very ordinary girl. When this girl was young, she lived with her mother and father. Sadly, her mother died, leaving her with only her kind father."

Milly stopped swinging her legs and said, "I think I know this one. It's the story of the cinder girl. Mama told it to us. But tell it anyway."

Mae nodded in agreement. "Please tell us. You tell the stories different than Mama. It will be like a new story. Plus, I love this story."

Em agreed to tell it, adding details to the magical story like garnish on a fine dish. She conjured up new scenes, wishing the moment could never end. She finished her tale with, "They all lived happily ever after."

No one moved. All three were lost to their own worlds of imaginary princesses and princes. From their lofty perch so high above the world, they could almost believe that fairy tales were real.

"Mama sent me to check on you girls," Eliza called from below, pulling them from their daze.

"Eliza, come up. It's like being a bird," Mae said.

"I will not. I am far too much of a lady to be climbing trees. Honestly, the two of you are likely to grow up and become wild animals. Then who will want to marry you?"

"Have no fear. Two dashing young men will come along and marry Miss Mae and Miss Milly. They are—"

Eliza gasped. "What are you doing back?"

Caleb sauntered toward them.

"What a surprise!" Eliza squealed and nearly jumped into his arms.

"I know. I thought we might be gone longer. The whole ride back I was sure I would come home to find you wringing your hands with worry." He looked at the tree a moment before heaving his body up onto the first branch. "Hello, Em. I should've known you'd be up here."

"What is that supposed to mean?" Eliza asked from below.

Caleb ducked under a branch so he could see down to Eliza. "It means she seems spry enough to climb the tree with the girls." Then, addressing everyone, he said, "How are all you ladies doing?"

Mae was first to reply. "We are quite well. Em was just telling us a story. She tells the best stories, but don't tell Mama that. She learned them on a very long train ride that she took with all of her friends. Doesn't that sound delightful?"

"I've heard of Miss Em's train ride." Caleb's eyes found hers. "But I had no idea she learned stories along the way. She will have to tell us all one now. It's been a long time since I heard a good story." Caleb sat back against the trunk, then gave her an expectant look. "I'm listening."

"I don't want to tell all my stories or there will be none left for another day. And since I told the girls one already, I will have to decline. No more stories today." Em smiled. "But it is good to have you back."

"Very well, no story today, but soon. I'd prefer a good adventure story." Caleb's brows came together. "Do you know any of those?"

Mae looked at Em. "Do you know adventure stories?"

Sounding shocked, Caleb asked, "What has she been filling your heads with if not adventure?"

"With princess stories. They are all so romantic. They are full of dancing and love and happily ever after. Sometimes there is even kissing. They're our favorite type of stories," Milly said, looking at him with dreamy eyes. "We've decided you are the Prince of Azure Springs."

Em had to grab hold of the nearest branch to keep herself from falling out of the tree.

"Is that so? Why, Em, I didn't know you thought I was a prince." He took off his hat and gave a partial bow that caused the girls to giggle. "I believe that is the nicest compliment I've ever received. What does that make you?"

His eyes were full of playfulness, his lip pulled up in a familiar half smile. Her heart leapt at the sight. In that moment she realized just how much she'd missed him.

Eliza had been stomping around beneath the tree. "It makes her the same ordinary Em she was before. Stop this nonsense and come down."

"Give us a moment, Eliza. I just returned and am enjoying the view from this tree. Come and see it yourself." Caleb looked down at her.

"Of course I'd love to sit beside you and see the view, but climbing hardly seems appropriate. I do try to be ladylike, unlike some people around here."

"Suit yourself," he said and turned his attention back to the girls. "Why don't you all tell me what I've missed? Has anything happened in Azure Springs while I was away?"

Milly stood up on her branch and looked around the trunk so she could see his face. "Em has a job. She starts tomorrow."

"I heard you were in the saloon with Silas this morning, Em. Is that where you'll be working? I hear he's not at all particular about who works there," Eliza said, her voice all sweet and innocent.

"You wouldn't work at the saloon, would you, Em?" Caleb's eyes were searching hers. "I know it's not my choice, but I don't think it's a good idea."

"I was in the saloon this morning, but not of my own doing. Silas cornered me and pulled me in. Whoever saw me must have missed my leaving. Had they seen it, they would know how I feel about working there. It's a shame—seeing Silas toppled over a chair, feet up, was quite a sight."

"This is a story we must hear. It sounds more like an adventure than a romance," Caleb said.

"I suppose it was an adventure." Em told her audience about her morning, sparing no details. "He never saw it coming. I don't think he expected a blow from a stick like me. And with him down, I left the saloon, walked away, and lived happily ever after." The little girls giggled.

Eliza let out a huff. "Well, I don't know why you even went in there at all. It was wrong, and I'm sure Mother will be terribly disappointed. Never would I set foot in that place, full of its cigar smoke and tainted women." Brushing a tendril of strawberry-blonde hair from her forehead, she said, "But you've done many things I wouldn't. I'm sure it's just your lack of breeding that puts you in such situations. With time I do hope you will learn."

Caleb shook his head. Em, mindful of the girls, bit back the snide remarks she so desperately wanted to zing back at Eliza. "I've had a different life. No denying that."

Eliza murmured something Em couldn't decipher.

"I think that's enough talk of saloons and Silas.

143

Tell us about the job you did find," Caleb said, diffusing the tension.

"Margaret Anders hired me. I'll be helping at the boardinghouse by cleaning and putting on the evening meal." Already forgetting the sting from Eliza's words, she smiled wide, grateful for her good fortune. "She said it's hard work, but it's a real job."

Eliza let out a gasp. "Mrs. Anders is an eccentric. She does what she pleases. Her food I've heard is decent enough, but why would you work there?"

"I need money, Eliza. She's given me a job, and even if she is different, she's willing to hire me. There is nothing morally wrong with the place. It's respectable work."

Cutting in ever so smoothly, Caleb said, "I eat there often. It's first rate. It gets pretty busy some nights. I tell you what, though, I don't envy you the dishes. I think you will do well there. Does anyone want to hear about my week?" Caleb knew how to keep the peace.

"Yes," they all said.

"We didn't catch them. But we will."

"You didn't catch them?" Milly's face fell. "You *always* catch the bad people."

"Don't give up on me yet, Miss Milly. I'll catch them. Just some take longer to catch, that's all." He shifted on the branch before going on. "We all met up like planned. There were twenty of us.

144

Most of us lawmen. Some of the men were just sharpshooters who had a personal stake in the pursuit. We learned a lot from being all together. Seems a couple people saw the men, and their descriptions match Em's. Another man didn't see their faces but heard them use the name Alroy. We all sat around sharing what we knew. These three have quite the reputation. They've robbed stagecoaches, wealthy houses, and even a bank."

Caleb pulled a giant leaf off the tree and twirled it around in his hand. Just twirling it, smiling all funny-like. Everyone waited. All eight eyes were locked on him. Looking up from his leaf, he chortled before saying, "Oh, did you want to hear more?"

"You shouldn't do that to us," Eliza said, crossing her arms.

"I was just having a bit of fun with you. After sharing all the information we had on the men, we pulled out a map and marked the places we knew they'd hit. It was a lot. They seemed to be moving steadily south and leaving a trail of crime behind them. We sent telegrams to all the law enforcement along the route. Then we spent a week tracking the criminals. We got close and then lost their trail when a storm hit. We're meeting back up in five days."

"Why do you sound so happy? It doesn't sound like you had any luck to me," Eliza said.

Em had planned to bite her tongue. She usually

kept quiet when the two were talking, letting them have their privacy. She was a guest and living off borrowed hospitality. This time, though, she could not sit placidly. "He did have luck. He learned more about them, found a whole group of others interested in bringing them in, and he has a plan. I think that is a big step closer."

"Exactly right. We'll get them—and soon. Plus, how could I not smile? I'm in a tree with three fine women. After a week of traveling with smelly men, it feels mighty nice. It's been a long week." Caleb looked tired. Em hadn't noticed when he had first climbed up.

Eliza resumed her pleasant voice. "I never doubted you would catch them. And we're all delighted to have you back. Come along, girls. Mama wants you to set the table for her."

Mae pouted. "Must we? It's so nice up here."

"Yes, you must. Em, I'm sure she could use your help as well," Eliza said as though Em were one of the seven-year-olds. "Hurry down."

"Of course." Em started climbing down after the girls until a strong hand stopped her.

"Em will be in shortly. I need to ask her a couple questions." Caleb started moving to the branch she was on. Her mouth went dry. Her heart beat faster as he neared.

Eliza pivoted away from the tree, then stomped toward the house, dragging the girls with her.

Caleb was beside her now. Not sure what to

do, Em avoided his gaze and looked at the back of the house, watching the girls go through the door.

"Was everything all right while I was gone?"

She swallowed hard and hoped her voice would come out normal. "It was just fine here. I've taken your pistol with me wherever I've gone, which hasn't been many places, except this morning when I decided to find a job. I made that trip on my own. For seven years I was nearly always alone and now I rarely am."

"Should've used that pistol on Silas for dragging you in there." Caleb rubbed his scruffy jaw. "He . . . didn't do anything he shouldn't, did he?"

"No. He did offer me a position *upstairs*. I've seen enough of that living on the city streets to know it's not a path I'll take—not ever." Then, realizing she'd just told him she'd lived on the streets, she changed the subject. "What do you need to ask me?"

"I have big news for you. And I'll tell you now because I've been eager to tell you most of the week. But first I want to hear how I became the Prince of Azure Springs." He threw the leaf he'd been holding at her. She caught it and held it in her lap.

"Very well. I'll tell you, but only because I'm eager to hear about your trip. The girls love stories of princes and princesses. I have told them

147

so many. I'm surprised I can remember them all. Mae and Milly are just little girls who believe dreams come true and magical things can happen. They want their own princes. But they don't want to move to a faraway castle because they love their mama and papa. They've been searching for a prince around here and have decided you are the Prince of Azure Springs."

"I see. Here I was thinking it was you who decided I was a prince. But really it was two seven-year-olds. Let me guess—they are both waiting for me to sweep them off their feet and carry them away to a castle." He rubbed the back of his neck. "I should be flattered."

"I've seen them staring awfully hard at you on your big horse, Amos, stars in their eyes." Em decided not to tell him that she too had dreamed of riding off on a horse like his.

"It looks like my parents will be disappointed. They've been pressing me for grandchildren. I'll have to write them tonight and tell them the fairest maidens are only seven and still have to grow up. Looks like I'll be disappointing them again." Caleb shrugged.

"Don't write them too quickly. They also think Eliza may be a princess."

"Ah, Eliza a princess. I hadn't thought of that. Who knew there was so much royalty right here in Azure Springs?"

Em looked around at the vast prairies and

gentle hills. Perhaps no real royalty resided here, but Em had discovered a kind family and a dear friend. "There seems to be more to this little prairie town than first meets the eye."

"Indeed there is." He was looking at the house. The playfulness gone. Was he thinking of Eliza? She wished she knew.

The silly conversation suddenly did not seem as fun and diverting. She was ready to be out of the tree and back in the house with everyone else. Dryly, she said, "Tell me your news."

"Don't sound too excited."

Em forced a smile. "I'm sorry. I do want to hear your news."

"When they told me one of the men's names was Alroy, I couldn't figure out why that name meant anything to me. Then a couple days later I remembered that I'd seen the name Alroy in the metal box."

He looked at her expectantly. Taking his lead, she smiled. "In the box? The one we found? I don't understand."

Caleb lowered his voice as though he were sharing a great secret. "Seems George and Gerda's son was named Alroy. Well, he wasn't really their son. At least not by birth. George and Gerda got him through the Aid Society. I'm not sure what it all means, but I do know that the two were connected. I wonder what type of relationship they had for Alroy to come back and kill his own guardian." Caleb looked excited about the clues starting to come together.

Em felt none of the excitement. "The Aid Society? Do you think George and Gerda got Alroy off an orphan train? What was the date on the paper?"

"I don't remember the exact date. I'll pull it out and look again. We can look tonight. Are you going to move to the room by the jail?"

"I don't know. I like it here with the Howells, but I don't want to be a burden. And if you are just leaving again . . ."

"You're right. Stay here—you'll be plenty safe. The gang is south, we know that. We'll get to them before they have a chance to head this way. But come meet me at the jail tomorrow morning before you go to work. We can dig through the papers together. Maybe something we read will help us figure out more pieces of the puzzle. Can you come at eight? I'll fit in a bit of a lesson for you too." Caleb jumped out of the tree. "I've been riding hard today and Amos needs that saddle off his back."

Em turned to scurry down the tree, but he reached out his arms and put them carefully around her waist to help her. "You ought to slow down."

"I'm feeling better all the time."

The two walked toward the house together.

"I think you'll like working with Mrs. Anders,"

Caleb said. "I've always admired her. Seems not enough women really live. But Mrs. Anders, I believe she does. If she loves a color, she wears it. If she likes a type of food, she eats it. If she wanted to climb a tree, I think she would. You two will get along well."

"I prayed for a way to find money. I don't know if you are a believing man or not, but I have no worries about working there. I think the job is an answer to my prayers."

"I'm a believing man. Although I confess I haven't prayed as often as I should." Caleb smiled down at her. "I will though. Tonight. Good day to you, Miss Em."

He started walking off. Before getting too far, he turned around and asked, "Is your name just Em?"

"Are you using a question?"

"Won't you just answer, because I've been wondering for over a week if it was? I thought perhaps your name was Emily or Emma."

Em felt a knot rise in her throat. He had been thinking of her all this time. He had been thinking of her! The other voice in her head reminded her it was his job to solve the case. Perhaps he thought knowing her name would help some- how.

"My family always called me Emmy. I knew that wasn't my real name, but I never thought to ask if Em was short for another name and then suddenly they were gone and I've been just plain Em ever since."

"Hmmm," he said as he walked away.

Plain Em walked to the house. Why had she never asked? Distraught by the reminder that she was just Em and no longer anyone's Emmy, she entered the house.

Nine

Em woke before the sun was up. She knew it was too early to start her day. She was restless, though, and could not sleep. Afraid she would wake the girls, Em lay in her bed for what felt like several hours. Finally, when she could wait no longer, she rose and quietly walked to the window. The stars were just beginning to fade. Soon the house would wake. She could busy herself and the minutes would go faster.

When Em was a small girl and her pa was still alive, her mother had promised to teach her to read. Her father's death and her mother's long hours changed everything. After she arrived home from her full day as a maid, her mother was always so tired. So tired that Em stopped asking for lessons. But in her heart the desire to read never diminished. Often she'd seen letters and had wanted to understand them. Oh, how she hated feeling left out, that everyone knew what the words said and meant and she did not. Now today she would have her first lesson.

Mae stirred in her bed, the sheets rustling about her. The movement caused Milly to rouse, and soon both girls were slowly opening their eyes. Milly sat up and reached her arms high above her, stretching for the sky. Em walked over to them. "Good morning, girls."

"I was dreaming about the social. I wish it were tonight," Milly said while rubbing sleep from her eyes.

Em brushed the hair from her little friend's face. "Four nights is not long to wait."

"But it will seem like a very long time," Milly said. "When I'm excited, time goes so slow."

"That is a feeling I do understand," Em said, thinking of the much-anticipated reading lesson.

"Are you very excited too?" Mae asked. "Will it be hard for you to wait?"

Em wrinkled her nose. "Actually, I don't dance. I'm not nearly as excited as the both of you. Come along, you two, and get up. The time will pass quicker if we do not sit around feeling sorry that today is not the social." Em reached for little Mae's hands and pulled her up.

"Ah, Em, let me sleep a little more."

"I will not." She tickled the sleepy child, making her laugh. Her infectious giggles spread to her sister. Soon Em and the girls were all laughing as she pulled them from the bed. Each time she pried a girl off the mattress, the other crawled back in. Em ran around the bed as quickly as she could, pulling them up, then running around for the other girl. They giggled more—even Em, who was surprised by the newfound energy her healthy body possessed, laughed as she darted around the room.

Falling onto the bed herself, she declared, "I give up. I will send up your mama. She'll know how to get you two sleepyheads out of this bed." Em rose and marched for the door. Her dramatic steps brought about more laughter. Soon the girls were by her side.

"We're up. Don't make Mama come get us," Milly said.

Em helped them dress and make their bed. Satisfied that they had left the room presentable, they all went to join the family downstairs. Only breakfast stood between her and her lesson; she was so close. Walking past a sampler, Em looked at the letters. Soon she would read it and so many other words.

"Abigail, what can I do to help you this morning?" Em asked.

"Good morning, Em. Getting those two girls up and going is always a big help."

"I did have to work extra hard to get them up this morning."

"I thought I heard some commotion above us. Are you ready for your new position? I do worry about you working yourself too hard." Abigail stirred a pot with a wooden spoon while she spoke. "You will be careful?"

Em nodded, grateful for Abigail's concern.

"What time do you need to be there?" she asked, her hand never ceasing its stirring.

"Caleb would like me to meet him at eight. I work at twelve. But if you need me here, I can send a message to Caleb and stay."

"I have Mae and Milly to help me. You keep your plans with Caleb." Abigail's dimple appeared in her cheek. "He is a nice man, isn't he?"

Em didn't answer right away. She began setting the table, happy to be busy so she did not have to look into Abigail's eyes. If Abigail saw her face, she would know how much Caleb's friendship meant to her. "He is very good to help me and worry so much about my being safe."

"Indeed. It's very good of him to care about your safety. This is ready—let's gather everyone to the table."

The breakfast conversation was congenial. Abraham always asked how everyone slept and what the girls were going to do during the day. Em loved the shared meal and friendly faces.

"Em, do you need to do anything else before you leave?" Abigail asked.

"I thought you didn't work until twelve," Eliza said before Em could answer.

"Em has a meeting with Caleb this morning at eight. She will be going to work right after that." Directing her attention back to Em, Abigail said, "While you finish getting ready, I'll pack you an afternoon meal."

"You needn't do that." Em, uncomfortable taking additional charity, squirmed in her seat. Already she was unsure how she would ever repay them for their kindness. Eliza's cold expression wasn't making things any easier.

"I won't take no for an answer," Abigail said.

Abraham set down his fork. "I've seen her like this before. When my Abigail has made up her mind, there is no changing it. Best to just admit defeat."

"Very well. I appreciate it. Thank you both for all you've done." Em rose from the table and started gathering empty dishes. "You've been so good to me."

With her hand fisted, Em knocked on the jail-house door.

"Em, you're here. Come in," Caleb said, his eyes flashing with excitement as he grabbed her hand and pulled her inside. "I dug through the box more after leaving yesterday. Hurry in, I want to show you."

Em wished she could read now so she could share in the discovery. From across the desk, he pushed a paper toward her. "I can't read it." She started to push it back, but then realized it was a wanted poster. Taking a closer look at the old, yellowed paper, she was startled to see the face of the red-haired man. He was visibly younger, but it was him. The infamous Alroy.

"This is him. The red-haired man who killed George. What does it say?"

"Says WANTED FOR ROBBERY. There's no name. My guess is they only had a description to go off of at the time. I think George was looking for Alroy. The money in the bag has to be from the robberies. I'm not sure how George came by it. There are still missing pieces, but it seems like a clue to me."

Caleb took the poster back and shuffled through the other papers. He found the one he was looking for and pulled it from the stack. "Look here, it's a clipping from a newspaper. It's about a string of robberies from several years ago. I read it last night and the only thing anyone knew was that one of the men had red hair. I think George was keeping up on the crimes. Tracking him."

Em looked again at the picture. "All those years when he would leave, maybe he was really off looking for Alroy. He never said a word about him. Not even once. He wasn't much of a talker, though, and I wasn't big on asking him questions. George left often, and I never believed his story about checking traps. What else did you find in the box?"

"Most of the papers are just legal papers. The properties he has owned and sold. There was his marriage license, the papers from the Aid Society about Alroy. I checked the date. His was from 1862. Other than that, there are a few other newspaper clippings." He pulled out one other paper. "This one doesn't seem to have anything to do with the case . . ."

Em picked it up. "What is it?"

"I'll read it to you," he said, taking it back from her. "The top part says THE CHILDREN'S AID SOCIETY OF NEW YORK. Then here it says that this paper certifies that Em Cooper has been placed in the care of George Oliver. He signed that he would care and provide for you, look after your safety. Things like that. It's dated 1874."

Staring at the paper, she tried to remember him signing it. No memory of the paper came, but other details did. The day was a blur, a whirlwind of emotion. At the time her mind and heart were in Beckford with Lucy. She'd all but given up on a family wanting her, and with Lucy gone, she didn't care what happened to her. When George came and asked after her, none of it felt real.

"I suppose he would have filled out the paperwork on me." Em stared at the letters on the page. "Living here with the Howells, it almost seems like a different life."

Caleb took the packet of papers that were hers and set them before her. "I didn't look in here. I wanted to, but they're yours."

Em took them and held them tight against her chest. "Thank you."

"Let's get reading. Then we can see what's in there. Hopefully you're a quick learner. I've never been very patient when it comes to a mystery." His eyes twinkled. Nothing belittling or demeaning. She had been afraid he would make her feel inferior, lesser because of her ignorance.

For the next hour Caleb went over the sounds the letters made. Em tried to commit it all to memory. She stumbled a few times when he asked her what a letter said. "No, Em. That's a D, not a B. I told you that a minute ago."

Embarrassed but determined, she pressed on. Again she mixed the letters up. "I'm sorry, Caleb. I had hoped to be so good at this."

"Don't be too hard on yourself. It's not you I'm frustrated with. It just seems so unfair that I had years of schooling and you had none. That's what frustrates me." He pointed again to the letters. "Try again. I know you can learn it. I guess I'm just eager for you to be able to read."

She continued, doing much better now that his voice was calmer. Then he took out a stack of papers from the desk drawer. On the back of one of them, he wrote out the letters of the alphabet. "These are old posters. We don't need them any-more. When you have time, practice writing the letters on the back. Try and write them like the ones I wrote out. Soon we will be putting them together. And then you'll be able to write a letter to anyone you choose and read those papers you are holding so carefully."

Her eyes jumped to his when he said she would be able to write soon. He must have seen it. The longing she felt must have been visible to him. "I wish you would tell me who you want to write to," he said.

She remembered his plea from before that she just answer a question without him having to pry. "I want to write to my sister. I want to read a train ticket and signs and find my way to her. Her name is Lucy."

"You have a sister?" Caleb leaned in closer to her.

"I do. I haven't seen her in seven years, but I've thought of her every day since." Em felt emotion building within her. "Every day. Every single day." She fought against the tears that threatened to spill, but a few desperate ones crept from deep inside her. Shaking her head, she battled to regain control. Seven years she had held back these tears. Why did they have to betray her now?

Caleb came around the desk and knelt beside her. "Cry if you need to. Talk. Yell if it'll help." He reached a hand up and, using his calloused thumb, wiped a tear from her cheek. His tender touch only brought more tears.

Through the storm of emotion, she said, "I . . . I never cry."

"You ought to. I know I cried buckets of tears when I heard about my brothers. There's no shame in it."

Sniffling, she said, "We were on the same train. I thought we would be together. That a family would want us both." Em's voice grew stronger, less shaky, as she spoke. "There were so many children. We never even stood on a train platform until Beckford. When they finally lined us up for everyone to see they pinned numbers on us and separated us. The little children were at one end and the older ones at the opposite side. Lucy was seven and far down the line from me. She was crying, but even with tears on her face she was perfect. Everyone must have known it and wanted her."

Em stood, unable to hold still as she talked about the bitter memory. "People started coming, walking across the stage inspecting us like we were cattle. A big man stood in front of me. He asked me to open my mouth so he could see my teeth. I wouldn't do it. My stupid, stubborn pride. It has always plagued me." Pausing to take a deep breath, she looked at Caleb through her tears. "Some of the women from the Aid Society came up to me, trying to get me to comply. Finally I opened my mouth and let the man look me over. He never really wanted me. He was just having a good time harassing us all. Blasted man finally left the platform—he didn't take a child with him. He didn't want me or anyone else."

"What happened to Lucy?" Caleb asked as he stood up.

Em's hands were in tight fists by her sides and every muscle in her body was tense as she recalled the rest of that fateful day. "I don't know. She was off the stage and gone by the time the man stopped blocking my view. I ran off the platform looking for her, screaming her name and crying. A couple of the men came and carried me back on the train. I fought them the best I could, but they were too strong. I tried asking after her when we left Beckford. The women just told me that the records were confidential. All I know is she left the train in Beckford. And I have to get there. I have to." She wasn't sure how many times she had repeated her need to go. Caleb stood by her, listening to her mourn, waiting until she was ready to say more.

"For seven years I've thought of little other than how I could get there. It's what I lived for. Having no money, no ability to read, and no idea where I was living kept me from getting there sooner. I would have gone for her. I would have if I could have." Em braced herself against the back of the wooden chair she had been sitting in. "I wanted to find her. I really did."

"I believe you," he said softly. "It's not your fault."

"I have a job now, and once I've earned enough to repay the Howells and can get on a train, I'm going to find her. I thought of writing first, but I don't know who has her." With her story told, she let her shoulders stoop forward. The weight of her words pressed against her.

"Did the train stop often? How did you end up so much farther across Iowa than her?"

She faced him. "Look at me, Caleb. Look at me! I'm plain. I'm scarred." She pointed to her burn. Normally she did all she could to conceal it, but today was different. "Not to mention that I was twelve, angry, and broken. I stood with my number pinned on me at every station from Beckford to the one George picked me up at. No one wanted me." A painful laugh came then. "They wanted the others. Little boys and girls found homes at each stop. More children were separated, friendships torn apart. But they were wanted. Not me—no one wanted me. I'd accepted the fact that I'd be living on the streets again as soon as the train returned. Then at the end, when there was no one else to take, George took me and it was over. I failed. I failed Lucy. And now I have to find her. I have to fix it."

Caleb ran his hands through his hair. Then he looked hard at her and shook his head. "How did you fail? None of this was your fault. None of it. You were a child."

"I'd been taking care of Lucy her whole life. While my ma worked as a maid, I cared for her. Before my ma died, she told me to look after Lucy. I tried, but I didn't know how." The mood was dark, the despair palpable in the air. "I failed.

The only person who needed me and wanted me was taken, and I've not been able to find her."

"How long were you on the streets? Let it be my second question if you must," Caleb said.

Em took a deep breath and then gave him a weak smile. "Very well. My ma died after I had turned eleven and Lucy was six. We were no longer welcome in the tenement because we had no money to pay our share of the rent. We found an abandoned building and moved in there. For a couple months we lived off of food we found and what I could buy with the money we made selling newspapers and doing odd jobs."

"Even then you were clever," Caleb said.

"I tried, and yet there were certain things I refused to do. I saw them though. Other girls who lived on the streets told me how they made money. I even ventured over to where they did business while Lucy was sleeping one night. I knew then what my ma had warned me against, and I ran back the entire way to Lucy. I picked her up in my arms and held her that whole night. I knew somehow I had to find another way to survive. I had to take care of her, but I was too afraid to sell myself. I wonder now if I made the right choice." Em couldn't meet Caleb's eyes as she continued.

"The next day I stole. I never had before. And as good as the bread tasted, I hated myself for taking it. But Lucy seemed stronger that night, more alive. The food had been good for her. I hadn't noticed until then just how thin she'd become. I pushed my guilt away and began stealing more often. I never liked it, but I didn't know what else to do. Everything went along all right for a couple more weeks. Lucy turned seven and we spent a happy day together, just playing, pretending life was not such a heavy burden. We made dolls from sticks. Like the ones you found. It was all I could give her. I wanted so much to give her more. I wanted her to be happy like the little girls I saw playing outside with their families. Like Mae and Milly are."

Em hesitated. She needed to finish her tale, but it was hard putting the past into words and hearing them out loud. "On the way back to our shelter, we saw a public hanging. I covered Lucy's eyes and distracted her, but I watched. The boy who was swinging looked so young. I asked a man what had happened. He said the boy was twelve and old enough to know stealing was wrong. That night I imagined Lucy living on her own and me swinging from the gallows. The image was so real that I emptied my stomach because I felt so sick. And so afraid."

Caleb was near her, his hand on her shoulder. Had it been there long? Em was not sure. "We went to the Aid Society the next day. We'd heard of their trains and decided it was best. We spent a night there, only to have someone tell us there was a chance no one would take us together. We snuck off the next day because we were unwilling to risk losing each other. One more night was all we spent in our abandoned building. Everything was against us—the building caught fire in the night. Lucy's dress went up in flames. I put it out and pulled her from the building. When we were safe, I looked at my arm. It was mangled and raw." Em ran her hand along the gruesome scar. "I'd seen what could happen when injuries were left to fester. I was not so afraid of dying as I was of leaving Lucy all alone."

Caleb reached a hand down and touched the scar. His fingertips brushed across it. "Does it hurt you?"

"It did hurt, but now it's not so bad. It gets stiff and it's ugly. The memory hurts worse than the arm." Continuing her tale, she said, "I could think of no other way to protect Lucy. We went back to the Society and agreed to take their train. They told us there was one leaving soon. We spent only a couple of weeks at the home before we boarded the train and headed to Iowa. My arm festered and ached the entire time. But nothing hurt like being torn from Lucy."

They stood in silence. Caleb still rested a hand on her shoulder. Part of her welcomed his touch while the other part wanted to run and hide. Never had she imagined sharing her tragedy. What must he think of her now? Did he think she'd done right or did he blame her like she blamed herself?

She stepped away from his hand and moved for the door.

"Wait. You don't begin work for two more hours—where will you go?"

"I don't know. I'll just walk and try to lock it all back up. It's hard having a past like mine." Pressing a hand to her heart, she said, "It hurts, more than any burn. More than the pain of being hungry. More than being unwanted. I miss her. Every single day I miss her."

"But now I know, and you don't have to lock me out. I'll carry it with you." He stepped toward her. "Let me walk with you. Fresh air will do us both good."

"Your job is sheriff. You don't have to fix this. Even if you wanted to, you could not." Em opened the door and walked out.

Caleb followed.

Others were around them now. They walked in silence, away from the town and the people. The farther they got, the more alone they were—trees and shrubs their company. A trickling brook sounded in the distance while birds celebrated the day, naive to all pain, and a squirrel jumped from limb to limb. All so carefree.

Caleb was the first to speak. "When I was a boy, I wanted to live on a big spread of land. Big enough that I could look in any direction and not see anyone else. I wanted a big old tree growing in my yard and a brook. Being outside in the open, that was always my favorite." He was doing it again, using his words to make peace.

"I didn't know there were such wide-open spaces when I was a child," Em said. "I did love the time we lived in a room with only our family. And I liked going to the little parks with Lucy. She always said the grass under her feet felt like a carpet rolled out for a princess." Em smiled. It was the first time in a very long time she'd smiled at a memory of Lucy.

"What else did Lucy do?" His eyes looked deep into her own. She believed that he really wanted to know.

"Well, she loved to sing. She would sing to herself little made-up songs. She also loved stories. Just like Mae and Milly. The three of them would have gotten along well. Each night she begged me to tell her stories. Even when she was small she liked them. I remember telling her tales before she could talk and it would soothe her to sleep." Em stopped walking when they reached the brook. "She would have loved this. I know she would. I remember her splashing her feet in the puddles after the rain. This water is so clean—she would have been thrilled."

Caleb sat on a log and started taking his shoes off. "Let's go in. For Lucy. Let's go in for my brothers too."

Em felt a moment of hesitancy, then she thought again of Lucy and her puddles. She nodded in understanding. "For Lucy and your brothers," she said as she sat down next to him and unlaced her secondhand boots. "But I can only get my feet wet. I have work today."

He didn't respond, just gave her that same crooked smile she'd come to love. With her shoes off, she stood, ready to dip her feet in. Before she knew what was happening, big arms came around her—one around her waist, the other beneath her legs. She was in Caleb's arms. His grip firm. "Would Lucy want you getting only your feet wet?"

Not waiting for an answer, he spun in a quick circle, making her laugh despite her melancholy. He ran for the brook and then jumped in, their combined weight causing water to splash up over them. Em could feel drops of water on everything—even her nose. Caleb proceeded to stomp around in the brook with Em in his arms. Clinging to his neck, she laughed and laughed. He laughed too—a big, deep laugh that made his chest shake. He marched about in the creek, shouting proclamations such as, "This is for you, Lucy. This is for you, Reggie."

And then, for no reason at all, she cried. Laughter and tears were a strange combination. Burying her head in his neck, she tried to muffle the sound and sight of her emotion. Rather than let her down, he pulled her tighter. His marching slowed.

Soon it stopped completely. Caleb stood still—an island in the brook, holding her as she sobbed. Seven years' worth of tears rushed from her like a thrashing river.

When she finally lifted her face, their eyes met and she saw tears on his cheeks too. Unlike her, he did not hide them. Instead, he spun one last time, pulled her tight to him, and kissed her on the forehead. He held her for a brief moment longer before stepping out of the brook and setting her back on the log.

Bending his long legs, he sat beside her. He rested his elbows on his knees and put his head in his hands. She wanted to reach out and comfort him or ask what he was thinking, but she feared his response. Was he thinking of his brothers? Of Lucy? Was he regretting the kiss?

They sat silently, letting the warm sun dry their clothes. Em lost in thought. Where Caleb was, she was not sure.

At last Caleb lifted his head and looked up at the sun. "I think it's nearing twelve. Let's get back so Mrs. Anders isn't kept waiting."

Ten

"D on't work too hard," Caleb said before leaving Em at Margaret's door. Walking to the train station, he reflected on the morning. It hadn't gone as planned. Some of it had. He felt as though he was getting somewhere with Alroy and his gang. Then there was the reading lesson, which had gone well. He had no doubt Em would catch on quickly. She was smart, and it irked him that she'd never been given a chance as a child.

And then she'd let him in. Opened up about her pain, shared with him the burden she carried. Watching her struggle as she remembered had tortured him. Every part of him had wanted to do something, anything, to fix it. All the years of loneliness, the struggle she'd endured to survive, the misery of living apart from the only family she had—each piece of her story was tragic.

Kicking at the loose rocks on the road, he battled his own emotions. Life was full of so much suffering. So much pain and hardship. So many trials. As he thought about the despair and unfairness of it all, a drop of water that had managed to evade the heat of the sun—like a message from above—ran down his forehead. He pictured the brook. There they had not just mourned their losses but laughed and celebrated their loved ones. Leaning on each other for a moment had been good. More than good. Since meeting Em, he'd felt more connected to Reggie and Sam and Marvin. And she'd smiled, remembering Lucy. Em understood pain and loss, and he'd felt safe sharing with her.

He'd never expected to find a friend in her. But he had. And now he hoped his impulsive kiss would not frighten her off. He hadn't planned to do it; it'd been an instinct. Seeing her grief had made him want to help, even in some small way. What did she think of him now?

He worried over it the entire way to the train station.

"How much is a ticket to Beckford?" he asked the man behind the counter.

"Depending on the season, should cost you between six and seven dollars. Could be a little more or a little less if they change prices before you leave. When you planning on traveling?" the agent asked. His long mustache shook as he spoke.

"Not for a few months. Maybe longer."

"You're welcome to check back anytime and see if the fares have changed. And when you're ready, we'll get you booked." The man pulled out a little notebook and began writing in it. Caleb couldn't think of anything else to ask, so he walked away.

How long would it take Em to earn six dollars? Weeks or perhaps months, maybe longer—hopefully longer. No, that wasn't fair. He wanted her to find Lucy and yet he wasn't sure he wanted her to leave. Without meaning to, he'd become used to her. He enjoyed her. Plus, she needed help with her reading, and Mae and Milly would be sorry to have her gone.

As he headed back across town, he hoped she was enjoying her first day at work. He looked for her but did not see her as he walked past Margaret's boardinghouse.

For a moment he stared at the bright yellow house until he remembered all the many things he was supposed to be doing. He had a telegram to send and the Alroy case to work on.

But first he was going to have a word with Silas at the saloon. Today he'd remind the worthless man how women were supposed to be treated. Parts of his job gave him a great deal of personal pleasure.

"You're on time," Margaret said as she opened the door. "From now on, you just come right in. No need to knock."

Em stepped inside, ready to dive into whatever work Margaret needed done. She looked around for a spot to set the pail that held the meal Abigail had so lovingly packed for her.

Margaret must have noticed her darted glance. She stepped closer and looked into the pail. "That looks like it hasn't been touched. Best sit down and eat it quick before we start. Rumor is you were shot not so long ago. I won't have you losing strength on my account."

Margaret motioned her into the dining hall. Em took a seat on one of the long wooden benches and then began pulling out the contents of her meal. Bread, cheese, and meat. She paused when she pulled a napkin from the pail. Such a simple luxury. She placed it in her lap and began eating as quickly as she could so she could get to work.

"No need to swallow it all at once. I'll go and butter a roll and enjoy it with you."

When Margaret returned, she sat herself right next to Em. "It's been far too lonely since my Scarlett left. This place can get awfully busy, but it's usually a houseful of starving men who aren't much for conversation. Sometimes a woman just needs to sit and talk to another woman."

"I'll be glad for the company too. Although I'm not sure I'll have anything interesting to say," Em said between bites.

"Of course you will. I have a feeling you've a far more interesting story than most of the towns-people. You've probably seen things I never have." Margaret winked at her. "In fact, I think

I would be entertained just hearing about your morning."

Em gasped. Her morning of tears and memories and the brook. "I . . . it was . . ."

Margaret patted her hand. "You don't have to tell me now. But in time I hope we become dear friends. Then I'll tell you my secrets and you can tell me yours."

"I'd like that." Em tucked her napkin back into her pail. "I'm finished. What can I do first?"

Nodding her head, Margaret said, "The bedrooms. All of them need the sheets stripped from the beds. Then we'll boil them and hang them on the line. If we work quickly, we should be able to put them back on the beds before dinner."

"I can do that." Em nodded, then made her way up the stairs to the bedrooms and busied herself.

She worked hard and fast, her hands doing what she told them to as quickly as possible. Meanwhile, her mind constantly disobeyed her and wandered back to the brook.

Within her mind's eye she saw the clear water and the morning sun. She saw the trees and she saw Caleb. Handsome, kind Caleb. Men had always scared her, except for her father, but he'd been dead so long she had few memories of him. Caleb was different. He was big and strong like other men. Capable of tearing her apart if he wished or at the very least belittling her, making her feel worthless and unimportant, like other men she'd known. But he hadn't done that. He had held her, even when she cried. And then he'd kissed her, but not like the vicious kisses she'd witnessed in the city. No, his kiss had been full of kindness, as though he wanted to kiss the pain away.

Someday Caleb would find a beautiful princess to marry. They would live happily ever after just like in all the stories. Em hoped he would get his stretch of land for them to grow old on. Land with a tree and a brook. When he was married and settled, she would be happy for him. Of course she would, he was her friend. Friends are supposed to want good things for each other, aren't they? No matter what the future held for Caleb, Em knew she would hold the memory of being in his arms and the feel of his kiss on her forehead in her heart always.

Daydreaming as she worked, she allowed herself to pretend he had kissed her because he cared for her and thought she was the most eligible maiden.

"What has you smiling? Or do you always smile while you work?" Margaret asked, pulling Em from her fantasy.

"I . . . I'm just happy to have a job. Never have I had a job like this, with regular hours and pay."

"And I'm very glad to have you. But I think you're smiling about something more." Margaret tugged off the last sheet and together they walked through the house and out the door, settling in a spot behind the building to start washing and hanging them on the line. "I saw a similar look on my Scarlett's face only months before she up and married Benjamin. You aren't planning on running off with some beau are you?"

"Me? A beau?" Em was shocked that Margaret thought it even possible. "No, there's no one. I have no plans to ever marry."

"No plans to marry? Certainly you have plans to marry. Being married to a good man, toiling with him day in and day out. Laughing together about things no one else is a part of. All of it, the good and the bad, is where you find real joy."

Picturing her ma kissing her pa, Em frowned, knowing it was a fate not meant for her. "I'm sure there is joy in it. I don't doubt that. I'm just not convinced there will ever be a good man who wants me. And I've no desire to marry a man who's cruel just so I can share his name."

"Oh, nonsense. There will be a man out there who thinks you are the sun and the moon, the stars—everything. Judging by that smile, you've already met him." Margaret's wild curls bobbed as she spoke.

Em, flustered, tried to think of a way to turn the conversation. "Do you attend the socials?"

"I do. Everyone does. I don't even serve a meal on social nights. I tried to once, but no one came and I missed the fun. I won't be doing that again.

I was left with a mountain of food. I'm glad you brought it up. On the day of the social, we will clean but we won't be cooking. We'll work fast so we have plenty of time to freshen up before the fun."

"I suppose work cannot be my excuse for missing the social."

The cauldron was boiling. Margaret stirred the sheets with a big wooden paddle. "The socials are fun—all the young people love them. You will too. Is there someone you're looking forward to dancing with?"

Em stood by the drying line. "I won't be dancing. I never danced as a child and I certainly never danced during the years I lived near Hollow Creek. I don't know a thing about it. I'd only make a fool of myself. If I had my way, I'd stay away from the social entirely."

"Dancing isn't so hard. It's fun too. When Wyatt was alive, we danced every dance at the socials. He was so good at leading, and I felt like I was floating the whole night." Margaret's hand slowed. "Dancing with Wyatt was pure bliss."

"Wyatt was your husband?"

"Sure was. He died a few years back—same fever took him that took the Howells' boys. Now I have to wait for someone to ask me to dance and none of the other fellows are as good a partner as Wyatt was. I still go though." Margaret sighed. "Every time I go I feel a little closer to him. I don't want to forget him, so I look for anything that reminds me of him—and dancing always will." She pulled a sheet out with the paddle, dipped it in the bucket of cool water, wrung it out, and handed it to Em.

She hung it on the line, her mind drifting to her morning again. The brook and the memories of Lucy had made her sweet sister seem closer. "I think I understand your wanting to remember him. Wanting him to feel close."

"We all grieve differently. I want to have him all around me. I do too. In little ways he's all over this house. In fact, that's one reason I can never paint the house a different color."

"Because he loved the yellow?" Em asked.

Margaret laughed. "Because he hated it. I hired two men to paint the building while he was away. When he came back, he stood in front of it and stared. Then he asked me what in blazes I was thinking. When I told him I thought it was cheerful, he just laughed. Then he swooped me up in his giant arms and carried me inside. He told me he must love me more than he ought to, to let me keep the house that color."

Smiling up at the house, Margaret said, "I keep it yellow because every time I look at it I can hear his deep voice saying he loves me. Every day after that when Wyatt walked home, I'd see him pause in front of the house, shake his head, and laugh. The yellow reminds me of him."

What would it be like to share so much with a man?

Margaret added wood to the fire. "I like reminders of him. But not everyone grieves like me. Others close the door like Abigail. She tries to lock it all deep inside. Those boys were something special. She knows it and can't figure out how to remember them without hurting."

"What were their names?" Em asked.

"Ask her sometime. Maybe she needs to talk."

"Seems everyone has lost someone."

"I think we all did between the war and the fevers that came through here. How about you? Did you lose anyone?"

Em wiped her wet hands on her sides. "I've lost everyone. I'm hoping to find one of them though."

"You will. You'll find what it is you're looking for. I can see a fighting spirit in you. I don't think you'll give up until you do." After wringing out the last sheet, she handed it to Em. "Let's hurry with these so we can get started on our dinner preparations."

Shaking her hands in the air, Em hoped to find a little extra strength in them. The pile of potatoes she'd peeled already looked like enough to feed *all* of Azure Springs. And so many more were waiting to have their dirt-stained peels removed. How many people were they feeding?

"You'll get stronger. I hired you knowing the pile would be more than you could handle at first." Margaret was kneading bread. "You've done remarkably well. I thought those thin arms of yours would take weeks to build up strength."

Em picked up another potato and started scraping the skin from it. "I'll finish them, even today I will. But I hope to get faster."

"I believe it was providence that brought you here." Margaret's voice interrupted her peeling. "We two are a similar breed. A challenge always makes me want to fight harder. When Wyatt died, no one thought I could keep this place running. Every time they said I couldn't, I grew more determined. It's been years now and the deed's still mine."

"I haven't succeeded at everything I've set my mind to," Em said, scraping harder. "I wish I had."

"Yes, but you're a fighter. The future may not work out how you've planned or dreamed, but it will work out." Margaret had a way of making anything seem possible.

"I like to believe it will," Em said. "I daydream of happy endings for myself. I've hoped more since living here than I did before."

"You're here in Azure Springs with a job, and from what I overheard Abigail saying, you have endeared yourself in the hearts of that family." Margaret began shaping the dough. "It's easier to believe when we have people cheering us on."

"I have been blessed as of late. More than I deserve."

"Nonsense. You're entirely deserving. I don't know much of your story, but I know it's been a rough road for you. Keep enduring. Sometimes the steepest roads lead to the grandest views. Now, before the crowd arrives, I must warn you about a few of the regulars."

Em looked up.

"There are always a few strangers just passing through, and we will learn about them together. But there are some regulars you can count on. There's Old Man Garret. He's been coming every night since his wife died two months ago. He's harmless but doesn't hear well. Be sure to talk where he can see you so he can read your lips. His manners could use some brushing up, but he's a good man."

"How will I know him?"

"I'll introduce you to them as they come in. Reuben Dronley will more than likely be here. He's boarding over at the saloon. His house burnt down nearly a year ago, and he says he's going to rebuild but doesn't seem to be in a hurry to do so. If he's been drinking, he'll forget all his manners and might even cause a few problems. Don't wander off alone with him." Margaret pushed a few curls from her face, leaving a bit of flour on her already wild locks.

Em nodded. "I'll forgo the evening stroll."

"Sheriff Reynolds comes a couple times a week."

Em perked up at his name, then just as quickly ducked her head and went to work harder than before on the potatoes.

"So you know our fine sheriff? Of course you do. He's been chasing after the men who shot you." She could feel Margaret watching her as she spoke. "Do you find him as dashing as the other ladies in town do? How could you not? You'd have to be blind not to. Scarlett always swooned when he was in, until she met her own man. Something about Caleb Reynolds turns all the girls' heads."

Margaret didn't pressure Em for answers and went right on telling her about their other potential dinner guests. She told Em all about Spencer and Titus Weston who were twins and had lived together their entire lives and never married. Then there was Walter Pratt, a traveling surveyor who was in town for a couple weeks.

"Every night it's like having a dinner party and not knowing who to expect. Some nights the company is very pleasant, other nights you wonder when it will ever end." Margaret stepped back and admired her loaves of bread. "It won't be long before you know them all too."

They worked hard preparing the meal to feed the mob. The conversation and companionship were easy. Margaret had a laid-back and natural way of sparking conversation, and Em felt herself relax in the woman's company. The work was not as easy or natural. Instead, it was hard and tiring.

The dinner rush, as Margaret called it, was perfectly befitting of its title. Em rushed from the kitchen to the hall, carrying bowls of food and serving one man after another. A few women were present, but it was predominantly men. Margaret walked with Em around the table once—her serving beans and Em serving potatoes—and introduced her new employee to the guests.

These hungry men seemed to have bottomless pits where their stomachs should be. The crowd ate without ceasing until Margaret walked in from the kitchen carrying an empty pot. She banged on the pot with a wooden spoon, silencing the crowd. "Dinner is over—kitchen's closing up. Finish what's on your plate and be on your way."

The men groaned and scraped their plates, desperately trying to get one more forkful. They obeyed though. When not a crumb more could be found, they stood and patted their full bellies and readied to leave. Chair legs dragged across the floor as they left the table and made for the door. Some were gruff, rowdy men. Reuben staggered out, announcing his need of a drink despite the fact that he had clearly had too many before dinner.

Most thanked Margaret and complimented her cooking. A few were bold and asked Margaret what it would take for her to cook for just them. Like a seasoned warrior, she stayed perfectly calm, only laughing and pushing them toward the door.

The noise of the men leaving the large dining hall was tumultuous. They left quickly, though, and suddenly it was very quiet. Strangely quiet after the long meal. For a moment Em just stood there looking at the mess the group had left. The table had become a long mountain range of dishes.

Weary from the afternoon of hard labor, she was tempted with every fiber of her being to sit down and refuse to lift so much as one dish from the table. Margaret patted her on the shoulder. "It's not as bad as it looks. Never look at the whole table—it will be more than you can stomach. Instead, start at one end and carry an armload at a time. One dish, then another, and then somehow I come to get more and find they're all gone. Done for the night. That is the best feeling of the entire day." She pulled Em toward the table. "Let's get started. The sooner we start, the sooner you'll get to experience that moment."

Margaret followed her own advice. She picked up an awkward load of dishes and carried them back to the big wash basin in the kitchen. Em picked up her own load and, walking carefully and slowly, also made her way to the soapy water.

She had aching arms, shoulders, and fingers, a sore back, tired legs, and even a pounding head, but she had survived her first hours of work. Washing the dishes was hard at the end of the day, but Margaret stayed beside her the entire time, washing and drying in turn. A comfortable silence settled over the two as they worked. And then the moment came. The table was clear, the mountain range replaced by a smooth wooden plain.

With their hands on their hips, the two women stood side by side admiring the empty table.

"Do you feel it?" Margaret asked.

"I feel it," Em said while enjoying the sublime sense of accomplishment. "You were right. This moment was worth it."

As she walked back to the Howells', she knew she'd given a good day's work and was a step closer to Beckford. Hope and pride crept into her heart.

Lucy, I'm coming.

Eleven

Rolling her shoulders back and forth, Em tried to loosen the knots that were forming beneath her skin. Despite her efforts, she could feel her muscles rebelling against the day's hard work. Em walked slowly back to the Howells' after her fourth day at the boardinghouse. She could feel the tightness all through her shoulders and back. Muscles that had lain dormant were now shouting as they awoke from their long slumber. She'd always worked hard, but this work was new and her body was struggling to adjust.

She rubbed the muscles in her neck with her hands. It was a satisfying feeling—painful but rewarding. It meant she was closer to Beckford and repaying the Howells. It meant she was no longer stagnant. Instead of waiting for her chance, she was now seizing it.

Margaret had proved a patient and kind teacher. She expected a full day's work but held effort in the highest regard, and Em gave each task her all. During mundane jobs, Em reviewed letters and their sounds in her head. Already, after only four brief lessons, she was recognizing the letters she'd learned.

Caleb had seemed pleased with her progress, which made her heart soar. He had made no mention of the brook and neither had she. Instead, they had returned to being easy friends.

The newness of reading, the gratification of hard work, and the hope of seeing Lucy again filled her with an abundance of optimism. Each day she sprang from her bed, eager to see what lay ahead.

Tomorrow she would have to learn on her own. Caleb was meeting up with the other lawmen and would be gone for days or maybe even weeks.

Back at the Howells' house, Em eased herself into a tall straight-backed chair near the fireplace. Eliza stood with her back to her on the other side of the hearth.

"You're back early," Eliza said without even turning to face her.

"Margaret doesn't offer dinner when there's a social. I helped her clean and do laundry. That was it for today."

"You look tired. Are you sure she is not working you too hard?" Eliza asked while heating the iron.

"It's hard work—I can't deny that. I think I'll get used to it. I hope I do. I need the money." Allowing herself a moment of reprieve, she sank deeper into the chair. "Margaret is good company, which helps the time go quickly. My muscles might disagree with me, but I like the work even if it's hard."

"Perhaps you should stop spending your mornings with Caleb. Then you would not be so tired."

"He leaves tomorrow and I don't know when he'll return. My mornings will be free again." Em stood and began walking to find Abigail and make herself useful. Never would she allow herself too much idle time, not while she was living off the goodwill of others.

"He'll never care for you. Not the way you want him to," Eliza said over her shoulder as she smoothed her dress with the iron.

Em stopped. "I'm grateful to be his friend and indebted to him for his kindness, but I have no other expectations."

Eliza stepped away from the dress and the iron and moved toward her. "I've seen you looking at him. Your eyes follow him when he's here, and when he speaks you hang on his words. You care for him. I just hope you don't end up with a broken heart."

"Thank you for the concern," Em said through clenched teeth.

"There are other men. Men who are more suited to you. Mr. Harvel lost his wife and has children who need care. His last wife was not much to look at—appearances don't matter to him. He's not so horrible. Papa says he works hard and he has his own home and business. I think you'd be well suited."

"I'm not looking for a match." Em said each word slowly.

"Well, you can't live here forever, and Caleb won't marry you. You need to think of another plan."

Em turned and started to leave the room. A word of departure might be customary, but she could not speak another word. Leaving was all she could think to do. Otherwise her injured pride might get the better of her. But she wasn't quick enough.

"There are already rumors about you. If you don't want to hurt his reputation, you should leave him alone. Just go away."

Through the kitchen and out the back door she went. The house full of people always had been so comforting, but now she wanted to be alone. Her knees buckled beneath her once she reached the big tree. In a pathetic heap she sat with her face buried in her hands. She tried to get Eliza's words out of her head—*he'll never care for you, already rumors, leave him alone, go away*—but the words would not go.

What rumors? She had only been in town a short while and most of that time had been spent convalescing at the Howells' home. Nothing she'd done warranted gossip. The very idea of hurting Caleb's reputation sat ill with her. He was her friend—she'd never willfully hurt him. Why couldn't life move ahead easily for once?

"Em, come inside. The social begins soon and I have found the perfect dress for you to wear." Abigail was standing at the kitchen door looking out at her. Her hand was on her forehead, blocking the evening sun.

"I was thinking of staying back. I find I am quite worn out from work," Em said from her spot on the ground.

"He was right. That man seems to know you well. Stand up. You've got to come." Abigail motioned Em inside.

"What do you mean, he was right?"

"Caleb stopped by earlier. Said he had a feeling you would try to get out of the social. I'm to remind you you're under an obligation to attend. Something about your word and a shooting competition. All that aside, I believe you gave me your word as well."

She hated that Abigail was right on both accounts. She had given her word. Being under an obligation did not make going any easier.

"I suppose I did," Em said, walking toward her.

"I'm glad that's settled." Abigail took Em's hand and pulled her inside. "I got ready early so I'd have time to help you. Let's try on the dress and then I'll fix your hair." Abigail pulled back a little and looked her over. "What is it? Is something else wrong? Are you nervous to meet so many new people?"

"I suppose that is part of it." Em did her best to brighten her face. "I'll be fine."

"What else is it? You can trust me. Tell me what's weighing on you."

"I worry I am in the way here. That there is not a spot for me." Em chewed on her thumbnail while she tried to decide the right way to explain all she was feeling. "I sometimes think I'm settling in here, more than I ever have anywhere. Then I am reminded that I have no real home. I don't even have a place to run to when I've had a bad day."

Abigail took Em's face in her hands. "My dear, something has happened. You've been nothing but sunshine these last few days and now this. Has something happened with Caleb?"

Em shook her head. "Nothing has happened between Caleb and me. Nothing ever will." Surprised by how much despair was in her voice, Em placed a hand over her mouth and walked to the kitchen window and looked out.

"He is your friend. I've seen it. You didn't know him before, but he is so much more carefree since meeting you. You're good for him and he's good for you. Come now and let's get you ready. We can talk more while I do your hair." Abigail put a gentle hand on Em's shoulder. Without saying a word, Em followed.

Abigail took her into her own room and helped her dress. Never had Em had such exquisite fabric against her skin, and yet she found little pleasure in it. It was just another farce to go with all the rest. None of this was really hers.

Abigail seemed to sense her lingering despair and filled the air with conversation. She asked after Em's job and told about the girls' escapades. When there was a lull, Em asked, "What were your sons' names? You don't have to answer, but I've wondered."

A moment passed. Abigail wiped a tear from her face. It had come so fast that Em regretted her question, afraid she'd hurt her motherly friend. But remembering Margaret and her happiness that came from remembering Wyatt, she pressed on. "I have heard they were the finest boys."

"That they were. The very finest. Never had boys shown so much promise. They would have been fine men now, men who could do anything they dared to dream." Abigail took a thin strip of Em's hair and curled it. "Their names were Mathew and John."

"John was my father's name. He was a good man too."

"I had hoped to hear all about your parents one day. So your father was John. I agree it is a good name. My John was a little horseman. We had an old horse named Win that he rode every day. I never knew a boy could love an animal so much. He also loved the store. He would look over the catalogs and talk Abraham into buying the newest items. They usually sold too. Such a brilliant boy." Em glanced over her shoulder and was amazed to see a smile gracing Abigail's face. She was happy remembering.

"What of Mathew?"

"Mathew was my fair-haired boy. Freckles, like yours, were all along his nose. I have heard some criticize freckles, but I loved them. They looked as perfect on him as they look on you." Em touched her nose absently. Nothing was perfect about her—at least it had never been before. No, that wasn't true. Her mother had thought her perfect.

Abigail must have seen Em react. "Yes, Em, your freckles are perfect. Looks are a funny thing, very peculiar. Never waste any time disliking the ones you have. The right person will think they are the very definition of beautiful."

Could it be possible?

Em felt tears prick her own eyes. "My mother always loved the way I looked. At least she said she did. As the years have passed, I've wondered how she could have. I think perhaps she only told me she did so I'd not feel sorry for myself."

"Your mother truly thought you were beautiful. I'm sure of it. Don't doubt her words, not for a moment. Everyone who knows you, who really knows you, will love everything about you. Don't go shrugging your shoulders like you don't believe me. I'm right. Ask Abraham—I'm always right." Abigail reached behind her and grabbed a hand mirror. "What do you think of your hair? It's coming along nicely I think."

Tight ringlets framed her face. "It looks like hair from one of the girls' stories," Em said, turning her head from side to side.

"You've described it perfectly. And that is just what I was going for. Now you will be perfectly suited for your dance with the Prince of Azure Springs. The girls told me." Abigail winked at her. Then, surprising Em, she said, "If my boys were here, they would be his rivals. They were princes, both of them. The finest manners, the kindest hearts. I'm convinced all the girls would be chasing them if they were still here."

Abigail took Em's hand in hers and squeezed it. "Thank you for asking me about them. I'm learning to live without them. I miss them so badly. Every day I miss them and wish they were here. I long to hear them stomping down the stairs in the morning. I miss it all—the noise, the dirty shoes, the critters they were always catching. Things I never thought I would miss haunt me now." Wiping at her cheek, she said, "It was good to talk about them. To have someone ask about them."

Em brushed her hand across her forehead,

longing for her mother's kiss. "I'm not sure we ever learn to live without those we love. I think Margaret may be right. The secret is to learn to live with them as nearby as we can keep them. My parents are dead and my sister is in Beckford. I miss them every day. Only now am I learning the right way to remember them."

"I believe you and I shall learn together. We'll find a way to live with our loss and find happiness along the way," Abigail said as she gave Em's shoulder a squeeze.

"I would like that."

Abigail kissed Em's cheek. "I want you to know I have prayed prayers of gratitude for the good Lord leading you here, to me and to all of us. Tonight I will thank him again. And I will pray for your sister. Someday soon I hope you will tell me all about your family. We must hurry now." The friendly glimmer returned to her eyes. "Or you shall be late for the social."

Deserted by even Mae and Milly, Em stood as far in the shadows as possible. Abigail had made her feel beautiful, but now, surrounded by strangers, she felt only fear. She wished she could blend in with the tall oaks—become one of them and spend the evening observing all the lovely couples as they twirled around the dance floor. Em's dress was a pale blue, the color of a robin's egg. White lace ran along the bodice, cuffs, and hem. It was not a dress meant to blend in. Oh, but she wished she could.

The weather was ideal for an outdoor dance, warm with a refreshing breeze. A makeshift floor was set up behind the church. Tables of food and drinks lined the edges. Musicians played in the corner, their festive tunes filling the air.

Children frolicked together in the trees. Mae and Milly had vowed to spend the evening with Em, but once they approached the gathering they had looked so longingly at the cluster of children that Em had told them to run and play.

"What time is it, Mr. Fox?" the children were shouting. A large boy was acting as Mr. Fox. He replied with his back turned that it was eight o'clock. The mob of children all took eight steps closer to him. Again they shouted an inquiry about the time.

"Dinner time," the boy yelled as he turned and ran toward them. The children sped away, laughing as they went, hoping Mr. Fox would not catch them.

What fun they were having. Just as they should be. Glancing away from the game and back to the adults, Em felt everyone was enjoying themselves but her.

Quiet Abraham had swept the elegant Abigail onto the dance floor. For a man of his girth, he moved about gracefully. Other couples were all around them. Some she'd seen around town, but many were new to her. And then she saw him.

Caleb.

Since she had seen him last he had trimmed his thick, dark hair and shaved. He wore a navy-blue three-piece suit. Even cleaned up he had a ruggedness about him that could not be washed or cut away. Nature seemed to run through his veins. What would it feel like to be in his strong arms dancing across the wooden floor?

Holding Eliza in his arms, Caleb thought again of his parents' letter. *With each passing month we seem to feel the effects of age more acutely. Often we wonder if we will live long enough to see a grandchild enter this world. We wonder if our name will continue on or is the Reynolds name to be a thing of the past? There was a time we never doubted it. We were naive enough to believe we'd have a healthy posterity.*

Had his brothers lived, his parents would have a swarm of grandchildren already. As it was, he was their sole hope on that account. The truth was, he wanted a family too.

"Miss Eliza, am I the first to dance with you in your new dress?" Caleb asked, looking at his partner's charming face. "I must say it is every bit as fine as I'd heard."

"You are the first. And if you are quick to ask, you may be able to dance another with me."

He pulled her a little closer. "I'd count myself

lucky. Eliza Howell, may I have not only this dance but as many as I can properly claim?"

"I've promised several others a dance. But since you asked so politely, I'll save you the last dance and any others I can find you for. You are an exceptional dancer," Eliza said. "I'd dance with you all night if I could."

Always she seemed to do and say the right things. "Very well, I shall look forward to the last dance. Waiting will be hard, but I'll endure it." He flashed a pained look at her. She compensated him with a polite giggle. "Tell me, though, is it only my excellent dancing that has you wanting me for a partner?"

Looking up at him through long lashes, she smiled. "You are bold tonight."

A lull in the music forced them off the dance floor. Caleb kept his arm around Eliza's waist as they made their way through the crowd, off the dance floor, and to the edge of the field.

Eliza turned to face him. "You are different tonight, asking me such questions."

"I feel different. I hope that is not such a bad thing. But I still want my answer. Is it only my dancing you care for?"

Eliza put her hands on her hips and circled him playfully, appraising him. "Different suits you. And to answer your question, I think you are much more than a fine dancer."

Caleb offered her his arm and the couple

strolled together. "I was hoping you'd say that. When I return, will you do me the honor of accompanying me on a picnic?"

"Oh, Caleb, I would be delighted."

"I don't know when I'll return, but when I do, I'll take you out into the open prairie. I ride a lot and have seen some beautiful places." They were near the dance floor again.

Eliza had been beautiful before. Now all her features seemed to shine in triumph. "I will be waiting anxiously for your safe return." She cocked her head and smiled. "If you'll excuse me."

She squeezed his arm affectionately before darting off toward Olivia. Eliza grabbed Olivia's arm and pulled her to the edge of the dance floor. Caleb could not hear them, but they leaned their heads in near each other and he could tell they were whispering.

Caleb hadn't singled out a girl in such a long time. The whole ordeal made him rather jittery, a strange mix of excitement and nerves. When was the last time he'd courted a girl? Been alone with a girl? Well, he had spent time with Em. But that was different.

Where is Em? He'd forgotten all about her. Glancing around, he looked for her. She wasn't on the dance floor or by the food. Ever since she'd promised to come, he'd been planning to introduce her to everyone. Now he wasn't even sure where she was. While the other couples danced across the floor, lost in each other's arms, he meandered around looking for Em.

Eliza had been dancing with Darrel, but when the music ended, she started toward him, her hips swaying as she walked. "Eliza, have you seen Em?"

She shrugged. "No, I haven't seen her. I know she doesn't dance. She doesn't do a lot of things she ought to. Perhaps she is playing with Mae and Milly. Or talking with Mr. Harvel. Did you check with him? I think they would make an excellent match."

"Why would she be with Mr. Harvel? He is twice her age and boring." He stepped quickly away from her. "I'll check for her by the girls."

Em leaned her weary back against a tree. The night was slowly dragging by. Watching the couples had proved somewhat entertaining, but after watching Caleb and Eliza walk arm in arm through the trees, she wanted nothing more than to return home and sink into her bed.

A group of girls near Em's age walked away from the dance floor and headed toward her sanctuary in the trees. She stood very still, unsure if she should make her presence known or wait in hope they walked past.

Soon they were close enough that Em could hear their conversation. A tall, red-haired girl said, "I heard she lived with a man in the woods for years. They were not married but lived like they were."

"I heard she goes to the saloon with Silas. Why is she here? The other tainted women don't come to the social. I'm surprised the Howells let her stay," a plump brunette said. "It's despicable. And the sheriff spends so much time with her. I'm sure he's only doing his duty, but it's not right."

"Did you see the way Eliza's old dresses hang on her? She's skin and bones. Even if she did fill in, I don't think she'd be very pretty." Chuckling and muted snickering cut at her like daggers.

"Of course she won't be pretty. She'll be lucky if anyone describes her as tolerable."

She wanted to run. Never had she expected anyone to say such hurtful things. Before waiting to hear anything else, she willed her legs to move her from the trees. As stealthily as possible, she walked away from the gossips, away from the crowd and the happy couples twirling in each other's arms. She'd come, that's all she had promised to do. She didn't have to stay.

Em walked until she ended up near the children, and then she got Milly's attention. "Milly, tell your mama I've gone home early. Tell her I wasn't feeling well."

Without waiting for the child to reply, she dashed away.

● ● ●

"Mrs. Anders, have you seen Em? I know she was here tonight, but I can't find her," Caleb inquired of Em's employer.

Margaret, with her analytical eyes, seemed to be reading into his soul. "She told me about her commitment to come tonight. Poor girl was so nervous. She didn't say it, but I could tell. All day she fidgeted, looking like she was in a daze."

"I'd meant to introduce her to everyone and help her make friends," Caleb said, guilt weighing heavy on his mind.

"But then you started dancing with Eliza and the rest of the world faded away." Patting him on the shoulder, she said, "A pretty face can be hard to see past. Be careful, though. All faces change with time. It's a good heart you want to be saddled with."

Not sure what she was trying to tell him, he asked again. "Have you seen her? I have to find her."

"I haven't seen her in some time. She was standing back in the trees, scared as a skittish deer. But that was a good half an hour ago."

"I'll keep looking." Caleb bid her a good night and continued his search.

Walking past a group of women, he heard them speak Em's name. "That Em girl the Howells took in is nothing but a tramp. Living with a man for years. She's a wretched sinner. And to think she has the nerve to show up at a place like this with good, respectable people. How will we ever explain such wickedness to our children?"

Rage boiled within him. How dare they say such things? None of them even knew her. She needed a friend, not this. He should have been that friend. He should have stood beside her and steadied her nerves. Shoving his hands deep into his pockets, he turned from the women and walked to Abigail.

"Have you seen Em?"

"Did you not see her? I was hoping you would. The dear girl looked so fetching tonight with her hair up. And the blue of her dress brought out her eyes." Pointing in the direction of her home, Abigail said, "Milly just ran over and told me Em went home. Abraham and I will get the girls and follow shortly. I hate the idea of her home alone." Abigail sighed. "I wish she'd stayed and made a few friends."

Caleb let out his own sigh. "She does need friends. Please tell her I'm sorry I missed her tonight."

"I'll tell her. Be safe while you're away. And if it's not asking too much, would you walk Eliza home? I can send Abraham back if you're unable."

"I'll see her home."

Caleb should have enjoyed the rest of the social. Conversation never ran dry, and he'd had a partner for every dance and Eliza in his arms for the final number. She'd smiled sweetly at him, laughed at the right moments, and flirted with expertise. He'd tried hard to reciprocate the good manners, but Em was on his mind the entire time.

He felt like a cad. How could he have been so insensitive? He knew she'd been nervous. Berating himself, he felt worse as the night wore on.

Once the last note played and the final dance ended, he took Eliza's arm and led her to the road home. His long legs set the pace as he whisked her away from the crowd.

"We needn't hurry so. It's such a lovely night," Eliza said, struggling to keep up with him.

Caleb looked up at the clear sky, shook his head, and kept walking—slowing only slightly. "I have to set out early tomorrow. It's best if I just see you straight home."

Eliza let a disgruntled groan escape. "I wish this whole mess with Em was over. I'm sick of the whole thing. If she hadn't shown up, you wouldn't be leaving and we could have our picnic sooner. She's been nothing but trouble." Eliza pouted like a child. He half expected her to stomp her foot and cry.

Caleb didn't say anything, but silently he thought about her words. It was true Em had come with a passel of trouble. Bandits now threatened his town. Until he apprehended them, he would not get a good night's sleep. Even knowing what misfortune she'd brought did not change that he was glad she had come. Never would he wish her away, back to her barn and rats, back to her lonely existence. Everything in him wanted to help her. Something genuine about her drew him in. She'd changed him over the last few weeks, and he was grateful for it. Did Eliza not see any of the good in her? Did she have no compassion?

Caleb knew Eliza wanted to talk, to have his attention, by the way she tried to slow their pace. He cleared his throat, buying himself some time while he tried to think of the right thing to say. When nothing came to him, he urged her forward. "Let's get home. We'll have more time to talk when I get back." He knew he sounded gruff, but he was ready for the night to end.

Once they were on the front steps of Eliza's house, he softened his voice and said, "Take care of yourself while I'm away. I'll look forward to seeing you when I return."

She bid him a good night and went into the house, leaving him in the bright moonlight. For no reason at all he walked behind the house and looked at the big tree. Realizing he was looking for Em, he whispered her name into the darkness. He waited but heard nothing. He called out once more. She wasn't there. He would have plenty of time to think of a proper apology while he was gone.

Twelve

In the two weeks since the social, Em had cut her potato-peeling time in half. From work she went directly home to the Howells', where she played with the girls and helped around the house as much as she could. Listening to her few coins clang together brought some pleasure. But even the happy noise and gratification that came from living with a purpose were not enough to keep the hours from dragging by.

Margaret often looked at her with knowing eyes, but she hadn't asked what was wrong. Abigail fussed over her and often inquired if she was sick. Em insisted she was well. Physically she was—her limbs no longer looked like those of a frail bird and her gunshot wound, though still red and rough, was much improved. Her muscles were also strong from days of hard work. She was sick, though, deep in her heart and did not know how to heal herself.

Never had she imagined gossip hurting so badly. The rumors were untrue, but they stung. As she walked through town, she questioned who had heard the rumors. She kept her head down and tried not to look at anyone. Even serving dinner she wondered if all the patrons believed the horrible stories.

Knowing others were whispering about her made it hard for her to walk with her head held high. But more than the rumors kept her awake late into the night. Caleb was gone and, unlike his previous absence, she didn't know if she should long for his return. He'd been a dear friend, or so she'd thought. But then at the social he'd not even cared enough to say hello. What would he be like when he returned? Would he be a friend to her?

"Have you had time to change the sheets in the upstairs room?" Margaret asked one afternoon.

"I just finished it. I was about to start on the meal preparations, unless you have something else you would rather I do."

"No. In fact, I was hoping you would be up for a walk. I put soup on the stove earlier. It's simmering away. The bread is already rising. What I would really love is to get out of the sweltering kitchen. Will you join me?"

"Of course." Em took off her apron and hung it over the back of a chair.

"I'm glad you agreed," Margaret said, struggling to untie her own apron. "It's always nicer having company."

The two women left their aprons and work behind and stepped out into the afternoon sunshine. And then they strolled side by side like true friends do.

"When I first moved to Azure Springs, there was only one main road. No side streets," Margaret said as she looked around the town.

"I didn't realize it'd grown so much."

"It has. It's a good place with good people. Sometimes they forget themselves though. These little towns don't change fast enough for some folks. There are too many ordinary days with nothing remarkable happening. There are always a few people who want something exciting to happen daily just so they'll have something to amuse themselves with. They loved these robberies and were all abuzz when you came." Margaret paused.

When Em chose not to speak, Margaret continued. "When I painted my house yellow, the town was in an uproar. Oh, it was great fun. They whispered and pointed. They made up stories about why I would do such a thing. And then one day they stopped talking about it. Guess they realized it was yellow because I liked yellow. That wasn't much of a story, so they moved on. Some people just haven't learned the secret."

Em's eyebrows rose. "The secret?"

"Yep, the secret. I'll tell you because we are much the same. Only I have been around longer. Here it is. The secret is that you have to find a way to enjoy life on the ordinary days. You have to enjoy the little things, like yellow houses with bright red doors. You have to enjoy the sound of the door opening when your man gets home. The laughing of little ones. Those things are more fun than gossip, but it takes a trained mind to soak them in. These folks who waste their time talking about you and me, they are the ones missing out. Not us."

"I may not be much of a gossip, but I've also never painted a house yellow. I haven't done much of anything." Em wasn't sure she was all that much like Margaret.

"Yellow may not be your color. Someday you might just paint a house blue . . . or pink. Wouldn't that get the ladies talking?"

Em pursed her lips. "Perhaps I'll do that very thing someday."

"Whatever you do, don't stop living now just because a few women got to talking about something they know nothing about. You keep your head up and keep living and soon enough they'll stop talking. In fact, I think you'll find a friendly face among them before long." Margaret's voice sounded so confident, like it really could be possible.

Em looked down the street at the other pedestrians. "I thought I was past caring what others thought. But their words hurt."

"When we really live, we risk the pain. But you'll work through it."

They reached the end of the main street and turned back. Em held her head a little higher.

"Margaret, may I ask you something?"

"You may ask me anything. Absolutely anything."

"How do you think I could repay the Howells for their kindness? I've thought about it and haven't been able to come up with the right thing. I'd planned to give them money, and I will if that is the only way. But then I'm not sure I'll ever have enough to leave or live off of."

"Knowing Abigail, she'll insist you do nothing. I've been indebted to others before for their kindness. I wish there were an easy answer to your question, but I've found the answer is different every time. Once a woman took us in when a snowstorm trapped our train. Rather than leave people on board, the townspeople took in families. My husband spent the whole time we were there splitting kindling and fixing porch railings. The Howells are not in need of home repairs and they are not lacking in money. I'll think on it, but you're the one who will know the right thing to do."

"I wish I had more to offer them. I'll keep thinking." Em felt ever so grateful for this woman who had remained a friend to her. "Thank you, Margaret. For the job and the friendship. You seem to always have the right words. Lately I've felt so lost and alone. Even today walking to the boardinghouse I wondered just how to find my place in this town. Again you have been just what I needed. My prayers seem to be answered by you so often."

Margaret laughed aloud. Em balked, confused. Finally the laughter stopped and Margaret said, "My little friend, prayers are funny like that. It is easy to see the times others answer our own prayers, but so often we don't realize we too are the answer to someone's prayer. When Scarlett married and left, I had so much work to do, but worse than that was how quiet the kitchen was. And then you came knocking on my door like the angel you are."

Margaret put an arm around Em's shoulder and pulled her close. The pair walked back to the boardinghouse leaning on each other.

Work passed quickly that afternoon, the hands on the old clock moving at regular speed once again. Em found herself enjoying little things about her work—the sound of the soup simmering and the smell of the fresh loaves of bread. Even the sound of the men scraping their plates made Em smile. No gossip could take those little things away from her.

After her work was finished, Em walked back to the Howells' with her back straight and her head up. She was eager to take Mae and Milly in her arms and twirl them about just so she could hear them giggle and to watch Abigail sew in the evening light and to listen to the rustle of Abraham's pages when he turned them. Even Eliza she did not dread being around. Em decided it was better to believe Eliza was good—a good person who just didn't understand *the secret* to finding happiness.

Days later Em still found herself smiling. A bit of peace had worked its way into her heart. She no longer cowered from onlookers' eyes as she passed. Let them say what they would, she knew her own story and they would not steal the measure of joy she'd found.

When Em left the boardinghouse a little after six like she did most evenings, her spirits soared as she thought of her hard day's work and the coins in her pocket. Thinking of Lucy brought a lightness to her step.

Em looked at the letters on the buildings as she walked. Knowing the sounds the letters made, she had begun putting them together by accident a couple weeks ago while baking with Margaret. Her eyes had found some now-familiar letters as she reached for the tin of baking soda. She made the sound quickly for each letter and then stared at the can. In her mind she heard the word *soda*. Looking at another can, she made the sounds over and over until they came together to make a word. Some were hard, but she soon knew what all the tins in the kitchen said. Now she was taking on the town and its signs. Caleb would be so proud! Or would he? It had been so long since she had seen him, she wasn't sure what he would think.

It didn't matter—not now, not today. What he thought could wait. *H-O-T-E-L.* She sounded out the letters and put them together. *Hotel*—another word. Another piece of her freedom.

I read it, Ma. You always said I would be able to. I'm not stuck in the woods anymore. I'm going to find her.

Caleb searched around the base of the tall oak tree. At last he found it. The perfect twig. Sitting back in the tall summer grass, he twisted the thin branch around the others in his hand. Holding it up in the bright sunshine, he inspected his work. Not too bad for his first stick person. Would it make Em smile? Would he get to hear her little bird laugh? Would it bring a tear? If it did, he knew she would bite her lip as she tried to hold back her emotions. Or would she pull her brows together and give him the same puzzled look he'd gotten when they first started reading lessons?

He put the man in his pack and swung himself up into the saddle. A few more hours and he would be back in Azure Springs. These weeks had been rewarding. Two of the three suspects had been apprehended and were on their way to Brigley, where they would stand trial. Only Alroy had evaded capture.

For days they'd followed his trail only to have summer rains wash away any tracks. Caleb wanted to wrap this case up and to know Alroy was no longer a threat to Em. He was ready for it to be over. For now he would have to be content spending as much time in Azure Springs as he could. Once any sign of Alroy surfaced, he would head out again. There was no way he was going to let this case stay open and hang over his head. He would finish it.

The nights on the trail had been a time of reflection for Caleb—hours of quiet, gazing at the stars, often offering up his heart to the heavens. Wondering about and pondering the past. A few wasted moments asking what if. What if his brothers had lived? Would he have followed the same course in life? Did he enjoy what he was doing or was he trying to prove something?

The future hung heavy on his mind as well. He thought of Eliza. Beautiful Eliza. What would a future with her be like? Was that what he wanted? Everything felt so different and uncertain now. For years he'd known the course his life would take, and he had his goals laid out before him. Something had changed, causing him to feel uncertain about his life's path.

Guiding Amos into Azure Springs as the sun crept low into the sky, Caleb savored the feeling of coming home. As weary as he was, he knew he would not be able to rest a wink if he did not see Em first. But seeing Em likely meant seeing Eliza. Why was he worried about seeing Eliza? After all, he was contemplating courting her. He brushed away the worry as he reined in Amos in front of the Howells' home.

"Caleb, you're back. We've missed you around town." Abigail was sitting on the front porch enjoying the setting sun with Abraham.

"I just rode in. I was hoping to see Em and let her know how the ride went," Caleb said as he dismounted. "If it's not too late."

"Not too late at all. My guess is she is up telling Mae and Milly stories. Those two would keep Em all to themselves if they could." Abigail smiled at him.

"Well, I heard one of her stories once," Abraham said. "Felt like a little boy again. I'd say that girl has a gift—a great many gifts. She's a treasure." Caleb was surprised Abraham had so much to say—and about Em.

Eliza suddenly came through the door. She looked right at her parents, not noticing Caleb. "Mama, Em is up there telling the girls stories. They hang on her every word and don't even listen when I talk. She's not even family and she—"

Abigail cleared her throat. Eliza stopped midsentence and looked around. Noticing Caleb, she let out a little squeal. "Oh, Caleb." Her voice was sweet now, no trace of the venom she had displayed just seconds ago. "You've come home—and to see me."

"I just arrived," he said, brushing at the dust that clung to his pant legs.

Prancing toward him, Eliza looked ready to jump into his arms. "And you came to see me first. I'm flattered. Oh, now that you are back, we can finally go on our picnic."

Picnic! He would have to honor his promise. The thought of an afternoon alone with Eliza did not hold its former appeal. Hiding his feelings, he simply nodded in her direction and said, "We'll have to find a time for our outing. Tonight I've come to see Em. I'd like to tell her the news."

"Surely you want to tell us all your news," Eliza said.

Abigail stood up and put her hand on Eliza's arm. "Go and fetch Em. Let Caleb speak to her. He said he needs to. I'm sure he has reasons. He's home now, and once he's rested up I'm sure we will all see lots of him. Go on." The order was gentle but firm.

"Very well." Eliza walked back into the house.

Caleb hoped Eliza was kind to Em when she fetched her. He couldn't understand why she disliked Em so. Could she not see Em deserved and needed kindness?

"Eliza was very sick when our boys were. I was so afraid I would lose her," Abigail said when Eliza was out of earshot.

"I hadn't realized that. I'm glad she pulled through," Caleb said.

"We were both so glad. Maybe too glad. We spoiled that girl. We gave her constant praise. Bought her what she wanted. I didn't have the heart to ever tell her no, not after what she'd been through," Abigail said as Abraham rose from the chair and stood next to his wife. "We hadn't realized what we'd done. Not until Em came. No one has ever spoiled her. Seeing the two together. Both the same age." Abigail reached over and took Abraham's hand.

Abraham took a deep breath. "We both have seen it. We always said Eliza was just young. But she is no younger than Em. And Em knows how to love others, how to give and work hard. She knows how to be grateful."

Shifting uncomfortably, Caleb looked at Abigail and Abraham. They loved their daughters. He'd never questioned that—no one would. He wasn't sure how to respond to such a confession. "I'm sure you've done your best."

"We love our Eliza. Always, always we have and always we will. It just seems you should know a little more about her. She'll learn. I trust she will. Especially now that we see it and can help her. We've prayed nightly to know how to raise our girls. When Em showed up here, we had no idea she'd be such a help to us. We thought we were helping her." Abigail sighed.

"Little did we know. Em has changed so many things, opened our eyes to issues we were blind to." Tears overflowed from Abigail's eyes. "I'm sorry, Caleb. I'm not sure where that all came from. We're so happy you're back and safe."

Caleb, pushing the toe of his shoe around in the dirt, said, "I'm glad to be back. And I'm grateful Em hasn't been a burden."

Silence filled the air, broken only by the sound of footsteps in the house. Em walked through the front door. Caleb felt his breath catch in his chest. She looked different. He stammered a hello, then stood staring at her like a dunce. Why hadn't he felt this awkward with Eliza? Was it because he knew he owed Em an apology? A long overdue apology.

Abigail, the saint, rescued the moment. "Em, Caleb is going to take you for a walk and tell you all about his trip."

Finally Em looked up at his face, uncertainty in her azure eyes. "Very well." Her voice was calm. "I'd like to hear about the case."

What was he supposed to do now? He knew how to behave but was suddenly unsure of himself. Abraham helped him this time. "Well . . . the sun is getting mighty low. Better take her arm and head on out so you can be back before it's too dark out."

Take her arm, that's right. Caleb smiled at Abraham, grateful for the help, before stepping toward Em and offering his arm. She took it. Her hand tucked in his elbow sent a strange shiver through him. Eliza came to the porch as they turned away from the house. Frustrated pleas to go too echoed behind them. They rounded a corner and her voice faded away.

Alone.

It was his chance to apologize. Stalling, he listened to the sound of distant coyotes waking for the night as they yapped and yowled and distracted him from what he knew he must do.

"I always thought coyotes sounded like women and children screaming," Caleb said.

"I was twelve the first time I heard them. I was sleeping in the barn at George's. I felt so afraid," Em said, and she moved a little closer to him.

Caleb reached across his body and patted her small hand. "I'm sorry you were afraid." He stopped and mustered his courage. "There was nothing I could have done then. I didn't know you. If I had, I hope I would have done something. I hope I would have taken you away and given George a piece of my mind." Wishing he could somehow go back and put it all right, he balled his hand into a fist. Heat rose to his face. "I know you now, though, and I failed you when you needed me."

"It's not your fault," Em said, looking up into his face.

Again he wanted to know what was different.

221

Where was the plain girl he'd first met? The girl with the harsh cheekbones and dull eyes.

"It wasn't my fault with the coyotes—no one can quiet them. But not finding you at the social? That was my fault, and it has weighed on me since I left town. I was not the friend you needed. I was selfish and careless and you suffered for it."

"It was only a social. A small thing."

"No, it wasn't. It was your chance to make friends and have fun. To dance and get to know people. You've been deprived of so much—it was your chance. If only I had taken you around and made introductions. I could have stopped people's wagging tongues and helped you feel at home. I'm sorry," he said, his voice quiet and remorseful. "Can you forgive me?"

"It was only one chance. There will be other times for me to socialize. And you needn't feel bad that I didn't dance. I don't know how to dance. I've never danced before, and besides—"

Caleb put a finger to her lips. "Hush—stop being so noble. It was wrong of me, and I expected you to give me an earful, make me beg for forgiveness and grovel at your feet. I'll do it." Dramatically, he knelt.

"Stand up, you are forgiven already. If I did all those things, making you grovel and such, I would need your forgiveness and then where would we be?" Em held out a hand to him.

Chuckling under his breath, he grasped her outstretched hand and stood. "You surprise me again. I've been worrying all this time about making the right kind of apology. Wondering how I would ever earn your forgiveness, and you gave it so easily."

"You've been good to me. Helped me to learn, worried about my well-being. You even helped me to cry—something I wasn't sure I was capable of doing. I admit I was afraid at the social. And then I overheard horrible gossip. I was wishing for an arm to hold, but that was not your fault. You owed me nothing. And you've given me so much already."

Caleb's heart felt lighter than it had the weeks he had been away. "I did indeed owe you something. As your friend I owed you a great deal. Plus, I may have forgotten to tell you, but I meant to promise you a dance." He smiled. "Are you sure I did not?"

"I am certain. I would have remembered that. Had you asked me for a dance, I would've told you I don't dance. I would remember that."

He put his hand on her brow. "Are you sick? Have you been ill while I was away?"

"No, of course not. I've been in good health. The best I've known for years. Why do you ask?"

He moved his hand to her chin and tilted her face this way and that, inspecting her. "You must have been sick. A very serious sickness that causes you to forget the most important things. In fact, you may have forgotten, but I remember promising you a dance. Since you left the social early, you'll have to dance with me now so that I'll be able to sleep knowing my promise has been fulfilled."

"I don't dance," she said. "Not a step. I would look like an awkward bird if I ever attempted it."

He bent near her and whispered into her ear, "Tonight you will learn."

He was so near he could smell the scent of her skin. So near he could see her swallow.

"I don't know if I can," she said, her voice a whisper.

"Every girl I've ever met loves to dance, and if you promise not to tell, I'll confess something to you."

"Very well, I promise." Her eyes twinkled in the last light of day.

"I love dancing. I always have. I never would admit it as a boy. No boys admit such things. But there is a certain thrill about it. You move to the music, each separate but not. Trust me, you'll enjoy it."

Em looked up at him. "Margaret says it's like floating."

"Hmmm . . ." Caleb leaned in and tapped the tip of her nose. "Floating, you say? I'll be sure to hold you tight. Being as light as you are, you may just float away."

224

"I'm not nearly so light anymore."

Since her time in Azure Springs, she had softened. Where sharp bones had once protruded, she now had subtle curves. Food had made a difference, but she remained slender.

"I'll hold on tight just in case. I'm not willing to risk you floating off into this night sky." Putting his big hands around her waist, he lifted her high into the air. "You're right—you're not nearly as light as you once were. But I'll still hold on. A person can't be too careful." He set her down and bowed.

Then he extended his hand. "Come, dance with me."

After she took his hand, he held hers a moment and ran his thumb over her knuckles. It was so much smaller than his, but somehow it seemed just the right size. Then he pulled her into his arms.

"There's no music," she whispered, her cheeks flushed.

He looked into her eyes. Without speaking, he began stepping in a small circle, humming whatever notes came into his mind. Not once did his eyes leave hers. Margaret was right—dancing was like floating. Like leaving the earth and all its worries and escaping to a realm that existed for just the two of them.

She knew no steps and he didn't teach her. He just held her, moving as he hummed. Somehow they moved together. Round and round, under the stars. His gaze left her eyes and found her lips. Pink and inviting. Never had he wanted to kiss someone as much as he did at that moment. *But why? Is it pity? It couldn't be anything else, could it?* Dropping his hands, he moved away from her, knowing pity was not an adequate reason.

"It's getting late. I . . . I told Abraham . . . I told him I would have you back before it was too dark, and I haven't even told you about my trip yet." He wondered what was happening to him. Too many nights on the trail must have affected him.

Em looked hurt. "It is getting late. Tell me of your trip. I have wondered about it often."

They walked side by side, leaving plenty of space between them. He neglected to offer his arm. Too confused by his feelings to know how to behave, he walked and talked, barely acknowledging her. Rapidly he told his tale of the places he'd been, the men he'd gone with, and the eventual capture of two of the bandits.

"We caught them in the bluffs outside of Herston. They were camping when we came on them. Alroy got away. He's still out there."

He stopped, put a hand on each of her shoulders, and spoke directly to her. His voice carried new intensity. "Em, he's out there." He pulled his lips into a tight line and swallowed hard before going on. "He's out there and he's bad. I knew he was bad, but I didn't know he was this bad."

"I'll be all right."

"You don't understand. We believe he's connected to other crimes. Not just George. Other evil deeds. Em, we think he's done horrible things. He takes what he wants. Do you know what I'm saying?"

She nodded. "I know."

Caleb gritted his teeth. "I'll catch him. Then this will all be over. He won't hurt you. I won't let him hurt anyone." He moved his hands from her shoulders to her face. "I'll catch him. You'll be safe."

Putting a slender hand on his sleeve, she said, "I know you will. I've never doubted."

When Em and Caleb returned to the Howells', Abigail and Abraham were still sitting on the porch. After a few moments of small talk, Caleb left them all. He rode away, alone with his thoughts. Unsure why he felt the way he did.

Thirteen

Troubled and confused, Em slept little that night. When at last sleep did come, she dreamed she was in the arms of a prince. Twirling around and around, floating. The feeling was enchanting—and just like her stories, it was not real. Disappointed to find it only a dream, she lay awake. For how long, she was not sure. What she did know was when the new day began, she did not feel rested.

Working with Margaret later that day was difficult. She wanted desperately to sit down, lean her head back, and sleep. Instead, she worked harder, hoping to distract her weary body and tired mind.

"I heard Caleb Reynolds was back in town," Margaret said.

Em didn't look up from the bread she was kneading. "He is. Just back yesterday."

"Have you seen him?"

"Briefly. He stopped by the Howells' to let us know two of the men have been apprehended."

"That's all he came to tell you? I thought it was something more exciting. Judging by the way you've been darting about like a nervous worker bee all afternoon, I thought he had either proclaimed himself sweet on you or told you he had no such feelings for you."

Em pulled her hands from the bowl and tried to pull off the dough stuck between her fingers. "He doesn't care for me. Not that way. At least I don't think he does. I don't think he ever could." Frustrated with the dough, she groaned and brushed her hands on her apron. "I never counted on anyone caring for me like that. And yet, I was fool enough to hope. Is it so wrong to dream?"

Margaret laughed a deep laugh, her whole body shaking. Her curls bobbing with each whoop. "Oh, my dear girl. We all think there is no one for us. Even Eliza and Olivia wonder it at times. I'm positive they do."

"It's not funny. I don't have their looks or your confidence. I am poor and plain. Caleb even admitted as much when we first met."

"Settle down," Margaret said from across the room. "Your appearance may not turn all men's heads, but it will turn someone's. Besides, you have plenty of gifts. Different from others, but they're gifts that the right man will treasure. So, tell me, did he say how he feels about you?"

"Well, no, not exactly. He told me he owed me a dance and we danced. Margaret, I have never danced before and it was just like you said. I was floating. For a few glorious moments I was floating under the stars without a single worry. Then he pulled away and acted as if it had never happened. I tossed about all last night, trying to decide what to make of it, and I came to no conclusions." Em pushed a strand of straw-colored hair away from her face. Dough stuck to it, provoking another groan.

Margaret walked to her and picked the dough from her hair. "This has got you all stirred up. Relax. You don't need to understand it all right now—and neither does he. He's your friend, you know that much. Enjoy it."

"You're right, I'm sure. I've never felt this flustered before. I think about him so often throughout the day and even at night. I am either thinking of him or telling myself not to."

Margaret put her hands on Em's face. "Enjoy that too. Enjoy it all."

Noise, so much noise. Before she even walked into the dining hall, Em knew there was a crowd. Hefting a bowl of potatoes in her arms, she pushed the door open and stepped into the busy room. She saw a few regulars, a traveling family, and several men she had never seen before. She stopped her scan of the room when she spotted Caleb. He was looking at her. Their eyes locked for just a moment before she pulled her gaze away and busied herself serving potatoes. With her heart racing, she started at the opposite side of the room.

She served a bald man with a mustache. Then the traveling family. A group of dirty railroad workers were next. Slowly she piled potatoes onto the plate of a guest who looked more like a little boy than a full-grown man. Only two plates were between her and Caleb now. She couldn't avoid him.

And then she was standing at his side.

"Potatoes?" she asked, eyes on her feet.

"I'd love potatoes."

She gave him a large scoop. As she stepped to serve the next patron, she felt something slide into her apron pocket. Startled, she looked to Caleb. He winked at her. "Just something I picked up on the trail."

Not wanting to draw attention to them, she gave him a half smile and walked on. For an hour and a half she served food. Each time she stood near him, he made small talk with her. Pleasant, easy talk. It infuriated her that he could be so . . . normal.

At last the night was nearly done. Well, not done. A mountain of dishes still needed scrubbing. But the food was gone and soon the crowd would leave. Dishes were the only chore between her and her pillow. Rolling her sleeves up, she prepared herself for the task ahead.

Margaret entered the dining room with a large,

empty pan in her hand. Like always, she banged on it and announced that the kitchen was closing up and the meal was over. The noisy crowd left reluctantly, leaving Margaret and Em alone with the dishes. No, it was not just Margaret and Em. Caleb remained in the room and leaned casually against the wall. The same twisted smile on his face.

"Mrs. Anders. Em. That was a fine meal."

Margaret wiped her hands on her apron and began stacking up plates. "Glad you liked it. Don't get any ideas though. You may be a fine sheriff and you may have been sleeping under the stars, eating who knows what for the last several weeks, but it makes no difference. The kitchen is closed and I'm not feeding you one more bite."

"Why, Mrs. Anders, do I look like a man begging for food?" Not waiting for a reply, he said, "As much as I could use another piece of that pie, that's not what I was after with my compliment. It *was* a delicious meal. I was hoping if I waited long enough I might have a word alone with Em."

"This girl can wash dishes twice as fast as anyone I know and you want to whisk her off right now? Leave all this work for the poor widow woman?"

Em spoke up then. "I'll finish before I leave."

"I knew you were loyal. Never doubted you.

It's this scoundrel I'm accusing." Margaret pointed a finger at Caleb. Em would have balked at her words if she had not been working with Margaret all this time. She knew her now well enough to know she was having fun.

"Mrs. Anders, what kind of a man do you think I am? I would never try to sneak Em off. I was hoping you would let me help scrub these dishes. If the dishes were done, you would let her go, wouldn't you?" Caleb asked, already stacking up dishes so high Em feared he would drop them.

"I'm a smart woman. I never turn down free labor. Get busy, you two young 'uns." With that, Margaret left them in the dining hall and went to the kitchen.

Em started stacking dishes as Caleb worked beside her. "I'm sorry it's been so long since we had a reading lesson. I was hoping we could begin again tomorrow."

Despite her early hesitancy around him, she beamed now. "Oh, I have something to show you. Come with me." She took her pile into the kitchen and he followed. When they entered the kitchen, Margaret left and went back to the dining hall, leaving them alone again.

Em set her stack on the counter and pointed to a can. "I was practicing my letter sounds a while back. I tried to make the sounds of all the letters I saw while I worked. I made these sounds and in my head I heard *soda* and—"

"And then all around you, you saw words," he said.

"I did. I read everything I could in the kitchen. There are words I stumble over. Lots in fact, but most I can figure out. Then I started walking down the street, finding words to read. A few days ago I picked up Abraham's newspaper and for the first time in my life it looked like more than ants crawling across the paper." Em sank her hands into the warm water and started scrubbing plates. "I haven't read my mother's papers yet. I want to and I will. I think I'm scared to though. I've waited so long and spent so many hours wondering what they say. I suppose I'm reluctant—nervous to have the moment here and gone."

She took the plate she had been scrubbing, dipped it in a rinse bucket, and handed it to Caleb. He took it without waiting for instructions and dried it. "I knew you would be able to read. I had no idea it would come *so* quickly though," he said.

"It's not easy. I sound like Mae and Milly when I read, but I find every day it comes a little easier. My letters look better too. I'll show you . . . tomorrow."

"Good. I was afraid I'd scared you off. I wouldn't want that. We'll have to meet tomorrow at eight and do our lesson quickly. I promised Eliza an outing and am to meet her at eleven."

Caleb dried another dish and returned it to its spot in the cupboard.

Keep washing, Em told herself. Coaxing her hands to keep moving, she washed in silence. Afraid her voice would give away her disappointment.

Caleb, equally silent, dried each dish beside her.

When she could trust her voice again, she said, "I'll be there at eight. Eliza will be happy to spend the day with you. She's talked of little else during your absence."

"Eight it is." Smoothly changing the subject, he asked, "Did you like your gift? I admit it was harder to make than I'd expected."

"Oh! I was so busy with the dinner rush that I forgot." She eagerly dried her hands and was about to reach in her pocket when his hand came over hers.

"Finish up here. Look later. It's nothing much anyway."

"Very well. I'll wait."

She worked faster, curious to see her gift but also eager to be done with dishes. Margaret finally reappeared in the kitchen. Eyeing her nearly clean kitchen, she said, "A fine pair you two are. If there is ever a dish-washing competition, be sure to enter as a team."

"A competition as teammates. That's a brilliant idea." Caleb winked at her. "Normally I just compete against Em. It works out well though. She says she'll beat me one day, but so far I've won every time."

Em grabbed the towel she had just wiped her hands on and whipped him in the side with it. "I *will* beat you someday." She set down the towel and brushed her hands on her apron.

"Did you just do what I think you did?" He laughed. Then he grabbed a cup of water from the counter and splashed it at her.

Shrieking, she grabbed the towel and got him again.

Margaret stepped between them. "Before you destroy my almost-finished kitchen—leave!" Turning to Caleb, she said, "Take this girl home and tell Abigail to put her right to bed. I can tell by her eyes she didn't sleep a wink last night. Something had her tossing and turning." Then, facing Em, she said, "I'll finish up here. You two go on."

"No, I'll finish," Em said, reaching for another dirty dish.

"Out!" Margaret pointed to the door. "Go on, out with the two of you."

Caleb grabbed Em's hand before she could insist on staying. He smiled a thank-you at Margaret and the two set out.

Once they were alone on the street, he asked, "What kept you up?"

Em shrugged. "I suppose it was the excitement

of my first dance. Or maybe it was Mae talking in her sleep. It's hard to say."

"So the twins don't even stop talking when they sleep? I should have guessed."

"Can I look at my gift now?" Em asked.

"Well, if you want to. It's nothing fancy. Just something I put together on the trail." Caleb rubbed his hand absently over his stubble. He looked embarrassed—timid, even. Not his normal confident self.

Em reached into her pocket and felt for the gift with her fingers. Without even seeing it, she knew Caleb had made a man out of sticks for her. A little man, just like she'd made for Lucy. She pulled it out and turned it back and forth in her hand admiring it. Little legs and arms, even a head with fuzzy hair made from some sort of moss she'd never seen before. He was right, it was not fancy. But she loved it. She pressed it to her heart. "It's perfect." With tears in her eyes, she whispered, "It is the kindest gift I've ever received."

"I kept thinking of Lucy while I was away. You were a good sister to her. Making that was no easy task."

Em looked at it again. "I'll treasure it. Thank you."

"You're most welcome."

As they continued toward the Howells', Em read—in her head—the words on the buildings they passed in town. He must have seen her eyes scanning the buildings. "What does that one say?" he asked, pointing to the single-story building on the corner.

"That one took me three days to figure out. But I believe it says 'millinery,' and under that it says 'premade' and 'made to order.' "

"Very good."

He asked her several others. Each time she was right. The walk was much too short, and they were almost at the Howells' long before she was ready to say good night.

Nearing the porch, Caleb stopped. "Em, about last night, I—"

"Caleb, I wasn't expecting to see you until tomorrow!" Eliza's voice broke into his sentence.

"Ah, Eliza. I'll be by tomorrow. I ate at the boardinghouse and thought I'd see Em safely home."

"She carries that pistol with her everywhere. I don't think she needs any protection from you." Eliza pointed to the basket Em was carrying.

"It's true—I have your pistol with me," Em said quietly. "Do you want it back?" She fumbled with her basket.

His hand came over hers. "Keep it. Until Alroy's brought in, I feel better knowing you have it."

Em nodded and took back her hand. "I better hurry in so I can see the girls before they go to bed. I plan to tell them the story of Rose Red tonight."

She ducked her head and scurried up the porch and through the door, leaving Caleb and Eliza alone outside. Then she stuck her hand in her pocket, tucking it around the little stick man.

Fourteen

"Abraham, will you send word to Caleb to let him know I won't be meeting him today?" Em asked while heating water on the stove. Mae had woken up sick. It didn't seem very serious to Em, but Abigail had insisted the doctor come.

"Of course." He began fastening his shoes. "It's good of you to stay with Abigail. She worries something awful when the children are sick."

"It's the least I can do."

He looked up at her. "But it's more than most would do. I'll let Caleb know."

All morning Em helped around the house, bouncing between the kitchen and the girls' room. Often she heard Eliza readying herself for her outing with Caleb. Not once did she enter the girls' room to see how her sister was faring. Instead, she fretted over missing gloves and the color of her bonnet. It took all of Em's willpower not to rush downstairs and tell Eliza to grow up and think of someone other than herself.

When eleven o'clock finally rolled around, Em could not resist scooting her chair near the little girls' window. She watched as Caleb rode up on Amos. Good old Amos—she longed to pet his soft nose. Caleb was clean shaven and wore the same handsome suit he'd worn at the social. Seeing him ride up like a prince, she berated herself for ever believing he might care for her.

Eliza came out of the house with her hair in ringlets tucked under an ornate bonnet of the most delicate violet. Her dress, the latest fashion, was custom-made to fit her curves perfectly. Em forced her eyes away. She couldn't look one moment more at perfect Eliza. It only reminded her of every curve she did not have. Watching only hurt.

"Mae, would you like me to tell you another story? I've remembered one you've never heard about a girl who lived with her parents deep in the woods where the ogres roamed."

Mae's tired eyes lit up, looking more alive than they had all morning. "Please tell it," the little girl said.

And so Em sat beside her, holding her hand and whispering her stories. She felt a warmth deep within her. The same warmth that had penetrated her heart as a girl when she'd held Lucy's hand.

"I love you, Mae," she whispered when the girl had drifted off to sleep. Em sat watching her. Grateful and afraid of the love she'd found with these good people.

241

At quarter to noon, Abigail insisted Em get ready for work. "You must go. I'll be fine here with the girls and Margaret depends on you."

"If she needs someone to sit with her tonight, I'll gladly do it," Em said, looking at the still-sleeping Mae.

"You're so good with them. Go now and let her rest. Hopefully she wakes feeling better." Abigail shooed her from the room.

Obediently, Em left for work. Her heart wasn't in it though. A sinking feeling made it hard for her to even focus on the words around her as she walked. Something felt wrong. Was it because Caleb was with Eliza? She scanned the town as she walked, wondering if she would see the couple.

She tried to be happy for them. But all she felt was a twisting in her gut.

"You're coming with me," a man's voice said from out of nowhere, startling her. Then the man reached around her and pulled her tight against him. His strong arms knocked the basket—with the hidden gun inside—from her hands and to the ground.

Shooting pain raced through her as the man twisted her arm behind her back and dragged her around the corner of the mercantile. Then up in the air she went as he threw her onto a horse. Finally understanding what was happening to her, she kicked and screamed, fighting to escape. She bit and clawed at the man as she tried to fend him off, but his strength was too much for her. He quickly hopped up on the horse behind her and rode off.

His arm around her waist was so tight that she felt short of breath. The world spun. Before she passed out, her head tipped back against the man and under his cap she saw tufts of red hair. A wicked smile spread across his face, showing a missing front tooth. Alroy. Then she went weak.

"I think I've left my post neglected long enough." Caleb rose from the log he and Eliza had been sitting on.

Eliza did not rise. "You could stay a little longer. Nothing ever happens in Azure Springs anyway."

"If only that were true," Caleb said, fighting the urge to roll his eyes.

Finally she stood up and walked over to him, putting her hand on his arm. "But if you head back, I don't know when I'll get you alone again." Her lips turned downward into an alluring pout.

"All the same, I have to return." He busied himself gathering up the remains of their picnic lunch and putting them in the saddlebags.

Letting out a little huff of frustration, she too began gathering their belongings. "Perhaps I'll have to cause some trouble around town. Then you'd have to take me in, lock me up, and make sure I was never left alone."

"I'm sure a *lady* like yourself would do no such thing." Caleb tried to remain pleasant. Pleasant was a challenge though. All he wanted to do was be free of Eliza and her flirtatious ways. Their time together had felt so artificial. Like a scripted performance, nothing real about it. He found his mind wandering to Em, wondering what she would have talked about if it had been the two of them together all afternoon. He knew he would have felt relaxed in her presence.

He'd played the part of a gentleman very well all through the meal, but he was ready to be Caleb again. "Amos is loaded up. Let's head back."

He offered Eliza his hand, ready to help her onto the tall horse. She took it and held it, making no move for Amos. "When you leave me at home, there will be such a crowd around. Let's say our farewell here. It's so quiet and peaceful, so romantic." And then she turned her little heart-shaped face up at him and waited.

His pulse was running rampant at the sight of her obvious intentions. *What am I to do?* He should want to kiss her, to take her in his arms. Not long ago he would have thought himself lucky to have a beautiful girl asking for his affection.

Clearing his throat, he let go of her hand, took a step back, and dropped his arms to his sides. "Thank you for an enjoyable picnic, Eliza."

Piercing eyes studied him. "That is your farewell?" Hands on hips, she challenged him.

"It . . . it has been nice. I must be getting back now," he said.

Eliza dramatically stepped toward Amos and attempted to pull herself up onto him. Caleb stuck his thumbs in his belt loops and watched. When she failed on her third attempt, he scooped her up and put her into the saddle. Without looking back at him, she smoothed her skirts and pointed her nose straight ahead.

As they rode back toward the Howells' home, Eliza sat in silence, moping. Caleb knew he should try to smooth things over but was afraid he would laugh if he opened his mouth. She called herself a grown woman but threw a fit like a child.

At the Howells' he hopped off Amos and helped her down. Like a cat, she darted for the door. His stride was long, though, and he caught hold of her before she disappeared into the house. "Hold up."

"I've nothing more to say to you. You've made yourself clear. You don't care for me." Anger, not hurt, blazed in her eyes. "How am I supposed to tell Olivia and all the other girls that the picnic went? Shall I let them all know you are not a gentleman? That you feigned affection, led my heart astray, only to hurt me?"

Caleb rubbed his freshly shaven chin as he searched for the right words. "I suppose you can tell the girls whatever you want about our time together. Shall I tell everyone you are a spoiled brat who needs a few good switches to the backside?"

"Ooohhh! How could you even say that?" She stomped her foot but did not walk away. "How dare you."

"Come now, Eliza. You're ready to tell the town I was no gentleman, all because I didn't give you the kisses you were wanting. Do you even care for me or did you just like the idea of whispering to all the girls about our picnic under the trees—making them jealous?"

Surprised he didn't see steam rising from her furious head, he kept talking. "Let's be honest with each other. Let's both stop pretending. The truth is I admire your family. I hope to always be welcome here. Few places feel as much like a real home as yours. It's full of good people. You are a beautiful woman and I thought perhaps there could be something more. But it's not going to work."

Eliza still didn't respond. Her eyes were now downcast.

"I include you in the list of good people in this home." He wished she would look at him. "Like I said, I hope to always be welcome here. But you and I would not make a very good match. Not as anything more than friends."

Eliza looked up. "But why?"

"Because we're too different. I am not the right person to make you happy. And—I need someone else too. Truth is, I'm figuring it out." Caleb put a soft hand on her shoulder. "Can we be friends?"

"Is it Em? Homely, plain Em who has you running from me?" Eliza spit the words at him. "It's because of her, isn't it? If she'd never come, things could be different. You and I could have a future."

"Be fair." Caleb let his hand drop from her shoulder. "Spending time with Em has helped me realize the type of woman I hope to end up with. But I think I would have realized we were not a good match even without her. I only regret it took me this long to see it. I never meant to hurt you." He shook his head and reminded himself that Eliza did not choose to be spoiled.

"What is so wrong with me?"

"Well, I don't know that there is anything *wrong* with you. There may be plenty of men out there who would be happy their whole life to have a woman like you on their arm. But I need someone who sees other people as important, with needs and feelings too. Your mama is one of those people. Em is too. I don't know who the right girl is for me, but I do know she will be someone kind and giving. Someone I can laugh with and be myself around." Were his words explaining what he felt? He hoped so. "I couldn't live my whole life worrying about saying the right things."

"I could be like my mama. I could," Eliza said. "If you'd give me a chance, I could be like that."

"I think you could—and I hope you will be. When you are, if you are, some good man will get himself a real gem."

With the anger gone, replaced by remorse, she said, "But that man won't be you?"

"No, it won't be me. But I hope I'm your friend and that I'll get to see you happy with whoever that man is."

Eliza nodded. "Thank you, Caleb. For not being afraid to tell me what you really think." She went into the house and left him on the porch with his own thoughts.

Did I do the right thing? Then, laughing to himself, he thought of his parents as he hopped onto Amos and began the ride toward town. He pictured the devastation on their faces if they ever found out he'd turned down the belle of the town.

As he passed the boardinghouse, he spotted Margaret with her back to him, putting wash on the line. "Afternoon, Mrs. Anders," he shouted.

She turned toward him—her mouth full of

clothespins and her wild curls blowing in the wind—and waved. She took the clothespins from her mouth and shouted back. "Same to you. Where are you hiding Em? I can hardly get by without her. I've become so used to her help."

"Em?" He looked around absently as though he expected to see her emerge from the house.

"She has never been late before. I'm sure it has something to do with you," she said, her eyes sparkling with amusement. "You've become sweet on her? Am I right?"

"She didn't come in? Are you sure?" His insides twisted into a tight knot. Without knowing, he knew. Alroy had come back. "I'll find her."

"You better." Gone was the laughter from her eyes. "That girl is worth her weight in gold."

With no time to hear any more, he quickly rode to the Howells'. Once there, he jumped from Amos's back and ran to the door, his heart racing with fear and rage. *How had he let this happen?*

With fists knotted in balls, he banged on the door with all his might. He waited impatiently as perspiration ran down his forehead. Again he knocked, pounding, until he heard footsteps rushing to the door.

"What is it, Caleb?" Eliza said breathlessly.

"Em. Is she here? When did everyone see her last? I have to know."

"I don't know. I wasn't here. I was with you."

Caleb pushed past her and into the front room. "Abigail!"

"She's not here either. She went to the store to see Papa."

Caleb smacked the back of the sofa, groaned, and started for the door.

"Wait," Eliza said as she stepped in front of him.

"I can't wait. You might not care about Em, but I do, and I have to find her," he shouted in her face. "It's my fault—I should have been here." He brought his palm down hard on the sofa again.

Eliza's voice was gentle. Kinder than it had ever been before. "The girls are out back. They might know when she left."

He followed her lead. Without a word, they moved through the house and out the back door. Mae and Milly were sitting under their tree, each with a doll nestled in their lap. Little chatter bounced between them and their dolls.

"Girls, when did Em leave this morning?" Eliza asked.

He was glad she spoke. He felt completely out of control. Anger, dread, fear—they were all colliding throughout his mind and body like a vicious storm.

"Em stayed with me all morning because I was sick," Mae said. "I'm better now. She told me a fine story. Then mama made her leave and go to work. I heard her say she'd better go so she wouldn't be late."

"It looks like she was headed to work at the normal time," Eliza said.

"Thank you, Eliza. For asking them." He grabbed her hand. "I have to go now. I have to find her. Keep the girls safe."

She nodded. "I hope you find her. I really do."

He squeezed her hand tightly, forced a smile, and said, "It's good of you to say. Take these girls inside. I don't know what kind of trouble is coming."

Keep calm. Just keep calm.

It was just past one o'clock. An hour. A whole hour she'd been gone. She had disappeared somewhere between the Howells' and the boardinghouse. Retracing the steps she would have taken, he hurried through town, hoping to find a clue that would point him in the direction he should head.

He saw her basket lying overturned under the overhang of the mercantile, which was about a block from the boardinghouse. He picked it up and tore the napkin out of it. His gun. Blast. Em had no way to protect herself. He shook the basket in frustration, causing the stick man he'd given her to fall to the ground. Dropping to his knees, he scooped it up. His body shook, overcome with a deep and foreboding dread that felt worse than anything he'd ever known. He fought the urge to cry as he took the stick man in his hands.

Knowing that giving in to the storm of emotions would leave him useless, he fought to regain control, to think clearly. After rising from the ground, he shoved the gun and the stick man into his saddlebags. The basket remained over-turned—a silent testament to the atrocity.

Never had a crime felt so personal. Sure, he'd worried over other victims, mourned deaths, and lost sleep over tragedy. But this. This was different. He felt as if a part of himself were lost—stolen—and he had to rescue it.

From high on Amos, he looked in all directions. *Where would they go?* Digging his heels deeper than necessary into Amos, he set out. Destined for Hollow Creek.

"Let me be right," he prayed aloud. If he was wrong—no, he wouldn't think about that yet. His gut was all he had to go on. Amos was well rested, and he was big and fast. He could possibly overtake them.

Em, jolted awake, tried to reach out and steady herself, only to find her hands were not free— thick rope held them tightly together. She was only staying on the horse because Alroy had an arm around her waist. Appalled that she was so close to him, she straightened her back in a vain attempt to put some distance between their bodies, even if it was only a mere centimeter.

Responding to her movements, he spoke. "Decided to come to, did you?"

"Where are we going?" Em asked, her voice flat.

"Well, missy, if you must know, we're going back to George's. You're going to get me my money."

"George didn't talk to me much. I don't know anything. Did he talk to you?" Still no emotion. How quickly she slipped back into her old ways. All the years she'd lived with George she'd kept her features and words void of emotion. "I know you knew him."

"Sure, he talked. He and Gerda both talked. And they yelled and they whipped."

Em winced at the thought. George seemed so worn out when she was there. She'd always seen him as a tired old man. He had never tried to know her, let alone discipline her.

"I didn't know Gerda."

His arm tightened painfully around her as he pulled the horse to a stop. In a single movement, he jumped off the animal's back, dragging her with him. He dropped her on the ground and paced away from her. With her hands tied, it was a struggle to stand but she managed.

"You don't know nothin' about Gerda. Or what it was like."

"I don't claim to," Em said. "George never even talked of her. I only know her name."

"Gerda's dead, same as George." Alroy pulled a cigarette from his pocket. Fumbling with a match, he struggled to light it. The match blew out and he swore and threw it to the ground. Then he reached into his saddlebags and pulled out a length of rope.

Em meant to bite her tongue, to let him fume on his own, but words just came. "You killed Gerda too?"

He slapped her, knocking her down. With her face stinging and her vision blurry from the blow, she struggled to sit up. It was safer being able to see and anticipate his moves.

"I didn't kill Gerda," he said as he pushed her skirts up to her knees and tied her ankles together. "Well, I did, but not how you's thinkin' I did. And I wouldn't have killed George if he would have just let me be."

Maybe she could distract him?

"I came on a train. An orphan train. Is that how you came?" She asked the questions hoping he'd continue to talk.

Alroy didn't say anything. She filled the silence. "No one wanted me. No one but George, and I don't think he really wanted me. I'm not sure why he claimed me. Just used me to tend a few animals and fix his meals."

"You from the city?" Alroy asked.

"I am. I lived there until I was twelve. Are you from there?" Em's chest tightened as she realized their stories were not so different.

"My pa dropped me off with the Society when I

was eight. Said he had too many mouths to feed. I never set foot in the city again." He seemed calmer now, as he leaned against a tree and successfully lit a cigarette. "No one wanted me either."

"I haven't been back. I bet it's changed. I used to know my way around, but I'd probably feel lost there now."

" 'Course it's changed." Alroy spit, then wiped his mouth with the back of his hand. "Everyone kept living without us." He was looking at his feet. Em pictured him as a little boy. A hurt little boy, all alone and afraid.

"I lived in George's barn for seven years—just barely getting by—only to end up in a town with people who had real lives. People who were living." Em tried to loosen the rough rope on her wrists that was cutting her skin. "It's taken me some getting used to. No one understands what it's been like."

"I started living my life too. Just different than some folks. I got tired of waiting for good things to come my way and decided to take a little. Figured I was owed a few easy breaks." Alroy sat down on a log then and scratched his head. Scratched it hard, his nails fighting a battle with the vermin that must have lived on his scalp. "I ain't been sorry."

"Is the money you're hoping to find your easy break?"

"Other people got plenty. I took some, enough so I could get away and start over. That's all it was supposed to be. Stuff happened. It got out of hand, that's all. But I need that money now. I got to get out of here."

Risking rousing his anger, she asked, "Why did George have it?"

"After Gerda died, I took off, joined up with Bill and Morris. I did the bank job with them. We hid the money. We was gonna split it up, and I was gonna go west and start over. I heard you could get your own land. Problem was, George never knew how to keep out of my business." Again his nails dug into his scalp. His voice was full of venom when he spoke again. "George was tracking me ever since I ran. He snuck into camp and took the money. We threw some fists around, but somehow George made off with it. He ruined everything."

"And you think he still has it?" Em asked. "He didn't live like he had any money."

Alroy looked at her like she was foolish. "'Course he has it. Don't you know nothing 'bout George?"

Fighting the urge to laugh, she bit her bottom lip. It was a strange time to laugh, tied here in the woods with a desperate man, but the question was bizarre. George had barely fed her, barely clothed her, barely spoken to her. "I don't know much of anything about him. The man cared nothing for me. Not even enough to tell me about his past. He came and went as he pleased. Ours was a strange relationship—if you could even call it that."

"Well, he didn't want the money. He wanted me. Every year he chased me. Always on my trail. When I was a boy, he would beat me and tell me he was teaching me. Took sick pleasure from it. I know he did. I saw it in his eyes—they would light up with evil excitement. The devil was behind it, I was sure of it. He wanted that money so he could rub my face in it and teach me another lesson. He knew someday I'd need it and come back looking for it. Then he'd teach me about stealin' and about killin'."

"But you said you didn't kill Gerda?" Em shook her head, confused. "Why didn't he just let you go?"

He rose, anger burning in his eyes, and walked toward her with his hands fisted. She tightened her muscles and braced for another blow. But he held back. "You just the same as me. We both got nothin'. Nothin'." He relaxed some. "I didn't kill Gerda. Well, I didn't murder Gerda. George told me to clean the guns. It's his fault, really. He didn't tell me one of 'em was loaded. When it went off, the bullet struck her in the heart, and just like that she was gone. I might've wished her dead often enough, but I never planned to kill her."

"Did you tell George what happened?"

He sneered at her. "The George I lived with never listened to me. I ran. And I been running ever since."

Silence settled between them.

"I'm sorry," Em said. If he hadn't seemed so hostile, she would have said more.

"Sorry. That don't change nothin'. I'll be running for the rest of my life. And if they catch me, I'll swing from the gallows. Your little *sorry* won't help me."

"It may not. But I am sorry. You were dealt a poor hand." She envisioned the little boys she'd ridden the train with. They were Alroys too. Just little boys with uncertain futures and troublesome pasts. Little boys who had held her hand and with tear-filled eyes questioned their futures. She felt a wave of grief rush over her and silently prayed that her companions on the train had found good homes, that they'd been loved. She hoped they'd found better roofs to sleep under than Alroy had. A few stray tears escaped the corners of her eyes. She too had known desperation.

Grabbing her arm, he pulled her to standing. "Don't go crying on me. I made my choices. I'll take whatever is coming."

"You were only eight," Em said quietly.

"Don't matter none now. What matters is getting me that money so I can ride on outta here," Alroy snapped. He shoved her down once more. She rolled and sat.

Through clenched teeth she said, "I won't be able to get on the horse unless you untie me."

Grumbling, Alroy pulled out a knife. "I'll cut the rope off your feet, but don't be getting no ideas. You'll be getting me my money. I got plenty of dead people on my record—one more won't make a bit of difference." He pushed her skirts to her knees, then he grabbed the ropes with one hand and held the knife in the other.

Em, trying to ignore how close he was to her, focused on a tree in the distance. "Thank you," she said, averting her eyes from what he was doing.

Alroy flew from his bending position in front of her and landed flat on the ground a couple feet away.

What is happening? And then she knew. Caleb.

He was now on top of Alroy, struggling to get the knife from his hand. Alroy was a big man with a temper that matched his fiery hair. Roaring like a bear, he struggled underneath Caleb until he finally exerted himself enough and broke free and jumped to his feet. Knife still in hand, he slashed at Caleb, who was now on the defense.

Both men were moving so quickly that Em could not get a good look at Caleb's wound, but blood seeped from him. She tried desperately to free herself from the bindings so she could help.

If only Caleb had waited a moment longer, she thought, wishing that Alroy had freed her legs. The harder she tried to loosen them, the more the ropes cut into her wrists and ankles. She had to do something. She would not be a spectator, not of Caleb's death.

Caleb used his long legs and kicked Alroy. Em cringed as Alroy fell to the ground. The knife he'd clung to so resiliently during the scuffle flew from his hand, landing somewhere in the underbrush. Alroy rose up again and both men made a dash for the knife. Like two raging dragons they attacked each other, leaving trampled ferns and summer grass in their wake. Fierce tempers and rage drove them at each other again and again. Each motivated by his own ambitions—one to run, one to bring justice.

The tight ropes that bound Em kept her from following after the men as they raged against each other. Flashes of them came into and out of her line of sight. Alroy was on top now. He had his hands around Caleb's throat. Grunting and breathing hard, Alroy looked near victory.

"No!" Em shouted. "Let him go."

Would her dear friend be the next victim? Pulling harder against her restraints, she fought for a way to help. Tears burned her eyes and blurred her vision as she tried to make them stop.

Regaining some composure, she was able to see

again. Caleb had pulled a leg out from beneath Alroy and used it to pry Alroy's grip loose. Caleb gasped for air. Twisting beneath Alroy, he broke away and both men stood again. Caleb turned quickly and the full force of his fist connected with Alroy's jaw. Em again shuddered as blood ran down Alroy's face. The man stumbled about only to receive another blow. Judging by the sound this blow made, she knew it had been backed by even more force. Again, he staggered. Em, hoping it would all be over, waited for him to fall.

However, something seemed to snap back alive in Alroy. Was he remembering all the cruel atrocities of his life? Like a deranged animal, he headed for Caleb. All sanity was gone from his eyes. Caleb must have seen it too. Taking a rapid step back, he seemed caught off guard by the menacing and evil look his pursuer now possessed.

"Turn yourself in. End this," Caleb said.

"So I can swing for my crimes? I'd rather go down with a fight," Alroy said, fury flashing across his face. "And take you with me."

More punches, more blood.

Em had been working her ropes against a rough log while the two men attacked one another. At last she freed one hand and was able to untie the other bindings quickly. She looked about, wondering where Alroy's knife was. The two seemed to have forgotten about it in the chaos. She ran to the spot she had last seen it, praying she would find it. She crawled in the underbrush and felt for it with her hands. Another silent prayer and she saw the sun reflect from the blade. She grabbed it.

Then she stomped toward the men, the knife gripped tight in her hand. "Stop this."

Being so near Alroy made her shake. The look in his eyes was like that of a monster from a nightmare.

"Feisty one, aren't you?" He jumped at her, overtaking her and grabbing the knife. Caleb acted just as quickly. He dove for Alroy's legs, pushing Alroy's feet out from under him and knocking him to the ground.

Then Alroy did not move. Em looked at Caleb, her eyes wide.

Neither spoke. Both watched, waiting for the monster to rise again and the fight to go on. But Alroy remained belly down on the ground.

"Is he—is he dead?" Em whispered, unable to take her eyes off the man.

Caleb came to her side and slowly turned her away from the sight. Wrapping his big arms around her, he pulled her close and tucked her head into his shoulder so she did not have to look. "He fell on his blade. He did this. You hear me?" He was shaking too, trembling against her. "He did this. It's not your fault."

"He was a boy. Just a boy," she said through her tears. "He rode the train when he was boy."

Caleb ran his hand up and down her back. "Hush, it was not your fault. None of it was."

"You don't understand. He was just a boy," she said again.

Caleb held her tighter and let her cry.

She tilted her tear-stained face up at him and asked, "What if you hadn't come?" Then she stepped away from him. Her arms wrapped around her middle, she stumbled a few steps and then emptied her stomach. With her back to him, she asked again, "What if you hadn't come?"

"I did come." He put a hand on her back. "I did come. And you're safe. I told you I would make this right. I meant it and now you are. You're safe, Em." His voice was so smooth, so soothing. He turned her toward him. Then with his thumb, he wiped a tear from her face. "You're safe. It's not your fault." Over and over he reassured her. "You're safe. You're free now, free of Alroy and of George. You're safe and you're free."

He put a hand on her elbow and led her back to Amos. "It's getting late. We have to ride so we can get back to town."

She stood motionless. Afraid to look at Alroy. Caleb pulled a carrot from his saddlebags and handed it to her. "Feed Amos this while you wait for me." Em obeyed, grateful for the distraction.

Caleb lifted Alroy and slung him across the

back of the lifeless man's horse. Then he tied the horse to Amos.

"Look ahead while we ride and don't think about what's behind you. Let me help you up." He reached for her but stopped. "Your wrists are bleeding."

Em looked down to see much more blood than she'd realized. But she was too numb to feel any pain. "I'll be fine for the ride. I can clean up at the Howells'. So can you."

"Me?"

"Your nose. I think it may be broken." He wiped his hand across his face and it came away painted in blood. Then he looked at his shirt. Brilliant red covered his left side. Even Em's dress carried the color from being so close to him.

She remembered the knife wound. "He cut you with his knife. Is it deep?"

"It's not bad. Only my side, and it's little more than a scrape. I'll clean it in town."

Em reached out and touched his side where the wound was. She tore the fabric away and inspected the gash. "I'm sorry, Caleb. I'm sorry you ended up with this mess. I never meant for any of this . . ."

Pulling her against him again, he held her. "Don't be sorry. I haven't been for a single minute. I've been afraid, but I've not been sorry."

"But you're hurt. If I had been taken to

some other town, none of this ever would have happened to you."

"I'll heal just fine. I'm a better man because you showed up in Azure Springs." He put a dirty hand to her chin and looked into her eyes. "Don't you be wishing things had happened any other way. You're right where you're supposed to be. Come now, let's ride."

When the pair were safely in the saddle on good old Amos, Caleb put a protective arm around Em's waist. His touch reassured her, quite the opposite of what she'd felt from Alroy's touch. She leaned her head back against the prince's chest and allowed herself to feel safe. They rode back toward Azure Springs just as the sun was bidding farewell, declaring the end of the fateful day with exclamations of red and orange.

Fifteen

Caleb read the telegram twice before shoving it into his pocket and heading toward the boardinghouse. Looked like he was going to be heading out. Would he never get to enjoy a few days of uneventful bliss? Three busy days were all that had passed since Alroy had taken Em. The bruises on Caleb's nose were still a deep purple and already he was to leave again.

One thing would be different this time. At least he hoped it would be. If she was willing, he'd be taking Em with him. The judge wanted her to be a witness against the other two bandits. He also wanted Caleb to bring him the money they'd found. No one else could testify that the two men had been involved in George's murder but Em, plus she'd had a conversation with Alroy. She was a prime witness and these men were no petty thieves—her testimony would be pivotal. Convincing her it was her duty should be easy. But Caleb wanted Em along for other reasons too. The trip would be more fun with her by his side. And with her near him, he wouldn't have to worry about her well-being.

Margaret greeted him at the door. "What are you doing out and about? I heard it has only been a couple days since you had your nose smashed up." She looked him over. "It looks twice the size it normally does. Did you break it?"

Caleb touched his tender nose and winced a little. "Doctor says it will heal quickly, so long as I don't take any more shots to it. Em around?"

Margaret's face went very sober. All the laugh lines pulled tight, and then her eyes welled up with tears. "She's here." She sniffled loudly. "I'm sorry," she said, wiping her eyes. "It's just—I care so much and when she didn't come in the other day and I found out what happened, I was worried sick. I've wanted to tell you ever since that you did well. Thank you for bringing her back."

"It's my job, that's all." Caleb fiddled with the button on his vest as he waited for her to invite him in.

"It's more than your job. At the very least, she is your friend. And you saved her. She's my sweet little friend too. Stop pretending you don't care a snip for her." Margaret fished out a bright handkerchief from her apron pocket and blew her nose. "The thought of my dear girl suffering at the hands of that man. It just makes my blood boil."

Margaret motioned for him to follow her. "Come in. She's inside. I told her to go home and sleep, but she's insisted on working every day. I'm worried about her swollen wrists and ankles, but she says she's fine. I never would have guessed that dirty little thing they brought in from the woods would be so tough. She's always surprising me."

Caleb stepped into the boardinghouse. The smell of fresh-baked bread greeted him. His stomach growled, reminding him that he'd not eaten at all that day. He'd been too busy sending messages and making arrangements for his upcoming trip. Come to think of it, he hadn't eaten a real meal since his picnic with Eliza. The picnic felt like a lifetime ago.

Margaret narrowed her eyes at him. "I heard your stomach growling and it won't do in my house. Come along."

He didn't argue, only followed. Em was sitting on a three-legged stool in the kitchen peeling potatoes. Her purple-blue eyes looked up at him, and then her potato dropped to the floor. "Oh," she said while scrambling to fetch it.

"Are you all right, Em?" Caleb asked.

Standing, she smiled. "Of course. I did that on purpose." She put the potato with the others and walked toward him. "Your nose. It's every color of the rainbow now. Does it hurt you much? Is your side healing?"

He touched his nose. "It's just a little tender. Looks worse than it feels. My side was not deep.

It doesn't pain me. It's you I'm worried about. Why did you not take a little time to recover? The shock of it all and your wrists—you should have."

"I couldn't miss work."

"Of course you could have," Margaret said from behind the counter where she was slicing bread. "I even told you to."

"I think you'll have to miss a bit of work. We're heading out on a trip," Caleb said.

"A trip? I can't go on a trip. Not yet at least."

He pulled the telegram from his pocket. "Judge's orders. They want you to come and witness against the two other men who were with Alroy. They also want me to bring in any evidence we have against them. You're the only one who can confirm their involvement in George's murder. And you can tell the court what Alroy said to you in the woods. They need you there."

Em hesitated. "How long will we be away?"

"She can be gone as long as she needs to be," Margaret said as she brought a thick slice of buttered bread to Caleb. "But don't you even think about leaving until you've eaten."

"I can't leave you with all this work," Em said to Margaret.

"Don't you worry about me. I had a new girl ask me about a job just the other day. I can find an extra set of hands to help while you're away."

Margaret grinned at Em. "But I doubt any will work like you do."

Em looked down, but Caleb could see the pink on her cheeks.

"There's no train for at least a day or two. But then we'll head out. We'll be near my parents' home. I'd like to stop in, if it's all right with you. We could be gone several days, maybe even a week or two."

Em sighed. "I would love to meet your parents. But weeks? I'll never earn enough money if I'm not here to work. Besides, we can't travel alone."

"I thought of that. But it's different than traveling. I'll be escorting you to the trial. I've done that many times, and this isn't any different. Besides, I'm with the law. We get our own set of rules." He winked at her.

"I'll go. I'll be glad to help. It's just unexpected, that's all." Em busied herself with peeling again, but Caleb could tell she was worried about the setback. He ate his bread silently, then he rose, thanked Margaret, and bid Em a good day.

He crossed town to the small train station, where he bought two tickets east. They would testify and then stop at his parents' home for a short respite from the journey. Looking down at the tickets, he suddenly felt his stomach churn. Never had he brought a girl home to his parents. He'd often pictured the day he did. In his fantasies, a beautiful girl—nervous and anxious to meet his family—clung to his arm. In his mind, his mother pulled him aside and told him what a lovely girl he'd brought home. Then his father patted his back and told him what a fine man he'd become and how proud he was.

What would they say about Em? He remembered what he thought about her when he first met her. But she was so different now. Besides, it didn't matter what they thought. He was only bringing her because she had to testify. Surely his parents would understand that.

In the evening, he stopped by the Howells' to let Em know they would be leaving in two days. Abigail greeted him with a friendly hello when she opened the door.

"I know I already told you, but I must say it again. We are so grateful you got to Em when you did. I just keep thinking what could have happened to her. I don't know what I would have done if we had lost her." Abigail embraced him like any grateful mother would. "Bless you. Now, come in. I promise I won't get all sentimental every time you stop by."

"I was glad to get there when I did. Is she around?" he asked.

"She's upstairs. I'll fetch her in a moment. She's telling the girls one of Lucy's favorite stories. I pray for the day those two are reunited."

"You know about Lucy?"

"I didn't at first, but everything's changed.

We trust each other more and are helping each other. I have found in Em a balm for my grief. She asks me about the boys and listens to all the stories of their mischief. She wants to know everything. At first it was hard to talk about them, but now, finally, I can open their door and not cry, but smile and remember. I ask her about Lucy and she tells me. It has healed me in a way I did not know I needed healing." Abigail pulled him further into the house. "That darling girl has done so much good. Somehow she has convinced herself she owes us a debt— little does she know we are the ones indebted to her."

"Seems she was led to Azure Springs," Caleb said as he sat down.

Abigail brought him a cool drink of water and then left him alone while she worked in the kitchen. Propriety kept him from going up the stairs and listening to Em's story. He could picture the girls wide-eyed, hanging on her words as she took them to faraway places.

Minutes later, pattering little feet preluded the girls' approach. Mae and Milly descended the steps with dolls in hand, laughing about the evil witch and her magic mirror. Suddenly the quiet living room was alive with noise.

"Hi, Caleb," Milly said when she spotted him.

"Hello, ladies. How are you doing on this fine summer day?"

"We're doing well. Except for one thing." Milly held up a finger.

"What's that?"

"Em said she was going to go away." Milly looked near tears. "Will she come back?"

He twisted his hat around in his hands, trying to decide how to answer. He planned to bring Em back with him—he wanted her to come back. But would she come? She really wouldn't need to. She was healthy now and no longer *needed* the Howells. Their travels would take her closer to Beckford and Lucy. "Well, I suppose that's up to her. But if she is willing and has a mind to, I'll bring her back."

Mae walked over to his side. "We love Em. She plays with us and tells us stories. She's our friend. You must bring her back."

He patted her head full of curls. "I'll do all I can. Where is she?"

"She said she was coming," Mae said.

"Looking for me?" Em asked. No one had heard her enter the room.

"We were indeed," Caleb said. "I've come to tell you the train leaves in two days. Will you be ready by then?"

"Yes. My bag will be packed, but my heart might not ever be ready." She grabbed the girl closest to her and gave her a tight hug. "Oh, how I shall miss my Mae-berry and Milly-girl. I'll miss you so very much."

Both girls started pleading with her not to go. She bent low and pulled them into her arms. Em looked near tears, but her voice remained calm. "I must go. This is my chance to help. We can't let the Prince of Azure Springs have all the fun."

"Will you have a gun?" Mae asked.

"No, I'll only be telling a judge what happened so he can decide the best punishment for the bandits." Suddenly her eyes shot up and found Caleb's. "Why did you not have a gun with you when you came for me?"

Caleb shrugged.

"You always have a gun," Em said as she stood up. "What happened?"

"Well, I wasn't thinking real clear when I found out you were gone. I didn't have one with me because I'd been off picnicking all morning. I should have had one then too, but I was wearing my suit." He shifted in his chair and watched as the girls took a seat on the sofa. "Then I found your gun in the basket you dropped and put it in the saddlebag. I figured I could use that if I needed to."

Em looked confused. "Why didn't you use it? It would have been easier on your nose. Perhaps you could have taken him in unharmed."

"He would have fought either way. I don't doubt that. I saw the devil in his eyes." Knowing she was going to ask again about the gun, he said, "When I saw him in front of you . . . by your . . .

skirts." He leaned in for only her to hear. "I didn't realize he was about to cut the rope. I thought he had other intentions. I just ran for him. I didn't think to get the gun."

Em was silent a moment before saying, "Thank you for saving me. For coming when you did. You rescued me."

"I normally am a bit more levelheaded. I'm not sure what got into me," he said, making a mild attempt at saving his reputation.

"It's behind us now, and after we tell the story in court, we can close the door on it. And it's a door I have no plans of ever opening again. Though I'll always remember the feeling of being rescued." Em sat down between the girls and absently picked up one of their dolls. "Will we be near Beckford?"

Her simple question was all he needed to hear for him to know. Em would not be coming back with him. "We'll be much closer than we are now." Rising from his seat, he put his hat back on his head. "I'll be by later to talk more about the trip."

There were more plans to discuss, more preparations to make. But he had to leave. The Howells' home felt too hot and stuffy.

She's never coming back.

"Caleb, come in. We didn't expect to see you again so soon," Abigail said after she opened the door. Not even an hour had passed since his last visit.

"I realized there was more to talk about. Is Em around?"

"Eliza surprised us all and asked her to go for a walk," Abigail said, leading him into the living room. "The two have been gone a little over a quarter hour." She looked at the girls playing on the floor before sitting down.

Once again Caleb worried for Em, but not for her physical safety this time. He worried Eliza would cut into Em with her ruthless words. "Do you think they'll be gone long?"

Abigail looked out the window. "I'm not sure where they were headed or when they'll return. I believe Eliza has plans with Olivia before too long. But I am in no hurry for them to return. I am hoping a little of Em will rub off on my Eliza. I think it may have already. Something has been different these last few days. Ever since the day Em went missing."

Caleb fought back the sarcastic tone he wanted to use and tried to sound convincing. After all, people could change. "Perhaps they will become the best of friends."

"I do hope so. They've been slow to hit it off. Em tries hard though. And if she continues to overlook Eliza's snubs, there may be hope for them." Abigail picked up a bit of embroidery and added a few tiny knots. "I won't worry about that now. But it's a lovely idea, the two of them friends."

Not ready to think about that again, he said, "While I wait, would it be all right if I told the girls the adventure story I promised them?" Caleb sat himself next to the girls on the floor.

"They'd like that."

"Is there a princess?" Mae asked.

"No. Of course not. This is a swashbuckling pirate story. Sword fights, treasure." Caleb swung an imaginary sword through the air.

Milly squished up her nose. "But princesses are better than pirates."

"How about this. I'll tell you a pirate one today and someday I'll tell you a princess story."

"All right. We'll listen. But you better keep your promise," Mae said. "Em says a prince always keeps his word."

"That's right—he does. And since the royal title fell upon me, you need not fear. I will not forget that I owe my two favorite seven-year-olds a story with a princess in it. May I begin now?" Caleb asked his audience.

Milly gave Mae a sly look. "He'll keep his promise. I think we can trust him."

Mae nodded her agreement. "We're ready. Tell us your story."

He chuckled to himself before starting the tale. There was no princess, but the girls seemed pleased enough. They held their dolls close during the tense moments and laughed at the funny parts. Sensing their interest in the story, he embellished it with different voices and extra details. Lost in the world of pirates and buccaneers, he barely noticed Em and Eliza return. The two stood quietly in the doorway as he finished his tale.

". . . and that is how Ordinary Robert captured the infamous One-Eyed Jimmy."

"But what became of the fair maiden, Adele?" Mae asked.

"I told you she was rescued."

"Yes, but did she live happily ever after? Em's stories always end with happily ever after," Mae protested.

"Hmm. If Em's stories end with happily ever after, then mine shall too. Let me end it again."

Mae and Milly listened intently.

"Let's see. Now you know the tale of how Ordinary Robert captured the infamous One-Eyed Jimmy. Ordinary Robert returned to land and found the fair maiden Adele, and they lived happily ever after." The girls sat up straight, both looking ready to pounce on him.

"But . . . but that can't be all. You have to tell us *how* they fell in love," Milly said.

Eliza stepped into the room followed by Em. Eliza announced their entrance by saying, "Caleb, we were not expecting you."

"Shhh, Eliza! Caleb is telling us a story. He

is about to tell us the ending again," Mae said without even looking at Eliza, her eyes stuck on Caleb.

"I'm not telling it again. If my ending was not good enough, you will just have to make up the ending yourself or get Em to tell it to you."

A deep frown formed on Mae's face.

"Mae, pull yourself together," Eliza gently demanded of the little girl.

Caleb was surprised. Eliza normally snapped at her sisters.

"All right, Eliza. But Caleb promised us another story, so don't think you can steal him away from us."

Caleb stood. "I have to talk to Em a little about our trip. I can't tell any more stories today."

"But you promised us a princess story if we listened to the pirate story," Mae said.

"That I did. But I did not promise it would be today."

"I hope it's soon," Milly said.

Caleb nudged her under the chin. "Brighten up, little Milly. I'll keep my promise. But you might have to wait until I get back," he said as he turned to Em. "If you have a minute, I want to go over the itinerary and a few last-minute details. Then I'll leave you to pack."

"I'll help you," said Eliza. "I might even have a few dresses that will fit you now."

Caleb's brow rose.

Abigail, taking her eyes off her embroidery, looked puzzled too. "That is a splendid idea—and very kind of you, Eliza."

"I've plenty already," Em said. "You've all been too good to me."

"Nonsense. They will look perfect on you and no one is using them here," Abigail said.

Caleb was enjoying his time but had far too much to do before leaving to delay any longer. "Mae, Milly, thank you for a lovely time. Good to see you ladies as well," he said to Abigail and Eliza. Em followed him out onto the front porch.

"Off walking with Eliza? I hadn't expected that."

"Nor I. She's been kinder lately. Did you tell her to be?"

Caleb cleared his throat. "No. Not exactly."

"Now who is the mysterious one?"

"All right. I told her she wasn't right for me. That I couldn't be with someone who wasn't kind. I thought she would be angry, but maybe she is taking it to heart."

Em looked off into the distance. "She is changing. I believe she really is. Perhaps she will be a good match for you. She is beautiful."

"Naw, she's not for me. But she will make someone happy someday. Let's talk about the trip."

And they did.

Sixteen

You can do this. She took a huge gulp of air but still she felt like she was suffocating. *You can do this.*

Before she was ready to face it, she saw it up ahead. The platform. No matter how many times she told herself it was just a platform, that it was different this time, her heart refused to listen. Against her will it beat faster. Then her legs stopped and she stood rooted to the ground. Eyes focused on the benches, the worn boards.

Remembering.

Swept away by images of her younger self, her hand grasping Lucy's.

"It'll be all right," she had said as she gripped her sister's hand even tighter. Then she'd bent down and touched her sister's cheek. "We're going to ride a train and go to a beautiful place. We'll live on a farm with animals and plenty to eat. We'll have blankets on our beds, and someday I'll buy you a doll."

"I'm afraid," Lucy had said. A tear trickled down her face. "What if we get lost?"

"Look at the tracks. The train stays on those.

It knows exactly where it is going. Don't worry. I'll be right there beside you."

"Everyone file onto the train," an aid worker had hollered.

Obediently the children had pressed together as they crowded onto the train. Lucy's hand had slipped from hers as Em pushed her way through the other children.

And then there Lucy had been—at the edge of the crowd. Tears streaking down her face.

"You said you wouldn't leave me," Lucy had said.

Em's own tears had come then. "I'm sorry, Lucy."

Em hadn't let the little girl from her sight again, not until Beckford. And now here she stood again on a platform. Again making her way toward the train.

"I can't," she said as she stared ahead. "I just can't. I'm sorry. I thought I could, but I cannot."

Caleb regarded her without speaking.

Em wanted him to understand. "I want to go and help you. Is there no other way we can get there?"

"Well, we could ride on Amos, but that would take us too long. I already wired that we would be there for the trial. I think this is the only way." Caleb stepped closer to her. "I'll stay by you. You won't be alone."

"It was so long ago. And yet standing here

looking at the platform, it feels so fresh. I'm a child again and unwanted and afraid. I can almost feel Lucy's hand in my own, slipping from my grasp."

"This time will be different." He put a hand on her arm. "I won't leave you."

"I believe you. It's not that. It's just that—that was the worst time of my life. When they took Lucy, I ached so deeply. Caleb, it was worse than hunger, worse than nights in the cold. It was like dying. And now I'm afraid—I'm not strong enough."

"But you are closer to her now than you have been before. This train ride will not tear you from her. It will take you closer to her." Caleb's voice was soothing.

"I don't want to feel that pain again. I'm finally living. I finally have people I care about."

"Em." He brushed his hand against her cheek. "Look at me, Em."

Slowly she turned her head toward him.

"Em, I'll be here. We won't dwell on the painful thoughts. When we're together, we can remember the good times. Let's talk about happy Lucy memories as we travel. We can look out the window and watch for good climbing trees. You won't feel like you did before. Not on this train ride. I won't let you." Caleb reached a hand to her. "Trust me. You don't have to do this alone."

Em stood a little taller and took a long, slow

breath. Then, pursing her lips together, she grasped his hand and nodded.

"We'll do it," he said, pressing his fingers tightly around her small hand. "We'll do it together."

Holding his hand, she felt less like an unwanted child. Drawing from his strength, she stepped onto the platform. One hurdle behind her. When the train arrived, he put a hand on her back and whispered, "Won't Mae and Milly be jealous? Another train ride, and this time you get to ride with a prince."

Em boarded the train thinking of her beloved little friends. A happy thought.

Once on board Caleb led them to a seat and promptly opened a window, letting in fresh air. Em marveled at the cushioned seats and wide aisles. This train was different from the train she had ridden as a child. Then she had spent the long hours crowded onto makeshift seats, shoulder to shoulder with other children. So snug sleep had been nearly impossible.

Caleb reached into his bag, dug around, and then pulled out three books. Em eyed him suspiciously. "What have you brought with you?"

He flashed his handsome smile. "I brought this one to practice your reading. We can't miss our lessons just because we're traveling. This one here," he said, holding a second, thicker book, "is so I can learn a princess fairy tale for the girls. I promised them one and can't let them down. You have them expecting happily-ever-after stories. And I aim to tell them a princess story so fine that they will stop telling me how much better your stories are than mine!"

"Always competing."

Picking up the final book from his stack, he said, "And this one is for me to read to you when you need to forget you're on a train."

Em reached out and took it from his hands. She studied the writing on the cover. Slowly she sounded out the gold embossed letters. The first word was *Jane*. He helped her with the second word, *Eyre. Jane Eyre.*

Caleb shrugged. "I've never read it, but my mother had it in her collection and picked it up often."

"Can we read it now?" Em asked.

"The train isn't even moving."

Em shrugged. "But I am ready to forget I am on the train. Please."

"You are as bad as Mae and Milly." Caleb laughed as he opened the book and started reading. Em sank deep into the seat, rested her back against the thick cushion, closed her eyes, and listened. Caleb's voice was smooth as he read and, without even having to try to escape, Em felt as though she were lost on the moors in England. She could see it all in her head. The grand old houses, the shameful school. She didn't feel like she was on a train at all. Only when he stopped reading did she remember.

"Why have you stopped?" Em sat up straight.

"I know the princes in your stories can do anything, but I, unfortunately, cannot. If I read one more page, I fear my voice will be completely gone."

Em sighed. "If only I could read better, then we would be able to find out what becomes of dear Jane. Do you think she will have to stay at that cold, awful school forever?"

"I hope not. That wouldn't make for a very good story. We'll have to pick it up again later." He put the book down and reached for the reader. "It's your turn. You keep practicing and you'll be able to read *Jane Eyre* on the return trip."

Looking out the window, she avoided his gaze. He set the book on her lap.

When she did read, she stumbled over words. Caleb placed a hand on hers. "Reading took me years to master. You'll be a scholar in no time. Tripping over the words is part of the journey."

"I'm twenty. I should think it was high time I learned to read. I long for the day I read as you do." She moved the book closer to her face, only to have it pushed away.

"You're twenty now? When was your birthday?"

"I don't know. I know my ma always told me I was a year older sometime around the beginning of summer. Since that has passed, I figure I'm a year older."

"I knew something was different about you." He brushed a strand of hair from her face. "You're practically an old maid." He laughed but stopped when she did not laugh with him.

She slumped back in her seat and said, "Someday I may be. I probably will be."

"Unlikely."

"I won't think about that now. Today I feel younger than I have in a long time."

Caleb picked up the book of fairy tales. "Since you are such a young thing, you will not mind me reading you a fairy tale."

"I thought your voice was in jeopardy."

"It seems to have returned."

Em made herself comfortable in the seat, eager to hear another story—something fanciful that would distract her and help pass the time. His arm came around her. She inched away but then stopped herself. He was offering her comfort. It was a gift. She let her head rest against his shoulder as he read the story of Hansel and Gretel. When he finished, he started in on another and then another. Soon Em was asleep and dreaming of a future that did not include becoming an old maid.

The afternoon continued much the same way. They talked of many things, the conversation easy and natural. Then they read.

"I'm surprised you know so many of these stories already," Caleb said when she again recognized a tale.

"When I rode the train as a child, we passed the time by telling stories. There are so many details I have forgotten, but the stories seem to have sealed themselves up tight in my mind and heart. That train ride was not like this one—the stories were the only escape. Lucy loved them too. I'm so anxious to see her."

Caleb swallowed hard. "I'm sorry it will take longer to earn the money for Beckford. I could buy your ticket."

"No. As kind as your offer is, I will not take any more charity. I'll find a way to get there. I know I will. This train is headed east. I have thought of finding work in a town along the way. My ticket would not cost as much then."

"Is that what you wish to do?"

Shaking her head, she spoke quickly. "I don't know. I'm not sure. I want to see her so badly. I have to see her." She looked out the window at the green hills. "Yes. It's what I want to do. It's what I must do. Only I want to see everyone in Azure Springs too. I want things I cannot have, but Lucy needs me."

"What of Mae and Milly? The Howells would be heartbroken to not get to say goodbye."

"I left a note with Abigail. I told her to read it to the girls if I did not return with you. I'm sure it is full of errors, but I hope it's clear enough. You will tell them why I couldn't come back, won't you? I love them so. Can you help them understand? You will tell them, yes?" Em quickly wiped a tear from her cheek. "I made a promise to my mother. I told her I would take care of Lucy." She felt the emotion becoming stronger in her voice. "I promised her, and now Lucy is all I have. All these years it's what I worked for. It's what I lived for."

He brushed away another tear and then let his hand rest on her cheek. "I know. We all know you must go to Beckford. It's only—Azure Springs will not be the same without you. We'll miss you."

Leaning against his hand, she said, "No one has ever missed me."

"Those two girls will. I know that."

Em looked away, unable to meet his eyes. Her heart ached in her chest. Oh, how she would miss Milly and Mae. In truth, she would miss more than them. She would miss Margaret, the Howells, even Eliza. The brook she and Caleb had stomped in and the tree they had climbed. The jail where he had finally taught her letters and the mirror in which she had seen her face clearly for the first time. She would miss so many things. Mostly she would miss Caleb. The very thought of never seeing him seemed like a burden too heavy to carry.

"I'll miss them too," she said. Then she sat in silence as the train chugged along the track. Her back to him, she pretended to sleep.

"Em, wake up. This is our stop." It was late in the evening when they arrived in Brigley. Caleb gently shook her shoulder. For hours he'd watched her sleep, wondering what life would be like when she was no longer in Azure Springs. Would life be as fun without her to laugh with? Read with? Learn with?

"I didn't mean to sleep." Em rubbed her eyes.

"It's late. I'm glad you got some rest." He started gathering their belongings. "The telegram said two rooms were reserved for us at the Spright Hotel. I've seen it before—it's not a far walk."

Em picked up her small carpetbag and followed him off the train. Brigley was much bigger than Azure Springs. Even in the dim evening light the ornate courthouse was easy to spot. Stone columns stood as sentinels all along its front. They passed a library, two millineries, a dry goods store, and three saloons. Neither Caleb nor Em expressed any interest in exploring the town. Traveling had a way of wearing a body out.

Caleb opened the door of the hotel and they were greeted by hard marble floors and a crystal chandelier. A young man stood behind a counter. "Can I help you?"

"Yes, there should be two rooms reserved for us. Caleb Reynolds is the name." The boy looked at a registry book before him.

"Yes, sir. Two rooms. I'll take you if you're ready."

They followed the boy up the curved stairway to the second floor. "Right this way, please."

Around a corner, the boy stopped at the first room. Caleb motioned for Em to go on in. "I'll see you in the morning," he said before leaving her.

"Good night, Caleb." She stepped through the doorway, out of his sight.

Across the hall was his room. He opened the door and surveyed a sturdy bed, a wardrobe, and other amenities. He hoped Em's room was as nice. Judging by the grandeur of the hotel, it likely was. Such a difference from the barn she'd lived in. He wanted her to always have a warm bed and plenty to eat. Would anyone make sure that happened for her if she didn't return to Azure Springs? Without the Howells, where would she stay?

In the dark of night he lay in bed struggling to sleep. His thoughts repeatedly went to Em, no matter how hard he tried to think of other things. After finally pulling himself from the soft bed, he knelt on the floor and offered a plea that someone would watch out for her. That she would have food to eat and a roof over her head. More than just food and shelter—that wasn't enough. His stomach twisted in knots as he thought of the dull look she'd had in her eyes when they'd first met. *Let her live, not just survive,* he prayed.

Stretching her arms above her, Em opened her eyes. Sun poured through the heavy, leaded window and danced gracefully across the room. Judging by the position of the sun, it was early morning. Allowing herself the luxury of waking slowly in a room all her own, she lay in bed content and rejuvenated. The sun rose higher, its rays now entering through an upper pane. Then she got out of bed and readied herself for the day. Caleb had not told her what time to meet him. She dressed hurriedly, afraid of keeping him waiting. She tiptoed across the hall and tapped on his door. Then stepping away from it, she wondered if she should turn back. What would he think of her coming to his room?

Frozen in her spot, she waited. She was about to flee when the door opened. Caleb was dressed, but his hair was a mess and he looked as if he'd been sleeping only moments before.

"Good morning to you, Em. You're a fine sight," he said, then covered his mouth as he yawned. "Did your stomach wake you?"

"No, it was the beautiful sunshine. The room was so pleasant compared with the constant jostling of the train. But now that you mention it, my stomach is ready to be filled." She looked down the hall, again uncertain how to behave. "Shall I eat alone or are you going to join me?"

"Of course I'll join you. We two are traveling companions. Let me go and wash some sleep from my face. I'll meet you in the lobby."

"Very well. I'll see you in a moment." With that she practically skipped down the staircase. He wanted to dine with her!

When he joined her at the bottom of the stairs moments later, she still felt like smiling. He offered his arm and the pair walked to the dining room. All through breakfast she smiled, pretending in her mind that Caleb Reynolds was more than her traveling companion.

"You must tell me what it is that is making you smile without stopping," Caleb said as he forked his breakfast ham. "That last bite I was sure would fall right out. You smiled while chewing. Tell me your secret."

"There's no secret. I can't put it into words. I just woke this morning and felt like it was a good day. Aren't I allowed to be happy? Do you ever feel that way when you wake—that life is good?"

"Usually I wake and start thinking of everything I need to do. But maybe if I spend more time with you, I'll wake up grinning from ear to ear. You did get me to jump in the brook and climb trees. Who knows what's possible."

"Ah, the brook and the trees." Putting her

napkin on the table, she eyed him. "I think it's time for another wager. I need a victory. Today could be my day."

"Just needing one won't get you one. What do you have in mind?" Caleb asked, his eyes already sparkling. It was the same look she had seen before when they had competed.

"I'm not certain. What time do we have to be at the courthouse?"

"Not until two." He pulled out a pocket watch. "It's only half past seven. Looks like we have a few hours to cause some mischief."

"We've already climbed trees and shot guns. I lost both of those, although I don't think the rules were in my favor. Let's head outside of town," Em said, already starting for the door.

Caleb set his napkin on the table and followed. "It won't take any convincing to get me away from town. Come on, end the suspense. What do you have in mind?"

"I'm still thinking. I'll let you know when I know."

"Fair enough."

Slowly they made their way through the town. Occasionally they remarked about the size of the town or stopped and peered in a window to comment on the goods they saw.

"Azure Springs needs a library," Em said, looking longingly at the shelves of books she saw through one window. "Someday I am going to read my way through everything I can get my hands on."

"It won't be long. You're learning much quicker than I had expected."

The sun was radiant, shining down on them as they walked. Once they were out of town, Em stopped occasionally to pick a wildflower or point out a bird she saw. She knew few of their names but had a good eye for spotting them.

"It's been too long since I took the time to enjoy nature," Caleb said.

"See there?" Em asked, pointing to a muddy patch near a creek that had many little pools.

"I see mud. You thinking of bathing in it? I don't think that will go over well with the judge."

Em smacked him playfully. "No, I am not going to bathe in it. There was a spot just like this near Hollow Creek. My days were so monotonous. I'd catch frogs. I had no one to compete with but myself. I'm willing to wager I can catch more frogs than you." Em scrunched up her nose and surveyed the mud. All she'd worried about was picking a challenge she thought she could win. Hopefully she would have time to clean up before going to the courthouse.

Caleb rubbed his hand along his jaw. "I haven't caught frogs in years. You sure you don't want to just climb that giant oak? Or run a quick race?"

"I thought of that, but with your height I think you'll be able to go higher. I need a win, and I think I might be able to get a victory this time." Em rolled up the sleeves on her dress. She would not back down. "Do you dare?"

Following her lead, he rolled his sleeves and nodded. "I'll take the challenge. What are the stakes?"

"If I win, I get to ask you three questions."

"And if I win?" Caleb asked.

Em tried to think of something she was willing to lose. Finally she shrugged. "What do you want?"

"I still have one question, so I'll pick something different. Don't look so surprised. I remember, and I plan to use it." He walked around the wet bank. "If I win, you let me pay for your ticket to Beckford."

"I can't let you pay."

"You can if I win." He set his hat on a log. "It's what I want."

Em looked to the east, toward Beckford. "All right. Half an hour. When you catch a frog, you have to run it down to the stream so you don't catch it again."

"Now I'm in real trouble. I'd hoped to catch the same frog over and over. If I'm even lucky enough to catch one." He looked at his pocket watch. "It's nearly eight thirty. Should we begin now?"

"Yes."

Em knew where to find the slimy little critters

and easily pulled a frog from the muddy bank. Holding it high, she shouted, "See here? This little one wasn't so hard to find."

"Ha. I'll find my own before long." He bent over and pulled at the tall grass along the bank. Minutes passed and he hadn't found a single frog. Em pulled up another. Again she smirked, enjoying her advantage.

Ten minutes later and Em's calves were wet, but she had pulled three frogs from the bank and Caleb was still desperately searching for his first.

When fifteen minutes had passed, Em held up a large frog. Laughing, she threw back her head, brushed her hair from her face, and held it out for him to see. "I believe that makes four for me. I see why you like competing so well. Victory does feel g—" Down she went into the mud. Black water splashed over her. "Ooohhh!"

Trying to wipe the mud from her face with her muddy hands only made the dilemma that much worse. "I suppose that is what I deserve for showing such confidence."

Caleb tried to stifle a laugh, but the sight of her sitting covered in mud was too much. He reached out a hand. "Help up?"

"I think now that I'm down here I ought to look for more frogs. They may not even notice me coming. I blend in so well." She scooped up a handful of mud and then watched it splash back down.

"I hear some people pay good money to bathe in mud."

"I've always been up on the current fashions," Em said. "I don't know why you don't join me. I think you would enjoy it."

"Very fashionable. In fact, I knew it the day I met you. I thought, there is a modern woman." Caleb grinned. "I happen to have an appointment with a judge later today. Otherwise I'd definitely follow your lead."

She groaned then. The judge! "Funny, very funny. That statement would only be true if the fashion was to be thin and plain—and sadly it is not." Wishing she hadn't brought up his long-ago comment, she reached out and grabbed his hand. "Get me out of this mudhole. I've got to face the judge too."

He pulled her to her feet.

"How much time have we left?"

"We have eight minutes. Seems you have wasted several minutes playing in the mud," Caleb said.

"I fear I may lose now. How many frogs have you caught? I seem to have lost count." Em tried to keep her face serious, but a smile threatened at the corners of her mouth.

"I admit defeat." He bowed low to her. "You are a far better frog catcher than I am. I concede."

"Victory!" She squealed and hopped around in the mud, only to fall back into it. The few places that had managed to escape the splatter of mud from her earlier fall were now covered. "Why did no catastrophes befall you when you won?"

"I suppose it is because I am so much more humble than you." He laughed as he pulled her again from the muddy hole.

"I will keep that in mind and be quieter about my boasting next time." She looked at her mud-caked dress and groaned again. "Oh, what will the judge think of me?"

"I think he better not see you that way. The hotel offers baths. If we hurry back, he may never know that his top witness spends her mornings swimming in the mud."

"Are you suggesting I need a bath? I thought a gentleman was never supposed to remark on a woman's appearance," Em said, trying to look insulted. Unable to keep a serious face, she shrugged. "Come to think of it, I agree—a bath is just the thing I need."

As they walked back toward town, Em asked, "If you love the quiet country so much, why did you become a sheriff? That's my first question."

"Well, my parents were so proud of my brothers for going off to war. Fighting for a cause. I guess I wanted them to be proud of me too. I was too young to join the army, but I could be a sheriff and fight for peace. That seemed a worthy cause."

"Are they proud?"

"I don't know. I like to think they are. They didn't say much about it. When I first wrote and told them, they wrote back and simply told me to be safe." Caleb reached over as they walked and picked a twig from her hair. "I think most of the choices I've made have been to make them proud. I know if my brothers had lived, my parents would be satisfied—and happy. I grew up listening to them talk about all the boys had done and were doing. When they died, that all stopped."

"Do you not think they sit at dinner now and talk of you and all you have done?" Em asked.

"I don't know." Caleb shook his head. "I hope they do."

"You should ask them. That's what Margaret would do. She would walk right up to them and ask, 'Are you proud of me?' "

"I'm sure she would. I don't think I could. I wouldn't know what to do if they said they were not. You'll understand when you meet them."

"What will they think of me?" Em looked at her filthy dress.

Caleb shrugged. "I'm sure they'll be welcoming."

"Everyone is looking at me." She ducked her head. "I wish everyone would disappear."

Caleb smirked at her. "They are all wondering what you've been doing this morning. They may gossip, but I'd be willing to wager—"

"No more wagers!"

"I wasn't *really* going to wager. I was just going to say I doubt any of them had nearly as fun a morning as we had." Caleb grinned and waved at a couple who were staring at them. They looked away quickly, causing him to smile broader. "Let them talk."

Em grabbed his arm from the air and shook her head. "You are not the one covered in mud. Let's just get back to the hotel."

Once there, he opened the door wide for her. She heard the attendant gasp when he saw her. She looked down and watched mud drip onto the marble floor.

Caleb motioned toward her. "I was told your hotel offers baths. I would like to arrange one for my guest. I think she is due for a soak in the tub, don't you agree?"

"I couldn't rightly say." He scowled while he spoke, eyes averted. "I'll have it drawn up right away."

Em went to her room to get a clean dress while Caleb went to his room to wash in the basin. He found that the mud came off easily with a good scrubbing. He went to the lobby to wait for Em— she had been gone for well over an hour. While he waited, he pictured her sitting in the mud. The image brought a smile to his face. Could she be any more unladylike?

And then there she was before him. Clean and

dressed in a lavender frock that he'd never seen before. Her hair was loose and wet against her shoulders. She looked lovely.

Had he just thought that about Em? About plain Em?

But he had thought it and he thought it still as he looked at her. Her thin frame and freckled face had once held no appeal. Today he saw her differently.

"No more mud?" he asked.

"I thought of leaving a little on but wasn't sure the judge would want to have to clean it from the courtroom."

"You look fine with or without the mud. I'm sure the judge will just be happy you're here," Caleb said.

"I'm glad I look good enough for the judge. Do we have time to dine before we go to the court?" Her eyes lost just a little of their sparkle.

He wished he were brave enough to call her lovely, or even beautiful. Were those words she'd ever heard before? Someone should tell her. But he could not. Those were not words he could say, not unless they were something more than friends.

"We have plenty of time. Come along," he said while leading her to the hotel dining room. Once there, he pulled out her chair and then sat across from her.

During their meal they spoke of the trial and what to expect. Em confessed she was feeling nervous about seeing Alroy's men again. He assured her he was there and that many other lawmen would be too.

"I'm not so much scared for myself. It's just that seeing them brings the past back, and I am glad it's over. Being in Azure Springs has been a new life for me."

"They can't take that from you. The Howells, Margaret, me. We are all real and not going anywhere."

"Sometimes I fear it's all a dream and I am still the girl who lives in the loft of a barn." Em folded her arms across her chest. "If it is a dream, I hope I never wake."

Caleb poked her cheek. "You feel real to me. And very little of that other girl exists. Her strength remains, but you don't even look the same. You were nothing but bones when I met you."

"You say strength, but I feel shakier now than I have before." Em wiped the corners of her mouth with her napkin, then stood.

"You'll do perfectly." Caleb stood and took her arm. "Let's head over now. Soon this will all be behind you. No more George. No more rats for dinner." He would make sure of it. Somehow he would.

The courthouse was a stately stone building. It boasted a dome ceiling and marble staircase.

Murals covered some of the walls and a statue of a man in chains stood in the front atrium. But Em was too preoccupied to appreciate it.

The court proceeding was not nearly as intimidating as she had imagined. Judge McConnel was kind and familiar with the case. He greeted Caleb like an old friend and her like a new one. Her time on the stand was brief. She recounted the details of George's murder and the injuries she'd suffered. Then she told about Alroy capturing her and the stories he'd confessed to her. Not once did she look at his men, Bill and Morris, while she sat on the stand. Instead, she looked to Caleb and spoke as though she were talking to him and him alone.

"Thank you for your testimony. You may be dismissed," Judge McConnel said. And just like that it was over. She left the stand and returned to her seat.

Caleb leaned over to her. "You did well," he whispered. "I never would have guessed you were nervous."

"I was. My knees were knocking together the whole time. I'm glad it's over."

Caleb slid closer. "Do you want to stay here and find out the judgment?"

"No. You stay and tell me. I don't think I care to listen." Em tiptoed from the room and made her way back to her hotel room.

Caleb rapped on her door not long after.

"It's over, Em. The men are going to hang."
He grabbed her hand and held it as he spoke.
"I know that's not a pleasant thought, but
they won't bother you ever again. It was the
judge's decision, not yours. You just told what
happened."

Em pulled her lips into a straight line. "Thank
you for telling me. I am glad they will never
hurt anyone, but I don't want to think about the
gallows."

"We won't speak of it again. But I must tell you
something else that happened in the courtroom."
Caleb waited.

When he did not tell her right away, she asked,
"Am I to guess it?"

"No. But you could use a question."

"All right, I will! I can tell by the look on your
face that it's a good surprise. My second question
is, What else happened in the courtroom?"

"That was easy. I would have told you without
using a question. I was only toying with you. Too
late now." His grin never left his face.

"Well, tell me already."

"I had to turn the bank money over to Judge
McConnel. He was responsible for its return. I
did, and then he handed me an envelope back.
I was surprised and asked what it was. He said
the bank had issued a reward for the capture
of the men or the return of their stolen goods."
Caleb reached into his pocket and pulled out the

envelope. "It's yours, Em. Two hundred dollars."

Em leaned hard against the wall. She felt weak in the knees. "It's mine?"

"All yours. George's land is yours too. I brought the papers with me and the judge agreed that you are considered the nearest kin. He signed it into your name."

The reality of his news struck her. The land meant nothing, but the money meant everything. "Lucy! I can go to Lucy. I don't have to wait. I can go to her now."

In between sobs of relief, she threw her arms around Caleb. "Lucy," she whispered again into his shoulder.

He patted her back. When her breathing returned to normal, he pulled away. "Will you come to my parents' first? I wired ahead and let them know I was bringing a guest. It's your choice, but I'd like the company. Then I'll help you get a ticket to Beckford."

"You *want* me to go to your parents' home?"

"I do. I want to show you the tree I climbed as a boy and the rocking chairs my parents sit in. I would like you to meet them." His voice had been so serious. He lightened it. "If you want to come."

Em thought a moment. "I *would* like to come. I'd like to climb your tree and meet your parents very much."

"We have rooms here tonight, but tomorrow we

will rent a buggy and go to visit them. They are hoping we stay at least a night or two."

"After that, what will you do?"

"I'd planned to return with you to Azure Springs. I suppose I'll return alone and take up being the sheriff again. I'm sure my deputy will be glad to have me back."

"I'm so close to Lucy. I need to go there." Em thought of her dream. The one she had so often. Riding the big horse with a prince behind her, going to get Lucy together. "Could you come to Beckford with me? Meet Lucy?"

Biting her lip, she waited for his response. Hoping she was not too forward.

At last he nodded and said, "I'll telegraph Alvin and see how things are in Azure Springs. If there is any way I can, I will. I'd like nothing better."

Throwing her arms around him again, she kissed his cheek and squealed. "We are going to find Lucy!"

Seventeen

And I thought the train was bumpy," Em said as they set off in the rented buggy. "This is going to wear sores clear through my backside."

"Maybe you ought to put a little more meat on your backside. Mine seems to be holding up just fine."

"I ate two desserts last night." Em smiled at the memory. They'd dined together in a little restaurant on the main street in Brigley. Caleb had treated her just the way she imagined he would have treated Eliza or Olivia. He'd had the finest manners and been so kind and attentive. The meal had been delicious. Even knowing she had money now, he insisted he pay. After eating they'd walked together in the perfect summer air. In many ways the trip felt like a dream, like her very own fairy tale.

"You did seem to enjoy your custard." Caleb snickered.

"I've never had anything so fancy. You kept insisting I eat whatever I wanted. I had no idea you were going to taunt me about it later."

"Whoa there. I wasn't jesting. I was glad to see

you eating and enjoying yourself. I figure you have years of sweets to catch up on. Maybe when you're all caught up, your backside won't hurt so much when you ride in a buggy."

"What was your favorite dessert as a child?" she asked.

"My mama made a pie out of blackberries. It's the kind I got in trouble for stealing. I can't eat a slice of it without feeling like a boy again. Best pie you ever tasted. What was your favorite?" Caleb snapped the reins, encouraging the horses through a puddle.

Em thought a moment. "We didn't have sweets much. But once my ma brought home a cream puff. The kitchen had made too many for a party. There were extras and the maids were able to bring them home. We all sat around looking at it before we finally bit into it. It was every bit as light and fluffy as it looked. I've always wanted to taste one again. I wonder if it would taste as good as I remember."

"Sounds like something else I would have snuck from the kitchen."

Up ahead a mother deer with two spotted babies crossed the road. Caleb slowed the buggy. "Some things you just never get tired of seeing. That's one of them."

They sat in silence watching the deer. The little ones went over to their mother and tried to suckle from her. She stood patient a moment or two before grazing on. Then the little ones jumped about in the tall grass.

"Today is one of those days," Caleb said as he leaned back in the seat.

"One of what days?"

"One of the ones when you are just grateful to be alive. Excited for what lies ahead." Caleb continued to watch the deer. "It's a good day."

"You didn't wake up thinking hard about what you had to do today?"

"Not this morning. Today I woke up to the birds singing and I wondered if you heard them too. It's a pretty nice way to start a day."

Em looked at the clear blue sky, the rolling hills, and the baby deer. It was a beautiful start to a day. Smiling contently, she leaned back in her seat and braced herself for the bumps ahead as Caleb signaled for the horses to move again.

"A bit farther and we'll be at my parents' home. My grandparents lived there before them." Caleb pointed to a cluster of trees on the horizon.

"It looks like a piece of paradise," Em said.

"I always thought it was one of the prettiest places in all of Iowa. You'll like it, I know you will. There is even a muddy creek a bit of a walk to the north if you need to take a quick dip." He winked at her, provoking a laugh.

The pace of her heart quickened as they neared the house. Nerves she hadn't felt earlier decided to act up. "Did you tell your parents why I am with you?"

"Yes, I told them I had to bring a witness to a court case and wanted to visit while I was nearby."

"You didn't even tell them I am a girl?"

"I didn't think it mattered." He urged the horses on.

"I suppose it doesn't. I'm just a traveling companion. Makes no difference whether I'm a boy or a girl." She folded her arms across her chest. "Of course it doesn't matter."

A large farmhouse appeared in a clearing up ahead. It had two neat stories stacked on top of each other and a wide front porch with two rockers. A neat little row of flowers bloomed around the porch.

Pointing to a spot in front of the house, Em whispered, "Your tree is perfect."

"I knew you would like it. Climb it with me later?"

"Yes."

Before another word could be spoken, a plump woman with gray hair twisted into a tight bun emerged from the home. Raising a hand above her eyes to block the sun, she looked at their approaching wagon. Moments later, she turned back into the house.

"She went to get Pa," Caleb said.

Em wanted to see Caleb's pa emerge from the

house, but she couldn't take her eyes off Caleb. He had a new smile on his face. One she had never seen before. His "going home" smile. With his eyes still on the farmhouse, he reached over and took her hand in his.

When Em did finally look back to the porch, a tall, thin man stood next to the woman. He wore work clothes and a wide-brimmed hat. As they got closer, Em could tell his skin was dark from the sun. A hardworking man, just like her own pa had been. Different jobs, but she saw the similar marks of a life of labor.

Caleb stopped the buggy, walked around it, and helped her down before he even greeted his parents. He whispered in her ear, "I'm glad you're here." Together they closed the distance between them and the Reynoldses.

"Caleb, it's good to see you." Caleb's pa approached and offered his son a hand. Caleb took it in his own. While they shook hands, Caleb's pa looked at Em. "And who is your guest?"

"This is Em. She had to testify against a couple of bandits over in Brigley." Then, putting a hand on the small of Em's back, he said, "This here is my pa, Gideon Reynolds."

"It's nice to meet you," Em said.

"Same to you. This is my wife, Betty. She'll help you get settled in the house."

Betty stepped forward and patted Caleb on the

arm as she walked past. To Em she said, "It's been a long time since we had any company. Come along. I'll show you around."

Em followed the woman up the porch steps and into the house. The front room was perfectly tidy. Nothing was out of place. Em could not see even a speck of dust.

"The kitchen's that way," Betty said, pointing to her right as they walked through the immaculate house. The farther into the house she walked, the more Em felt she understood Caleb and his need to please. Judging by the home, these people had high expectations for themselves. Did they expect perfection from their son?

Once they were upstairs, Betty opened a door and ushered Em into a small room. "This will be your room while you're here. I hope it suits you."

Em walked past her to the window and spotted the mighty oak. "I like it very much. Thank you for hosting me."

Betty nodded. "Feel free to freshen up. I'll go and see Caleb while you get settled." She looked down at her feet as she shuffled from the room and closed the door behind her.

Em plopped on the bed and fretted, unsure if she should have come to meet Caleb's parents. Their welcome had not been cold, but it had not been warm either. Not sure how to freshen up when she was already in her best dress, she moved to the window and opened it, letting in the warm breeze.

Voices drifted up from below her window. Giving in to temptation, she leaned closer.

"You haven't been home in two years and now you arrive with a stranger and expect us to host you both like some hotel." The voice was Gideon's.

"No one stays in the boys' rooms. We never have guests because they are off-limits, and now my Sam's room has a girl staying in it." Betty had joined them. "Why didn't you tell us?"

"I'm sorry I haven't been home. I've been meaning to come. I wanted to come—but coming back has been hard for me. Anyway, she isn't some strange girl. Her name is Em," Caleb said. "And the boys would have liked her."

"She mean something to you?" Gideon asked.

"I've been helping her. I'm the sheriff in town—it's my job." Caleb paused. "She's more than that though."

"You got feelings for this girl?" Gideon asked.

Em was tempted to pull away from the window, unsure if she wanted to hear his reply. But she did not budge.

"She's not the kind of girl I ever planned to have feelings for. But there's something about her . . . ah, I don't know how I feel. She's been good for me. We talk about the hard things. It's helped me."

"Spending all this time together, traveling together, rumors will start. Better sort it all out." A chair creaked. "Walk with me to the fields. I want to show you my new irrigation system."

"All right, Pa."

Em listened as the two left the porch. She waited for her racing heart to calm before returning downstairs.

Betty and Em stood in the farmhouse kitchen. Together they'd prepped the evening meal. At first they'd peeled and chopped in silence. Em did her best to emulate Margaret and forced herself to start a conversation. After several minutes of small talk, Betty began to open up.

"When Caleb was a boy, he often brought in stray animals and even a few downtrodden neighbor children. I should not have treated you the way I did. I'm sorry my greeting wasn't friendlier." Betty's face softened some.

"You don't have to apologize. I'd like to know what Caleb was like as a boy. He's told me some."

"What has he told you?" Betty asked.

"That he was often causing mischief. Once he stole a blackberry pie and has loved it ever since. Says it reminds him of home and of you. He told me of climbing the tree in front of your house and taking care of animals. Mostly he talked of his brothers and how dear they were to him."

"I'm surprised he spoke of them." Betty wrung her hands together. "Gideon and I haven't been very good at speaking of the past. There's too much pain."

"I'm sorry for that. From what Caleb has told me, they were good men. He misses them."

Betty busied herself by pouring two tall glasses of water. "Sit with me on the porch. I'm sure you're tired from the ride out here and helping me in the kitchen. Tell me the truth about how my boy is doing."

The two sat down, and over the course of an hour, they reminisced about Caleb as a boy, laughing at his antics. Em told Betty what kind of a man her son had become. Betty's eyes glistened with pride as Em spoke of his honor, his sacrifice, and his kindness.

"I always thought Caleb would settle down on a little piece of land. Close enough so that he could come and see us. That boy loved being outside. Often he was up before me. I had to call him down from the tree to eat breakfast. I never thought he would take a job as a sheriff. He changed, though, when the boys died. I suppose we all did." Collecting the empty glasses, she stood. "Well, that was all a long time ago. It's just nice to have him home."

"Tell him that."

Betty looked at her for a long time. "Tell him? Does he think we don't want him?"

"He loves you both. I saw it in his eyes when we drove in. But he thinks he has to heal everyone, to live all the lives his brothers would have. He thinks he must fulfill all their dreams to make you proud. He's so busy doing it, he isn't living his own life." Em hoped she hadn't said too much.

Betty put a hand on Em's shoulder as she walked past into the house with the glasses. Em's eyes followed her.

After cleaning up the evening meal, the four sat and visited. When the conversation ran dry and the sun descended, Betty and Gideon retired for the night.

"Come to the tree with me," Caleb said, taking Em's hand in his own.

Fireflies darted around them when they stepped outside. He led her to the tree and boosted her up onto the first branch, then climbed up himself. He had planned to climb high, maybe even race Em, but instead he sat beside her on the sturdy first branch, slowly swinging his legs.

"Is it what you expected?" Em asked him. "Being home."

"In a way. My parents are hard on the outside and soft inside. They worry first and care later. I am only sorry they didn't do a better job of welcoming you."

"At first I thought your ma was cold and

prickly. But when we spoke on the porch while you were away, she just looked tired to me. She spoke of the boys, though, and of you when you were little. She even laughed."

"Did she tell you anything I should be embarrassed about?"

"Oh yes. Lots of great stories," Em teased. Then in a low voice, she went on. "She said she always thought you would live on the land. She thought you would visit often."

"She said that?"

"Yes. And she told me you have a history of bringing in stray animals and people. I suppose that is what they think I am."

Caleb nudged Em. "You're not a stray. With all your money, you are practically an heiress."

"Heiress? No. I'm much closer to a stray than an heiress." Changing the subject, she asked, "What did your father have to tell you?"

Caleb couldn't tell her. Not all of it, at least. His father had asked him questions about her. Questions that had him thinking. "Does she bring you happiness, make you laugh?" Gideon had asked. When Caleb confessed that she did, his father then asked, "Do you like who you are when you are with her?" Again Caleb answered in the affirmative. He confessed she was not what he had planned, that at first she was just a case to solve.

Then his father said something Caleb couldn't

get out of his head. "Our whole lives people try to tell us what beautiful is. As young boys we think we know exactly which women are the loveliest. Then we meet one who doesn't fit the mold and we know we were taught wrong our whole lives." While his pa talked, Caleb envisioned Em's freckled face. "Beauty is something we get to define. We may not see it right away, but when we do, we have trouble even remembering the other definition. We wonder how we were ever so misled. All we can see is the one person who defines it for us."

Then his father put a hand on his shoulder and said, "Don't let anyone else decide which kind of beautiful is right for you. You find a girl who brings out the best in you. Who you can see a happy future with. That's your kind of beautiful."

Realizing Em was waiting for an answer, Caleb said, "My pa wanted to show me the property. And ask how life in Azure Springs was."

Em picked up a leaf and tore little pieces off it. "I think there is more and you're not telling me."

"Look up. It's too dark to see now, but there's a branch near the top with a nest in it." Caleb pointed high in the tree.

"I can almost see it."

"Every year as a boy there was a nest in this tree and every year we climbed all the way to it and looked inside."

"You spent a lot of time in this tree," she said, still looking up.

"I did. But I haven't been up in it, not even once, since my last brother died. Not until now." Caleb ran his hand over the bark and then picked at the edges that stuck up. "You're good for me, Em. I told my pa that. That you have helped me to heal."

"I told your mother that you saved me."

Their eyes met then. Silent questions passed between them. But neither voiced an answer.

Caleb broke away first. He climbed down from the branch and then helped her to the ground. Somehow she had become his definition of beautiful. Yes, she had changed some—filled out and lost the sunken look. But it was he who had changed the most. He wanted to tell her. But how could he when the future was so uncertain? What good would it do to confess his heart when he didn't even know if she would ever return?

Eighteen

Em woke to rapping on her door. "You better get up," Caleb whispered. "My ma likes early risers."

She threw off the blankets, flew out of bed, and dressed in a hurry. Smoothing her hair, she opened the door and rushed down the stairs.

The family was sitting at the table, waiting for her to arrive to begin breakfast.

"I'm sorry I'm late," Em said.

"No need to apologize," Gideon said.

"Caleb, were you outside last night?" Betty asked in the same way Em would expect her to ask a child.

"I was indeed. I lured Em out and the two of us climbed the tree," Caleb answered in between bites of bacon.

"You climbed the tree? You climbed *your* tree?" Betty's brows rose. She cleared her throat before speaking again. "I thought I heard some noise. Reminds me of when the house was full of you boys. Seems I could never keep all four of you in bed."

Gideon leaned toward Betty. Em was fairly

sure the two were holding hands under the table.

She looked at Caleb—his eyes were on his parents as he spoke. "We did have trouble staying in. Especially in the summer when the sun was up so long." He sounded tentative. "It was usually Reggie's idea. The leader of the pack."

"You always thought you were so quiet, but we heard you. Heard you laughing into the night too. I always wondered what was so funny, but I knew if I asked I'd have to scold the lot of you for staying up so late." Betty did not laugh, but she looked less weary. "I just pretended I didn't hear. I was glad you all cared so much for one another."

"You heard us? But we were so careful." Caleb looked dumbfounded. "All these years I was sure you had no idea."

Gideon scooped another pile of eggs onto his plate. "I heard you too. Been far too quiet around here lately. We keep hoping one of these days you'll bring home a wagon full of babies to visit. Then you'll understand the other side of your trouble causing."

"Gideon!" Betty declared. "Don't say such things."

"Why not? It seems to me that we are finally saying things we should have said years ago. It feels good to talk openly. And you're always talking about babies and family. We might as well let Caleb in on the discussion."

Caleb put up his hand. "Enough. If I ever have a wagon full of babies, I'll bring them here. You have my word. I would want them to know their grandparents and fill this house with noise."

Betty smiled at her husband. Gideon continued to eat, but even he had a smile on his face in between bites. When his plate was empty, he stood. "I'll head on out to the field now. I'll be back in the afternoon."

A few bites later, Caleb stood. "I'll go out with him. Thank you for breakfast, Ma. And for the laugh."

Betty nodded. "That's a good son. Your pa works so hard out there. Em and I will get an afternoon meal cooking. And while we do it, we'll talk about the old days."

Caleb looked back from the doorway. His eyes met Em's. He mouthed "Thank you" to her before setting out to help his pa.

Em and Betty rose and effortlessly worked together to clear the table and wash the breakfast dishes. A comfortable silence settled between the two of them. "Tell me more," Em said after they'd cleaned everything up. "Tell me about Sam. Was he as much trouble as the rest?"

"They were all trouble. The best kind of trouble. I was always after them about something or other. Telling them to do this or do that. I sometimes wish I could go back and tell them all I loved them just the way they were." Betty took a slow, deep breath. "It all just went so quickly. The growing up years, then the war. Then one by one they left and never came home."

"I have regrets too." Em stirred her cup of tea, twirling the spoon around and around. "But I'm learning how to move beyond them. Caleb has helped me. The pain is not so intense now."

"You've done something for our Caleb. I know that. The last time he was here, he was so somber." Betty reached out a hand and put it on Em's. "I think you've been good for him."

"He's been good for me too. I guess we all get to learn together," Em said. "Maybe someday we'll have healed enough that we will be able to think of our losses and not ache."

"Having Caleb back—truly back, seeing him smile. I feel closer to all my sons than I have felt in years."

Em could sense that change. They had been there only a day, but the house was brighter. Em thought of her own life—it had changed quickly as well. These two good people, Betty and Gideon, were stepping out of mourning. They may have traveled a sorrowful road for years, but they were on a different path now. It had started with just a single step.

"It's beautiful here," Em said later in the day as she and Caleb walked over a lush green knoll.

"It's because of you."

"No. I haven't done a thing. I wish I could take credit for the beautiful grass and perfect blue sky." Em tried to breathe in the freshness of it.

"The sky might be out of your reach, but you did change things. You asked my mother about the boys. Whatever you said or something about the way you asked her, it cracked the shell she'd built around herself. Look." Caleb pointed to the front porch. There sitting in the two rockers were his parents. They had moved the rockers close together and were holding hands. "They don't think we can see them." Caleb put an arm around Em.

His words brushed against her ear. "That is a sight I have prayed to see. I just had it all wrong. I thought if I was a sheriff and bought a big house, they would be happy again. But that wasn't what they needed."

"It was having one of their boys return," Em said. "Seeing you smile and living. Seeing you happy. They needed you."

"No. Well, that was part of it. But it was letting the other boys live too. All around us. It's like they have been set free. I've felt them this time. The memories are all around us." Caleb picked off a stalk of the long summer grass. "They're here again. Just like they should be."

"But you were lost before too. Or so your mother says. She says you went with the others. Says her carefree baby boy changed. That the war took you away from her too." Em put a hand on his arm. "You came home. And what a perfect home it is."

Brushing a piece of stray hair from her face, he said, "I'll always be thankful that you came here. Abigail told me you answered her prayer and helped her heal. You've done so for me as well."

"Margaret told me that often we get so caught up in seeing our own prayers answered that we don't realize we are blessing others. That is how everyone has been for me. Seems she is more right than I realized." Then, letting her eyes travel across the property, she prayed the scene would stay in her memory forever. "We are leaving in the morning. Let's go and spend time with your parents."

Leaving was harder than Em had expected. The Reynoldses had not given her the best welcome, but less than two days later they were embracing her as they said an emotional farewell.

"Take care of yourself, Em. Write us and tell us about Lucy," Betty said.

"I will. I'll tell you everything. Thank you for having me."

"Oh, thank you. Remember, you are always welcome here. We so hope to see you again."

Gideon patted Caleb's back. "It was good having you home. I know you are a grown man, but having you back here felt like the old days.

Like our boy was home again. I'm sure proud of you. I—I've never been good at saying what I feel. But, well. You're a good man. A man who would make any father proud. You got a fine lady by your side. Bring her back sometime." He stepped away from his son. "Travel safely."

Caleb put his arm around Em as they walked away. His voice caught in his throat when he whispered to her, "He's proud of me. Did you hear it? My pa is proud of me."

"I heard. I know he meant it. I could feel it."

Loaded into the rented buggy, they were about to drive away when Betty came running toward them. "Em, thank you again for coming. And for everything."

Caleb slapped the reins on the horses and they set off. "I think my parents like you better than me."

"I didn't know it was a competition."

"Everything here always is!"

"Are you sad to go?" Em asked, looking back at the picturesque farmhouse nestled in the bluffs.

Caleb looked too, then shook his head. "I know I'll be back this time. It feels a little like the home I grew up in again."

Smaller and smaller the farmhouse became as they rode back toward Brigley.

"I'll talk to the ticket man about getting you on a train to Beckford when we get there," Caleb said.

"I'll use some of my money and stay at a hotel again tonight and the next too if there is not a train tomorrow. If there is any time this afternoon, I'll go and take a quick bath in the mud so I am looking my finest," Em said, trying to keep the mood light.

"I'd planned to spend the evening with you, but I suppose I'll spend it alone instead. No mud for me."

"Since it will be our last evening together, I can change my plans. I pick you over the mud."

Caleb smiled at her. "You'd change your plans for me?"

"Yes! I can give up a mud bath for you," Em said, knowing she would be willing to give up much more for him.

"I'll telegraph Alvin as soon as we are in Brigley. If it's still all right, I want to go to Beckford. I should know soon."

"With any luck, Alvin will only have Silas to complain about, and you will be able to come." Em hoped this wasn't their last evening together. Joking about their parting was one thing—actually living it was another.

"What will you do when you find Lucy?" Caleb asked.

"I don't know. I picture her being seven. If she were seven, I would take her in my arms and swing her around. Then pull her in tight and hold her until she squirmed away. It's hard for me to picture her fourteen," Em said. "I wonder how she remembers me. Is she angry that I left her? I know how I want it to be, but I don't know how it will be."

"What if the family is kind and loves her? She has lived half her life there." Caleb reached around and straightened the load behind them.

"Then I will move to Beckford and see her as much as I can. She's my only family. We have been lost to each other too long for me to just walk away." Em twirled the end of her braid in her hand. "If they're not kind, I will take her away. Somewhere safe."

He nodded his head but said nothing. When the lull grew too long, she pulled the reading book out and practiced aloud. He corrected her when she stumbled, but most of the words came smooth.

"You read so well. Have you thought of reading your mother's papers?" Caleb asked.

Em nodded. "I have thought of it. I nearly did the other night. But I'm so near Lucy, I've decided to wait. I'll read them with her."

"That's a fine idea. Even if she starts out angry over the past, it will not take her long to realize you have a good heart. I wouldn't worry." Caleb's voice was confident. Em stared at him while he drove, alternating between watching his strong hands guide the horses and studying his face. His face was the perfect combination of angles and smoothness. How was it she had become friends with such a handsome man? And such a good man.

Laughing to herself for staring, she said, "I think Lucy will take to you as well. She'll probably be as smitten as Mae and Milly are."

Sticking out his chest, he said in a deep voice, "Well, I am the Prince of Azure Springs, and if she was raised on your stories, she will be looking all over for a prince."

Shoving him, she laughed. "In my stories, the prince is always humble and gracious."

"Humble and gracious. I can do humble and gracious."

"Besides, it is Mae and Milly who call you a prince. That was not my idea."

He pulled his lips into a playful smirk. "I was certain you thought I was a prince as well."

"Don't look so smug." Her comment only made him do it more, until she finally conceded. "Oh, all right. I have thought you look a bit like a prince. But it still wasn't my idea."

A grin spread across his face. "I knew it. I knew you thought I was a prince."

"I want to use my third question."

"Better make it a good one—because it's all you get. This prince never changes the law."

"Very funny." She started to say more but stopped herself, suddenly afraid to hear the answer. Instead, she stared hard at an old barn they were passing. It looked like it was about to topple over, but other than that it was fairly unremarkable.

"I was only teasing. Ask me whatever you like," Caleb said. She turned her eyes to him.

When she still didn't speak, he pulled the reins—stopping the horses—and turned toward her. He looked her in the eyes and waited.

"It's nothing, really. I think I'll ask later," she said while fidgeting with the seat.

"Ask me. I'm curious now." Caleb looked serious. "You can trust me. I'll give you a serious answer."

"I know I can trust you. That's part of the problem. I know if I ask you, you'll tell me the truth. I don't know if I want to know the truth." Looking away, she said, "Let's drive. Forget I said anything."

He tapped his foot. "Em, if I have to return to Azure Springs, this could be your last chance."

"I'm sorry, Caleb. I can't ask it."

He sighed, clucked to the horses, and set off down the road again. Em picked up the reader and read more. She stumbled over many words as she went, unable to focus on the book.

Caleb reached over. "You don't have to ask me your question. But if you ever want to, you can. Put the book away a minute and look over there."

Caleb brought the buggy to a halt and together they watched as a fox and several kits played.

The little ones jumped back and forth and wrestled. One was so bold as to pounce on the mama fox. She snarled and nipped at him until he backed off. But then he came at her again. This time she wrestled him before walking off.

"This is what I miss. As a sheriff, I'm always on guard. Always looking for criminals. Out here I can set my spade down if I want and just stare at something good."

"Don't be a sheriff then. Fighting a battle with the earth seems like a plenty noble calling to me. Putting food on your table and on the plates of others—it's a quieter way. But it's a good way. Your ma and pa would be just as proud of you if you chose to work the ground."

Caleb started driving again. "Maybe I will. Of the two of us, you're the landowner."

"I had forgotten about that." Em didn't think she would ever return to Azure Springs. She would live near Lucy, or with Lucy, depending on what she found in Beckford. Where they would go, she wasn't sure. But living so near Azure Springs would be too hard if it meant watching Caleb with someone else. She would part ways with him and always remember him this way, as the dearest friend she had ever had.

In Brigley, Caleb hurried off to send his telegram, while Em trekked over to the hotel.

Caleb met her later in the day, note in hand.

"Alvin wrote back. Things are fine in Azure Springs. Said the only excitement has been a brawl at the saloon. Just like you suspected."

"You can come!" Em said, nearly jumping into his arms. "We don't have to say goodbye yet."

"Looks like Silas ended up with a broken leg from the brawl. As much as I'd enjoy seeing that, I hardly think it's a reason to skip out on Beckford." Then he waved two paper tickets in front of her. "I booked us both passage to Beckford. Let's go and get Lucy."

Nineteen

I never thought I would stand here again. It was right here that I saw her last." Em looked at her feet. The boards beneath them were faded and worn but still the same. "For seven years I have wondered about her, prayed for her, and dreamt of her."

"You ready?" Caleb asked as the two stepped off the platform.

"I've been ready all these years. Waiting for this day. And now I feel nervous and scared and excited and even afraid."

"Be excited. Your sister will love you. How could she not?"

Raising her head high, she looked from left to right, scanning what she could see of the town. "Where do we begin? How do we find her?"

"Let's go and find the preacher. You said the town preacher often orchestrated the adoptions. There's a chance he will know. If he is anything like our preacher, he knows just about everything about everyone." Caleb looked about and spotted a whitewashed steeple high on a little hill on the edge of town. "The church is that way."

Grabbing her hand, he pulled her forward. "We may as well start there. If he is not in, he might live close by."

On the way to the church, they passed a school. A young woman about Em's age stood on the steps ringing a bell. Children ran from the yard to the door. Was one of them Lucy? Did Lucy attend a school? A real school! Em walked faster, forcing her legs to move quickly up the hill. It seemed she could not get to the church fast enough.

Caleb kept up with her swift stride. Once they were at the door of the church, he grinned and said, "Knock."

Em did. She knocked louder than was necessary and then waited, swaying back and forth as she stood on the step. Fighting a battle with her many emotions. Then she knocked again. No answer. She knocked even louder then, banging and banging. Caleb closed a hand over her fist. "We'll find her Em, we will. This was just our first stop. Let's walk through town and ask around."

Knowing he was right but still rattled by the delay, she turned and started back to Main Street. Everyone she passed looked as though they were headed somewhere. Who could she ask? Who would know her Lucy?

She let Caleb lead the way as she clung to his arm. He got the attention of a man in a suit. "Sir, do you have a moment?"

The well-dressed man nodded. "You new in town? What can I do for you?"

"Yes, sir, we just arrived on the afternoon train. We're trying to find someone," Caleb answered.

"Well, I've been in this town fifteen years now. If they live around here, I'll know them," the man boasted. "Who're you looking for?"

"This here is Em and she was separated from her sister, Lucy, seven years ago. They rode into Beckford on an orphan train. Lucy was taken in by a family in this town."

The man smoothed his suit, then took a handkerchief from his pocket and wiped his bald head. "I remember a train coming through. Every couple of years a train full of kids stops here. I think I know of your Lucy. Better head down Oak Street. It's three streets that way"—he pointed to their right—"then turn left, and about a quarter mile on your right you'll find a farmhouse. Look for rosebushes in front. That's where the Oversons live. They should be able to help you." He blew his nose into his handkerchief, then tucked it away. "I'll be on my way then."

They thanked him and watched him go.

"Overson. That must be who took her." Em looked toward Oak Street. "It's so close, Caleb. Only a little over a quarter mile away." And then she cried. Right there on the street, she burst into tears.

"I'm sorry," she said as she wiped at her face.

Caleb wrapped a strong arm around her and pulled her to him. "Remember when you told me you never cry?" he whispered into her ear.

"I don't. I mean . . . I didn't, but now I do," she said through her sobs. "It's just that I'm going to see Lucy. Oh, Caleb, I have wanted this for so long." She pulled away and looked him in the eyes. "This is what kept me going all those years. The dream of this very day. It's here." More tears. "I'm a mess," she said as she tried to regain control. "I can't let her see me like this."

"She won't care. I bet she's dreamed of this day too." Caleb's words only brought more tears to Em's eyes. He guided her toward Oak Street then. "Come on, you weepy woman. Let's go find your sister."

They walked in silence through town. The house was easy to find, just as the man had said. A quarter mile down Oak Street, rosebushes—neatly trimmed all along the front of a two-story house—shot into view. The siding of the house was a soft blue with white trim, which gave it a sophisticated look. But what caught Em's eye was a swing hanging from a branch of a tall tree. Biting her lip, she again suppressed the emotion that was so near the surface. Had Lucy swung on that swing? Had she played in this yard?

"What do I say?" Em asked Caleb as they walked up to the door.

"Just tell them who you are. And ask about

Lucy. You've had seven years to think about this, and you don't know what to say?" Caleb sounded frustrated. Was he nervous too?

Em thought of snapping back, telling him he just didn't understand, but instead she took a deep breath. Waiting wouldn't give her any additional confidence, so she knocked on the door. The seconds she had to wait felt like an eternity, but they passed and the door opened.

A woman stood in the doorway. Her chestnut hair was pulled back into a braid and then wound around itself into a bun. Em met the woman's hazel eyes. "Can I help you?" the lady asked.

No words came. Caleb nudged her side, prompting her to speak. "Um, yes. I hope you can. We are looking—we are here to see Lucy."

"Lucy," the woman repeated.

"Do you know her? A man in town said you would be able to help us. I thought she lived here. She's my sister . . ." Em's rambling silenced only when the woman's arms came around her.

"Emmy? Is it you? After all these years, you've come."

Emmy! No one had called her that in years. Not since Lucy. This woman knew Lucy. She must or she would not know her name. "You know Lucy," Em whispered. Pulling away, she asked, "Where is she? Oh, please tell me. I've waited so long to see her."

"Come inside out of the sun," the woman said, her voice soft and gentle.

Em could hold back her emotion no longer. "No," she shouted. "Where is Lucy? Tell me where she is."

Caleb put a firm hand on her shoulder. "Em, it's all right. Let's go inside."

She pushed him away and approached the woman. "Is she at school? Is that where she is? Tell me. Tell me where my sister is." Her voice cracked when she spoke. "Please, please, tell me."

Mrs. Overson again put her arms around Em. Sobbing, Em buried her head in the woman's shoulder. She shook from the tears that came and came. Years worth of sobs racked her body. Mrs. Overson quietly said, "I'm sorry—I'm so sorry" over and over as she patted her back and let her cry. Em felt weak when she finally stepped away. She was weary from dreaming the same dream over and over only to have it play out so differently than she had ever imagined.

Twice she tried to ask but could not get her voice to work. At last Caleb asked for her. "What happened?"

Mrs. Overson took Em's hand and tried to lead her into the house, and this time she followed. "Sit down," she said as they stepped into the living room. "I can tell you're tired."

Caleb found a spot on the sofa. Em slowly

lowered herself and sat beside him. Then the woman stepped to a desk and pulled out a stick person and placed it in Em's hand. "Would it be all right if I started at the beginning?"

Unable to look away from the figure in her hands, Em simply nodded her head.

Mrs. Overson sat in a chair across from them. "Like so many others, my husband and I lost our children to the fevers that swept through. Our house was much too quiet. No sounds of little feet, no laughter. When I saw the sign about the orphan train coming through, I ran to town to tell Walt. I thought he might not want an orphan, but he surprised me by saying it sounded like a fine plan."

Mrs. Overson stood and looked out the window that faced town. "We were some of the first there the afternoon the train was due. We'd planned to find a boy, hoping he could help out around the place as he grew. But when the children walked on the stage, all I could see was this one perfect little girl. I knew many of the other couples at the station, and I was so afraid one of them would take her and work the little angel tirelessly on a farm."

She brushed a tear from her cheek. "I should have looked at the others. Taken more in. I could have, but all I could see was this little girl. My heart loved her the moment I saw her.

"We acted quickly and took her off that horrid

stage. Away from men like Max Welton and his kind. She screamed and cried, but we thought she was just afraid. Once we got her home, she started talking about Emmy." Mrs. Overson looked at Em. "Talking about you. By the time Lucy was calm enough to tell us about you, the train was gone. We thought we could calm her down, that she would be all right with time. But she wasn't. Two weeks later Walt took the train and asked about you at every stop. He was gone three weeks before returning home. We wrote letters then to the Aid Society. They said the files were confidential."

Mrs. Overson knelt in front of Em. "Forgive us. We wanted to find you. To make it right."

"I've never blamed you. Only myself for not being there with her. Tell me, was she happy? With time, was she happy?" Needing to draw strength from somewhere, Em reached for Caleb's hand.

Mrs. Overson stood up and walked to the mantel. She took down a small framed likeness and walked back to Em and handed it to her. "Lucy was happy. She made everyone around her happy. I often called her my sunshine girl. She lit up a room. She lit up every room she was ever in."

Em reverently held the image. There before her was the same little girl she had mothered and loved. The picture captured light in her eyes.

Cradling the frame to her chest, Em pressed her lips in a tight line as she struggled with the reality that her baby sister was gone. Sorrow—deep, painful sorrow—filled her heart. The ache battled with the overwhelming joy she felt knowing her dear Lucy had lived a good life. She'd been able to tell just by looking at the picture that Mrs. Overson's words were true. Lucy had been happy.

"What happened then?" Em managed to ask.

"For five blissful years we lived together. And in a way, you lived here too. Never did Lucy pray without mentioning you. She told us stories of your bravery and goodness. Fairy tales filled our house. Lucy told them, but first she would say, 'Emmy told me this story and now I'll tell it to you.' She wrote to you too. She said you would be so proud of her for knowing how to read and write. Someday she vowed to give her letters to you. Always—always she believed you would come back. And she was right."

"But I came too late," Em said as she looked again at the beautiful girl in the picture. "I lived for the day I would hold her again. And now she is gone. I was too late."

Caleb had been a silent observer until now. "But you came, and she knows you're here. I know she knows. You came, Em. It was all you could do."

"What took her?" Em asked.

"Sickness. Always sickness. It came quickly and took her in her sleep. I was beside her when she passed. Never has a child looked more peaceful. It was Walt and I who were in pain. Not Lucy. Again the house was so quiet. But we never regretted taking her in. Losing her was so hard, but loving her had been so easy."

Mrs. Overson walked to the door. "This house has been in our family for many years. Out back there is a white fence that borders our little resting place. Walt had a stone carved for Lucy's grave. Go and visit it. I know she would love your company. Come back though. I want to give you a few treasures. Little things I saved for you."

Em nodded before silently walking out of the house and to the gravesite. Little stones and crosses were nestled close together beneath a lush green tree. Stones jutting from the ground begged to be read and remembered. Three little stones all held the same year. Nelda, Mabel, and Thomas. Next to them was Clement, who must have been a grandfather. Then came LaVern. Em guessed by the dates that she was a grandmother. She stopped when she read the next stone. "Lucy, Our Sunshine Girl."

Em sat down next to Lucy's grave. At first she just stared, and then she wept, and then she begged her sister for forgiveness for not coming sooner. "I wanted to come—I wanted it so badly.

I'm sorry, Lucy. I'm sorry I missed so much." In desperation, she said, "Forgive me, Lucy. For not being here."

Then, laying herself next to the soft mound, she cried, "I love you, Lucy. I never stopped loving you."

When the minutes had multiplied, Em finally sat her tired body back up. Caleb, who Em had not heard come outside, cleared his throat. "I was hoping I might have a word as well."

Sniffling, Em said, "Of course. She would have wanted to meet you. I'm sorry I'm so emotional."

"Don't be. I told you how I cried when my brothers died. It's nothing to be ashamed of." He knelt by the grave and turned his attention to Lucy's gravestone. "Hello, Lucy." His voice was serious. "I've wanted to meet you. I'm sure you are someone awfully special. Having Em to raise you, how could you not be? I'm sorry we couldn't come sooner. But I want to thank you for keeping Em going when life was hard for her. I've found a true friend in her and have you to thank." He pulled a stray weed. "I like the name Sunshine Girl. I'll think of you whenever I feel the sun's warm rays."

Rubbing his stubble, he went on, his voice thick with emotion. "My brothers are up there with you. Tell them their baby brother misses them and thinks of them often. Tell them I'm doing better now. That I'm ready to start living my life again. Tell them that I sat in the oak again and I found someone I can beat in competitions. Don't worry about your sister. She may have cried enough to fill a rain barrel this week, but she's strong. And she's going to keep living too."

He stood then and pulled Em to her feet. "I saw Walt Overson come home a half hour or so ago. When you're ready, let's go and meet him."

Mr. and Mrs. Overson, or Walt and Olive, as they preferred to be called, invited Caleb and Em to stay with them. For two days they all talked of Lucy. Tears were shed, many tears. More than Em thought possible. But there was also laughter and joy.

"I've got to head back to Azure Springs," Caleb said the evening of their second night with the Oversons. "I'd like to stay longer, but I have an obligation to the town."

"When do you leave?" Em asked, not ready to say goodbye.

"I leave tomorrow morning. What will you do?"

"I don't know yet. I feel so close to Lucy here—it will be hard to go. I need to think. I've got to form a plan. I don't know how, but I know I must make new goals for my future."

Caleb brushed a hair from her face. "Come back to the Howells'. To Azure Springs."

"I can't live with them forever. I don't know

where I belong," Em said, eyes downcast. "This was my plan—to be here with Lucy—and now I have no course to follow."

"You will find a way. If I know anything about you, it is that you will fight on." Caleb looked away. His voice was shaky. "Will I see you again?"

Em waited to reply. She knew honesty was something Caleb valued and she wanted to give it to him. "I don't know."

"Tell me what your third question was going to be. Tell me before I leave."

She shook her head. "No, it would do no good."

"Write it down for me. Give me that gift before I leave." His eyes pleaded with her. "Give me that."

She nodded slowly. "I will. But don't answer it. I don't want to know, not anymore."

Twenty

Passengers disembarked from the train. Soon it would be time for Caleb to board and travel back to Azure Springs. Em was by his side, her bonnet strings blowing in the wind. Oh, how he would miss her.

She reached into her pocket and pulled out a note. "I'm not certain you'll be able to tell what the words are. But if you can, it's my third question and my farewell."

He took the slip of paper and started unfolding it.

"Stop!" Em grabbed it back from him. "You can't read it now. I don't want you to."

"Give that back." He tried to take it from her.

She held it behind her back. "No. Not until you tell me you won't read it until you're gone."

"Honestly, woman." He laughed as he tried to go behind her and snatch it away.

Standing tall, she turned and started from the platform with the note in hand.

"Oh, all right. I won't open it now. I'll wait."

Em walked right back to him and gave him the note. He was tempted to open it and read it just to spite her. But he resisted. This was time to say farewell, not tease her. He put the wrinkled note in his pocket.

"Will you write me? Tell me where you decide to go?" Caleb asked.

Em put her hands on the railing. "I'm learning. Even that note in your pocket took me most of the morning. I'm not sure my letters would make any sense."

"You'll get faster. Olive will help—I think she'd like to. At least tell me where you go," Caleb said. "I would always wonder if you didn't."

"I'll tell you as soon as I know. I think I'll stay here a while. Read through Lucy's letters, get to know the Oversons better. After that, I'll try to find something else to work for. Something to dream about."

Caleb nudged her under the chin. "I know you will find something. There is always Margaret's."

Em shook her head. "I think I need a fresh start."

"It won't be the same without you." He took his finger and ran it across the bridge of her nose. "Your freckles are like your very own constellation."

Em covered her nose.

He pulled her hand away. "Don't hide them. I want to remember them."

The whistle blew. It was time to load the train.

Time for them to part ways and go on with their lives.

"You have to go?"

"I do. I told them I'd be back." He bent down and kissed her freckled cheek. "Take care of yourself."

He left her then—standing on the train platform.

As he looked back through the train window, he saw her leaning on the platform rail. The look on her face made him want to abandon his responsibility—to flee the train and go to her.

Instead, he settled into his seat and pulled her note from his pocket. The penmanship was similar to that of a child, but she had written it herself and he was proud of her. Several errors were slashed through and written again. With a little deciphering, he was able to untangle her message.

Dear Caleb,
Thank you for being a friend to me. It has meant a great deal. Often I have dreamed of a friend like you. Someone I could trust. Someone I could laugh with. I will treasure the gift of friendship you have given me. I promised to write my third question, and so I will. But please don't answer it. I don't think I want to know, not anymore.

My question is, could anyone ever find me beautiful? As a friend I had wanted to know what you thought. Do you think anyone could ever love me like that? I stood on so many platforms, and no one ever wanted me. I believed no one ever could. And then a gunshot wound brought me to Azure Springs and I started to believe. I found hope in Azure Springs. I don't know what to think now or what to aim for.

Kiss Mae and Milly for me. Tell them a story.

Your friend,
Em

Resting his head against the seat, he closed his eyes. Could anyone find her beautiful? He did. Would someone else? Were there other men out there who would take the time to know her? If they did, they would discover she was beautiful. That she was the most perfect definition of beauty. Why hadn't he told her? He knew why. She needed to come back on her own. Leave Beckford on her own. He prayed she would. Fervently, he prayed.

Olive and Walt were so kind, and it eased her mind a great deal knowing such loving people had surrounded Lucy. Each day Em read through

Lucy's letters and diary, and listened to stories Olive told. Each testified of a life of love and laughter. Happy tears often spilled from Em's eyes as she read Lucy's letters or heard the sweet stories of her life.

One day, weeks after arriving in Beckford, she pulled a small stack of envelopes from the desk and sat down to read a letter from Lucy.

Dear Emmy,
It has been three years since I last saw you. I am ten now. I feel much older, just like you said I would. I have grown at least a foot since you saw me, and soon I'll be taller than Mama O. That is what I call Olive. She is good to me and loves me. I had planned to not love her, because you were my family. But I have come to love her. She says no one can be loved too much. I believe her. I wonder if anyone is loving you. I am and always will.

Mama O gave me a new dress for my birthday. It is yellow with white lace around the cuffs and collar. Every time I put it on, I think of you. The color reminds me of your hair. I think of your stories and of princesses. I know I am ten now and too big to believe your stories, but I love them and when I miss you, I think of them. It's a beautiful dress and I know you would love it.

Helen is coming this afternoon. She lives on Oak Street too and is my best friend. I have chores to do first and I want to get them done. When she comes, we are going to read up in the tree.

Love,
Lucy

Setting the letter aside, she wondered if she was living now. Summer was swiftly turning to fall. Em felt a pull inside her, something urging her to do more with her life. Needing a purpose, something to work for. She became antsy and restless. But if she left, would she still feel Lucy close to her like she did in this home?

"I'm grateful for the love you showed Lucy. And to you for welcoming me into your home," Em said to Olive that night.

"But now you must go and live your life," Olive said, finishing her thought for her.

"I owe it to Lucy to live. I believe she would want me to. I prayed so hard she was having a good life while we were apart—and she was. Now I think she is telling me I need to do the same." Em stood and ran her hand along the bed that had been Lucy's. "I only wish I knew what to do next."

"Why not return to Azure Springs? I saw the

way Caleb looked at you. I figure by now he is missing you sorely." Olive crinkled her nose in a delightful smile. "If I were you and had a man like that looking at me the way he looked at you, I wouldn't put so much distance between us. What's keeping the two of you apart?"

"I don't know that we could ever be more than mere friends," Em said.

"There are others there that love you too. Caleb mentioned a family that took you in."

Loved her too. Could Olive really believe that Caleb loved her? "There are others. The Howells have two little girls. They remind me of Lucy when she was little. I miss them, but I am afraid of going back. I haven't even written any of them. I don't know if I should return. What if Caleb doesn't love me? What if he loves another by now? Someday he will. I don't think I could watch that."

"But what if he does love you and you never go back? How will you ever truly live if you are too afraid to be where you need to be?" Olive smiled. "Sometimes we have to risk the pain."

"I want to be brave. I really do."

"You're braver than you think you are. We'll miss you when you're gone. You have been an answered prayer. It's been like having Lucy back for a little while."

"I feel so close to her here. I can almost imagine her growing up."

"You will always be welcome here. Always."

Two days later, Olive and Em stood side by side filling Em's carpetbag. "Wait a moment," Olive said when Em was about to buckle the latch.

Olive left the room for a moment and returned with a doll tucked under her arm. "Lucy loved this doll. She played with it for hours and hours, brushing her hair and dressing her. They had tea parties together and went for walks. Take her with you."

"This was Lucy's doll," Em said, touching the doll's smooth face. "It's beautiful. I can't take it."

"I insist. I know she would want you to have her. Consider it a gift from Lucy."

Em took the doll. She patted its little head and planted a kiss on its rosy face. "Thank you, Olive. For everything. Thank you for loving Lucy."

When the doll was safely tucked away, Em decided to visit Lucy's grave one more time before she left.

The grass was soft beneath her. The sky was blue above. A gentle breeze moved the trees, making the leaves rustle against it. This was a place Lucy would love.

"I have to go away now, Lucy. I think you understand. I can't stay here forever—it's not my home. I'm not sure where my home is, but I'm going to start by heading west to Azure Springs.

It's a small town, but the people are good. It took me a while to see that, but they are. There is a family with two little girls. They love my stories, just like you did. I think I'll start by telling them one. I've never told them the story of the beauty that loved the beast. I think they'll like it. You always did.

"I have a friend there too. He was here. He even said hello to you. I know if you were here, he would make you laugh. I want to see him again. After that, I don't know. But I know time is short, and with so much loss, I owe it to myself and others to live. So I'm going to. Olive says she puts flowers here all year. I'm glad you had her to love. Mama would be happy knowing you were with such good people."

Em pulled the faded packet of papers from her pocket. "This was Ma's. I've been waiting to open it with you. I thought we could read it together. See if there is anything important."

Sitting beside her sister's grave, she opened the packet. Her hand shook as she lifted the flap and pulled out the papers. Inside she found a note about a room to rent and a job listing from a newspaper. Under these was another clipping from a paper. This one told about an accident at the docks and the deaths of eight workers. No names appeared in the article, but Em was certain her father was one of the men.

A yellowed envelope caught her eye next.

Inside she found a letter written in neat little penmanship. It was signed, "Mary." Curious, Em began reading aloud.

Dear Viviette,
Your letter delighted me. What happy news, a baby girl. I hope to visit someday and meet your Emmeline myself.

Em stopped and stared at the words. Reading them again, she realized she had seen them correctly. Her name was Emmeline. Not just Em. Eager to learn more, she kept reading.

I have missed you these years since you have been away. I am sorry that Father and Mother will not welcome you. I thought John was a good man and I understand why you married him. They never speak of you, but I have seen Mother pull out your portrait and look at it when she thinks no one can see her.
I have been courting Edward Brentley. You remember him, I am sure. Father approves of the match. Just think, your baby sister could be Mrs. Brentley before long. I wish you could come.

The letter went on about other friends and social outings. There were more letters from

Mary. It was easy to piece some of it together. Mary was Em's aunt, and from the looks of it, she was the only member of the family who wrote to her mother after her marriage to John Cooper. Under the stack of letters from Mary, Em found a note written in a shaky hand.

My Beautiful Girls,

"Lucy, this is a letter to us. From Ma. She wrote us a letter." Excited, she read on.

I am very ill and I fear I will not be with you much longer. Life has been hard on us, but the moments of joy you brought to me have been worth every trial. I am proud of you both.

Emmy, my beautiful Emmy. I have loved you always. Keep fighting, dear girl. Fight for a better life. Fight for love. It's out there. Even in this harsh world, it is there. Not always where we expect it, but it's there. Find it, cherish it, sacrifice for it. I have such dreams for you, dreams where my freckled-face girl is treasured. Dreams where you smile and laugh. When I go, know that you are not alone. Don't be afraid. A way will provide itself for you. Live, Emmy, and love. That is what I wish for you.

Lucy, my baby. I have been gone from you so often. My heart aches at all I have missed and all I will miss. I have always known Emmy would care for you. She will find you a place where you are loved. I pray you stay the happy girl you are. Always brightening the world around you. Keep smiling. I know you will. Some dark corner of the world will be brighter because my Lucy was there.

I love you both. Your pa did too.

Love, Ma

For a moment she sat, letting her ma's words hang in the air. Then she gently patted the ground where Lucy lay. "She loved us, Lucy. I always knew she did. Hug her for me. Tell her I'm going to live and love. Tell her I will remember her every day. And please, stay as near me as you can. I need you. I always have."

She put the papers back into the packet and stood. Then she tucked it back into her pocket. Looking at the light dancing between the branches of the trees, Em put her hand out and let it fall across her skin. Like a kiss from heaven. Like a kiss from Lucy. Then, raising her eyes to the light, she said, "I love you too."

Twenty-One

"Anything for me?" Caleb asked Calvin at the post office.

Calvin turned and looked in a little square box. "Nope. Nothing today."

"Thanks for checking." He turned and left the small post office. Why hadn't she written? A letter should have come by now.

Margaret saw him as he passed the boarding-house on his way to the jail. She was outside washing sheets with Laura, the daughter from a family that was new to town. "Problems in Azure Springs?" she yelled as she walked toward him, leaving Laura to the laundry.

He approached. "No, ma'am. Why do you ask?"

"I just thought there must be something awfully wrong for you to look so distraught." Margaret hung a sheet on the line. "You spend enough time watching people and you start to understand them. At least a little."

"What do you understand about me?"

"Your whole world changed when that skinny stray was brought in. And now you miss her more than you thought you ever could," Margaret said matter-of-factly.

"You're right—you have learned a great deal from watching. She was nothing but a case to solve when she showed up. I'm not sure when it happened, but it all became something more." Caleb sighed. "I left her in Beckford so she could find her own way. I had thought she would come back or write. At least I had hoped she would. This wondering and not knowing, it's agony. I don't understand why she hasn't come back."

"And if she comes back?" Margaret raised her eyebrows. "What then?"

"I don't know."

"Well, you better know. If that girl comes back, it's because she thinks she can have a life here, but she won't wait forever. You have the time right now. Rather than moping around town, figure out what you'll say if you get the chance." Margaret was standing with her hands on her hips, looking ready to pounce on him. "Better decide what you want."

"Em said you were good at saying exactly what you thought."

"Life's too short to keep people wondering. You remember that when you see that girl of yours. Just because she doesn't look like the belle of the town doesn't mean that every man around is too dim-witted to leave her alone. Someone will see her beauty."

"I've worried over that."

Margaret laughed, her curls shaking with each breath. "Don't waste time worrying. Act."

Caleb brought his brows together, thinking hard. *What should I do?*

"Come in, Caleb," Eliza said. "How have you been?"

"I just got an earful from Margaret Anders. Other than that, not much has changed."

"No word from Em?"

"No. I checked on my way here. I was hoping I would have news to share. I know Mae and Milly would've been happy to hear something."

"We all would have." Eliza looked remorseful. "Sometimes you don't know a good thing until it's gone. The house hasn't been the same since she left. We're all hoping she comes back to town. Mama has a letter Em left. She showed it to me and Pa but hasn't shown the little girls. I think she's still hoping Em will return."

Mae ran in the back door and through the house to Caleb. "Do you notice anything different about me?"

He bent to her level and looked at her closely. "I know—you changed your hair?"

"No."

"You got a new bonnet?"

"No."

Milly came into the room then too. "The same

361

thing that happened to her happened to me."

"That is a fine clue. Aha, I know now—you've had a birthday."

"Yes," the girls said together.

Mae's smile faded. "And Em missed it. We had ice cream, and Em has never had it before."

Caleb was glad Em could not see the pain on the little girl's face. "I'm sure she wanted to be here."

"Why doesn't she come back?" Mae asked. "Did you really do your best to bring her home?"

"I wanted her to come, but she had to stay. At least for a while."

Her hands fell to her sides. "Do you think she will ever come back to us?"

Eliza answered this time. "We all hope she does. But Em has to do what is best for Em. She would want us to be happy here. So no sitting around feeling sorry for ourselves. Let's go and eat together."

The girls, still sullen, left them and went to the dining room.

"How have you been?" Caleb asked Eliza.

"I've been doing a lot of thinking. It's been hard. Realizing who I had become." She took a deep breath. "I have to tell you something . . ."

He waited.

"I'm not proud of this. It seemed harmless at the time, but it was cruel and hurtful." She stopped again. "This is so hard."

He said nothing, giving her the freedom to say what she would.

"I'll just say it. I started the rumors about Em when she lived here. I told the other girls in town. I didn't think about the harm it would cause her. But then when you woke me up to what I was becoming, I realized how wrong I was." Eliza's eyes were focused on the floor. "I'm so ashamed."

"You told the girls the stories? About Em and George? About the saloon? You started all of that?"

She nodded. "I was jealous and wanted her to go away. But now I want to tell her how sorry I am. I've told everyone I can think of that the stories weren't true. But I haven't told Em. What will she think of me?"

"She'll think you were wrong. But you are setting it right and that is all that matters now. She'll forgive you. She seems to have been born with an extra measure of grace."

"What do you think of me?" Eliza looked at him, her eyes begging for an honest answer.

"I think you're growing up. Your mama will be proud of who you're becoming." Caleb took her arm and led her to the dining room.

Before they entered, Eliza said, "I know why you love her."

He stopped. "Love her?"

"Yes, love her. I've seen it written across your

face. I had hoped you would look at me like you looked at her, but it wasn't meant to be. Where I saw unrefined manners and coarse clothing, you really saw her. I only wish I had seen her sooner." Eliza smiled then. "I hope she comes back for you. I thought I could make you happy, but I'm not Em."

"No, but you will be someone's Eliza."

They sat down to dinner then. He was grateful for this good family and their welcoming home.

When he walked back to the jail that night, he thought about Margaret and Eliza. What they had said to him had him thinking. He had been moping around for weeks now. He couldn't control whether Em came back, but he could decide what he would do if she did.

Twenty-Two

Home.

When had Azure Springs become home?

Em gathered her few belongings and moved toward the door, ready to get off the train. Finally the doors were opened and she set foot on Azure Springs soil. Everything looked welcoming to her. The buildings were just how she had left them. The trees had begun to change color but were right where they belonged. The saloon was noisy as she passed it. And there was the jail. Did she dare stop there first?

"Just knock," she told herself. And she obeyed—knocking, then waiting. Her heart pounded as the seconds ticked by. She raised her fist to knock again.

"Is that a stray?" she heard someone ask from behind. Turning, she saw Caleb strutting her way. There he was. Just as handsome as she had remembered.

"I am no stray." Waving her arms about, she declared, "This is my hometown and I don't plan to go anywhere."

He nodded as he looked her over. Then he put

a hand to her forehead. "You all right, Em? Last I saw you, you weren't sure where you belonged. I've been worried about you."

Pushing his hand away, she stood a little taller. "It's one of those happy days and your teasing won't change that. I woke knowing I was coming home and haven't stopped smiling since. And it's Emmeline, but you may call me Em for short."

"Emmeline, is it? That's a beautiful name." Then he stepped closer and took her hand in his. His touch sent her heart racing. "Beautiful name for a beautiful girl. The answer to your question is yes. Yes, there are men who will see you as beautiful and there are men who will think a lifetime is not enough time to spend with you."

Her breath caught in her chest. Her question. He'd answered it.

She stared at him with her mouth open. He thought she was beautiful! He reached over and pushed up on her chin. "Don't look so surprised. Tell me something, have you seen Mae and Milly yet? Or did you come here first?"

Em shook her head. "No, I haven't been there yet."

"Well, they cried buckets of tears when I came home without you. Let's go and see them. I owe them a story. And I think today is just the day to tell it to them." He took her bag and led her to the Howells' house.

As they walked, he asked her about her weeks

in Beckford. Em stopped thinking about his perfect answer to her question and told him about the letters from Lucy and the letter from her mother.

"I loved it there in Beckford. I loved Walt and Olive. I loved feeling close to Lucy, but something in me told me it was time to go. That I needed to find something other than the past to cling to."

He nodded. "So you came back here."

"It was hard for me to though. I was so afraid I would lose Lucy all over again when I left, and it did hurt walking away from her little grave, but I think she is here with me. I think she would want me to tell Mae and Milly more stories and create a life for myself."

"I think you're right." Standing in front of the Howells' door, he asked, "Are you ready to be pounced on by two overzealous twins?"

"I am. I am very ready."

He raised a hand and knocked. Before the door opened, he bent over and whispered in her ear, "I missed you, Emmy." And then he kissed her cheek.

When she brought her hand to her cheek, she felt as though the kiss were still there. A sweeter welcoming gift she could not imagine.

"You're back!" the two girls were screaming when the door opened. Instantly, they were on both sides of Em, pulling her inside and into the front room. They asked questions, hugged her, and laughed all at the same time.

"Hold up, girls. I know you have lots to say to Miss Emmeline, but I promised you a story and today is the day I'm going to tell it. Sit, you three, and listen."

On command they sat.

"This is a new story. It's a story about a prince. This prince received a decree from his father to find a fair maiden to marry. The prince looked far and wide hoping to find the fairest maiden of all to please his father, the king. There were several pretty girls in his kingdom. He looked them over, wondering which one he should offer his hand to."

"Did they have rosy complexions and fair skin?" Mae asked.

Caleb tried to keep a straight face. "Yes, there were lovely ladies just like that in the town. This prince tried to decide which of them was the fairest, but could not decide. For there was another that caught his eye. This maiden was different. She had a magical kind of beauty. The kind that can only be seen if you know how to truly look at a person. At first the prince had not seen it. He had thought her too plain." He looked up and caught Em's eye. He winked at her. "He thought her skinny and plain."

Mae interrupted again. "Why didn't he see her magical beauty?"

"He hadn't seen it because he had been misled by evil men who told him beauty had to look a certain way. But once, when he was high in a tree, he looked down at the girl and saw a sparkle in her eye. When he saw her again, he looked harder, trying to figure out what it was that made this maiden so different from all the rest. She laughed this time and the sound echoed through his mind. It was like the sound of birds singing to the morning sun. It was perfect. Every time after that, he found something else beautiful about the girl. He found that she was strong, honest, and brave. Did you know goodness is the fairest of all the beauties?"

Milly looked at him with dreamy eyes. "Am I good?"

"Indeed you are. And someday I am certain a man will see that goodness and carry you off to his castle. Now where was I?" He glanced at Em. She was sitting next to Mae with a far-off smile on her face, her hand absently running through the girl's hair.

"Ah, yes. He was finding more and more beauty in this girl. He discovered talents he'd not known she had. This girl could catch frogs and shoot guns."

"Guns! What kind of a story is this? That is not what princesses do," Mae said.

"It's very different from Em's stories. Are you sure this is a princess story?" Milly added.

"Let me finish. Shooting guns and catching frogs may not seem like what princesses do, but you'll have to believe me when I tell you this girl was a princess and the very fairest of all. One day everything changed for the prince. When he looked at the other maidens, they no longer held any charms. Only she did. And he knew that she was his true princess."

"Did the prince marry her?" Milly asked.

"The prince was scared because he loved her *so* much. He had to leave her for a time and feared he would never see her again," Caleb said. "He was miserable the entire time they were apart. He dragged his feet all over town, downtrodden and self-pitying."

"If he is afraid, how will he ever live happily ever after?" Milly questioned.

"He had been granted a gift. Three questions. Two were gone, but he had one remaining. These questions were special. If he asked them, the princess *had* to answer. He decided to save that final question, and when he was certain he could not live without knowing if the fair maiden would be his queen, he got down before her and pleaded with her to marry him."

"What did she say?" Mae asked, impatient for a happy ending.

Abigail entered the room. Or had she been there all along? "Em, I'm so glad you've returned. And I can't wait to hear all about your trip. But I think

I'll ask all about it after dinner. Girls, follow me into the kitchen."

"But Mama, we want to hear the end of the story," they both said.

"You'll hear it. But not until later. Come along now." Abigail gave them a look that told them not to question her.

The girls stomped out of the room, resigned to their fate.

Caleb knelt in front of Em. "I have one question left. I've saved it. I was too afraid to ask it. When you were gone and I feared you would never return, I vowed to use it if I ever saw you again."

Em tried to blink away the tears that were already coming to her eyes.

"You are the princess. The only girl who holds any charms for me. My third question is, Will you marry me? Live on the land with me, climb trees with me, dance with me. Will you be my wife?"

"Why?" Em reached out and put her hand to his cheek. "Why me?"

"Because when I think of what beautiful is, now I see you. I see freckles and yellow hair. You will always be what beautiful is to me. When your hair is gray—that will be my definition of lovely. No one else will ever be right for me. I want to grow old with someone I can laugh with. I don't want a woman who always says the right words and has forgotten how to have fun. I want a future with you. You told me you had decided to live. Live with me. Marry me, Em. Let me look for rays of sunshine with you."

The words from her mother's letter floated through her mind. *Live and love.* "Yes. My answer is yes. I will marry you." A little laugh escaped despite the tears. "My very own prince."

Two little heads crept from around the corner. "You are the princess, Em! I always thought you were the most beautiful and wonderful. You are a princess. And you get to marry the prince!"

Taking Mae in her arms, she twirled her around. "You are a princess too, little Mae-berry."

Setting Mae down, she planted a kiss on the top of Milly's head. "You too, Milly-girl."

Milly looked at her and said, "Now you will live happily ever after."

Caleb's voice boomed above the others. "We will. We will live happily ever after." He took Em in his arms then and kissed her. Closing her eyes, she felt just like she always dreamed a princess would.

Epilogue

Em, are you ready?"

"Yes. Let me just get John's coat and I'll be right along."

The three loaded into the wagon and headed into Azure Springs. The ride was bumpy as usual, but Caleb had bought Em a cushion to sit on and the bumps delighted John. Each rut brought a roar of laughter from the couple's two-year-old son.

"Do you think we will get there on time?" Em asked, looking at the sun as she tried to guess the hour.

"We will be the first there. I don't think anyone else in town is nearly as excited as you."

"I'm more nervous than I thought I would be," Em confessed as they bounced along.

Caleb took her hand in his. "Don't be. I think we will know what to do when we get there."

"But Caleb, how will I pick and not help them all?"

"Let's not worry yet. Let's just enjoy the day and embrace whatever is ahead." They rode on, giggling whenever they heard their son's laughter.

They arrived in Azure Springs early enough to visit with the Howells before the children arrived.

When the clock announced four in the afternoon, Em held Caleb's hand and together they made their way to the train depot. Lined up across the platform were wide-eyed children of all shapes and sizes. Some looked afraid, while others seemed excited. Each had a number pinned to their chest.

Suddenly, knowing what she must do, Em walked to a woman who was ushering the children onto the stage. "Have you any siblings?"

"We don't worry about relations. Just try to find homes for them all. Pick whoever you like," the woman said, her face void of expression.

Em looked at the rows of children as she walked away. A little girl with stringy brown hair was in tears. Crouching in front of her, Em met the girl's eyes. "My name is Em. What's your name?"

The girl raised her head a little. "I'm Bessie."

"I'm glad to meet you, Bessie. Why are you crying?"

"I want my sister."

Em felt her heart skip a beat. "Where is your sister?"

"Hattie is over there." She pointed a chubby finger down the line. "They won't let us stand together." Em followed the finger and saw a taller version of Bessie at the other end of the platform.

"Wait here, Bessie."

She ran to Caleb and told him about Bessie and Hattie.

Caleb scooped up John and together they returned to the rows of children. He squeezed Em's hand and whispered, "I knew you would know what to do. Let's go get our girls."

Em remembered her dream from long ago. The dream where she found Lucy. It had not come true. These girls were not Lucy. They lacked her perfect curls and bright eyes, but Lucy was there all around them. Em knew it, and the world felt right.

That night when Em tucked Bessie into bed, Em handed her the doll that Olive had given her. "This was my sister's doll. I want you to have it. But you must share it with Hattie."

"But Hattie is too big to play. She doesn't ever play. She doesn't even smile."

"Not now she doesn't, but she will. Here everyone plays. When you wake tomorrow, we will take you outside and show you many wonderful places to play. Hattie will remember how. I know she will."

Em stood and started to leave but then walked back to the little bed and knelt once more by its side. She kissed the girl's cheek and whispered, "Good night, princess."

Discussion Questions

1. When Em is first brought into the town of Azure Springs, she is slow to trust those around her. What causes her hesitancy? Is it justified? Have you ever entered a new situation and struggled to feel comfortable?
2. Caleb makes quick judgments when he meets Em based solely on her looks. How did his early judgments affect the story? Would their relationship have progressed differently if he'd been able to look past her outer shell sooner?
3. Abigail and Abraham Howell are very quick to welcome Em into their home. Why is it that some people are more eager to help others? Have you ever known anyone like that? Why was Eliza slower to embrace Em?
4. Abigail is still grieving the loss of her sons. Margaret grieves her husband. The women approach their losses very differently. Is there a right way to handle grief?
5. Lucy plays a significant role in the story. Em says that wanting to be with her is what kept her alive all those years. What people or things keep you going when life is hard?
6. Caleb spends a lot of his energy trying to

please his parents. In what ways was Caleb's desire misguided? Is it wrong to want to please others? Have you ever gone astray when you thought you were doing what was right?

7. How do your feelings toward Alroy change as you learn his story? What was it that kept Em from becoming hardened like Alroy?

8. Caleb's father, Gideon, talks to him about defining beauty. Do you agree or disagree that we have the power to choose our own definition of beautiful? Has society's definition of beauty ever caused difficulties in your life? How can we help those around us see their true worth?

9. Em decides to stay in Beckford even after Caleb returns to Azure Springs. What ultimately gives Em the courage to return? How would the story have been different if she'd been reunited with Lucy?

10. Margaret is often a voice of wisdom to both Caleb and Em. Who have you turned to when you've needed advice? What qualities must a mentor possess for you to listen to their advice?

11. Em has to learn to do more than just survive. Have you ever had periods of time when you've simply been getting by day after day? How did you get past that and learn to really "live" again?

12. Eliza's character goes through a difficult transformation. How did the way you felt about her change from the beginning of the book to the end?
13. The packet of letters from Em's ma plays a role in her healing. Is there someone from your past you wish you could speak to? What would you say? Or want to hear?
14. In the epilogue, Em and Caleb bring home sisters from an orphan train. How does this act bring the story full circle? Have you ever found beauty despite trials?

Acknowledgments

The Hope of Azure Springs is the second manuscript I've ever completed (someday I hope you'll see the first). Writing this book was a strange experience for me. In the beginning, I flew through it. The words just jumped onto the page. I felt like I knew Em from the very start. I knew her and I loved her. I found myself rooting for her as I wrote her story. Everything about the writing experience was ideal. Every writer loves it when the story just tells itself, and that's what this one was doing for me.

But then my son, who was four at the time, became very ill. One night I drove him to the hospital, and he was unresponsive and stiff. I was so afraid. After a lengthy hospital stay and weeks of tests, he was given the diagnosis of adrenoleukodystrophy. Our world changed that day. And though we were blessed to find out early enough to try treatments, it was daunting (and still is). For five months I didn't open *The Hope of Azure Springs*. I couldn't. It all felt so trivial in comparison to the battle my sweet boy was facing.

I remember when I finally opened my Word document—it felt strange and almost foreign.

I'd been so removed from it. There was a level of guilt just knowing that as I typed, the future was uncertain. And yet, I'd felt called back to it. So much of Em and Caleb's story was already written and I wanted to finish. I wanted something I could control, and writing their story was something I could take into my own hands. As I dove back in, I found Em's experiences of grief and tragedy more relatable than they had been before. I cried with her and cheered her on. Em learns to do more than survive—she learns to really live despite hard times. I had to discover that again as I went through my own trial.

I'm happy to report that my son is doing well. His road is uncertain, but he, like Em, is a fighter. He's one of my inspirations. In fact, his name is in this book along with all of his siblings' names. I have the greatest kids (call me biased if you wish). I want to thank them for being patient with me as I wandered down this new path called writing. They've been my biggest fans from the start. I hope they know I am grateful and they are my world.

This book couldn't have reached completion without the many people that read the early versions of it. Thank you, Mom, Anna, Stephanie, Heather, Leah, Amy, and anyone else I missed. Your feedback made Caleb and Em's story possible. You caught loose ends and called me out when I got off base—I love you for it.

I'm beyond grateful for my agent, Emily Sylvan Kim, and my editor, Lonnie Hull DuPont. You both were incredibly patient and kind as I peppered you with questions and tried to make sense of the publishing world. I couldn't have asked for better people to start this journey with. Everyone at Revell has been welcoming, helpful, and kind. They are amazing people. Good people.

My acknowledgments page would not be complete without thanking Tyler. He said to me one night, "You read so much, why don't you write a book?" And never once has he doubted that I'd be able to do it. Thank you for encouraging me in all I do.

Writing this book has been a pleasure. I thank the good Lord for giving me this gift and allowing me to share it with you.

It's my wish that this story touches other hearts like it touched mine as I wrote it.

About the Author

Rachel Fordham has long been fascinated by all things historical or, in the words of her children, "old stuff." Often the bits of history she discovered and loved were woven into bedtime tales. Despite her love for good stories, she didn't attempt writing a novel until her husband suggested it (and now she's so glad he did). Since that time, she's often been found typing or researching during naptime or while she waits in the school pickup line. In addition to her passion for storytelling, she enjoys reading, being outdoors, and seeing new places. Rachel lives with her husband and children on an island in Washington state. Visit her website (https://rachelfordham.com/) or Facebook page (https://www.facebook.com/RachelFordhamFans/) to learn more about her life and current projects.